Drawn *to* Jonah

A SCALLOP SHORES NOVEL

JENNIFER DeCUIR

CRIMSON
ROMANCE

F+W Media, Inc.

This edition published by
Crimson Romance
an imprint of F+W Media, Inc.
10151 Carver Road, Suite 200
Blue Ash, Ohio 45242
www.crimsonromance.com

ISBN 10: 1-4405-7341-7
ISBN 13: 978-1-4405-7341-5
eISBN 10: 1-4405-7342-5
eISBN 13: 978-1-4405-7342-2

Cover art © 123RF and iStockphoto.com/Dean Mitchell

Acknowledgments

Thank you to my family for putting up with strange schedules, pizza and cereal for dinner, and the occasional need to boot you out of the house so I could get some work done.

Much appreciation to Cathy DuVall, who never let me lose sight of my dreams.

Many thanks to Sarah Meyer and Cathy Ramisch for your unwavering support of my writing career. And for the many hours of childcare—definitely couldn't have done it without either of you.

Thanks to everyone on the ECWC committee (this year and last) for keeping me on course and showing me that hard work and determination really can pay off.

A huge thanks to Ms. Cherry Adair. Accepting your "Finish The Damn Book Challenge" forever changed my life. I am eternally grateful.

Thank you to my Canyon Girls. You've been there through all the ups and downs. Next round of drinks is on me!

Thanks to my one-man cheering squad, self-appointed business manager, and marketing guru, Joanna Brown.

And lastly, a giant thank you to Jennifer Bodenrader, who helped me out with a last minute editing snafu when I had to scramble for a new name for my town.

CHAPTER 1

If bad things really did come in threes, then a flat tire in a chilly October rainstorm rounded out the trifecta. Though a failed marriage and the death of her beloved grandmother certainly put this particular crimp in perspective. Quinn eased her BMW to the shoulder and prayed that she wasn't inviting more trouble by getting the wheels stuck in gooey, back roads mud. She leaned her head against the backrest and closed her eyes.

The engine was idling, the wipers barely able to keep up with the sheet of rain pouring steadily from the sky. Daylight was giving up its last gasp and Quinn was stranded on a road that didn't see much traffic at the best of times. This move back Scallop Shores, Maine, was not starting off well.

She rooted through the usual plethora of junk in her purse searching for her elusive cell phone. Of course it hid at the bottom. Quinn grimaced when her fingers came in contact with something sticky—she didn't want to know. Seconds later, fished the phone out of her bag. "Yes!"

The battery was dead. "No, no, no!" She threw the phone the floor, startling the cat in the kennel beside her, still sleepy kitty-downers. "I just charged this last night." The day off could not get any worse.

Distracted, she didn't realize she was no longer alone quiet rural road until a tall silhouette suddenly loomed driver's side window. Grizzabella, the cat, hissed. Quinn scr Her heart thudded in time with the thumping on her win the larger-than-life man tried to get her attention. How snuck up on her like that?

She twisted in her seat to look behind her. Sure enough white pickup truck had pulled to the edge of the road,

color still discernable against the bright autumn wardrobe that dressed the trees lining the road. Squinting, Quinn could make out someone else in the truck.

The city girl in her balked at the idea of opening her window, even an inch, to talk to this man. But the small-town girl, the one raised right here, remembered that folks in Scallop Shores helped each other out. Even if it meant getting a thorough dousing while waiting to do a good deed. She lowered the window.

"Got yourself into a bind, huh? Pop the trunk, I'll get the spare out." He grinned, showing dazzling teeth, and Quinn thought it unfair that one man could have been gifted with so many gorgeous features.

"I can get out. Do you want me to get out? Maybe I could help." Quinn shoved a knuckle into her mouth to stop the blathering.

Raking a large hand through his soggy dark hair, the stranger tossed her an amused stare and shook his head. When she just sat there, he nodded toward the button that would release the trunk. Oh yeah.

Quinn sunk low in her seat, embarrassed that she'd gotten so flustered over a good-looking stranger. He was just a man. She scooted back up and checked out what was going on through the rearview mirror. He hefted out the spare tire and jack and slammed the trunk closed. He really was big. Tall, broad-shouldered, pec muscles clearly defined by the soaked-through T-shirt that clung like a second skin.

Sure her assessment through the rearview mirror had been covert, Quinn nearly squealed when the stranger stopped to stare back at her. Even in the fading twilight, she could see just how icy blue his eyes were. There was nothing icy about the slow heat that spread through her veins when their eyes met.

She squirmed in her seat, trying to ignore this physical reaction that she had no time or use for. Relief flooded through her as she spied her sketchpad on the passenger seat. She snatched it like a

To my darling daughter: While I saw myself as just a stay-at-home mom, you told everyone you knew that your mom had a job as a writer. Your faith in me means the world. Never stop believing in fairies.

lifeline. Switching on the overhead light and flipping to an empty sheet, she braced the little notebook against the bouncing of the car as it was jacked up. Quinn started to draw. She always started with the eyes. What would hers say right now?

Relief. Things hadn't worked out. Marriage wasn't for everyone. Coming back to the small New England town where she was raised was the perfect place to start over. She was better off alone.

Her thoughts wandered until a tap on her window made her jump again. She lowered it just a crack.

"Making sure you'll have a positive ID for the police?" He lowered his gaze to the drawing in her lap. Quinn looked down in horror to see the stranger's face staring back at her.

"I, uh, sketch when I'm bored." She'd meant to say nervous but didn't want him to know how much he'd affected her. She ripped the page out of the book and passed it through the space in the window. "Here, take it."

He took the picture, staring at it curiously.

"I'd really like to give you something for your time." *Oh good lord, could that have come out any more suggestive?* Quinn felt her cheeks grow warm again.

"I was raised not to expect anything for helping someone in need."

"Then I hope to return the favor someday."

He raised an eyebrow. "You're going to change a flat on my truck?" Chuckling, he headed back to his own vehicle.

That wasn't what she'd meant! He had deliberately misunderstood her. Quinn turned around in her seat, but he was already getting into his truck. He pulled up alongside her car and rolled down the passenger side window.

"Have a nice trip."

He'd noticed the New York plates then.

Well, she was done with New York City. She was done with broken dreams. And she was especially done with men. Quinn Baker was starting over—and she was in Scallop Shores to stay.

• • •

Did he really look that cranky? He looked mean. She made him look mean. Jonah threw the sketch back on the kitchen table where he'd been staring at it, off and on, since they got home earlier.

"What do you think, Cuteness? Do I look like a grouch?" He turned to Lily, fresh out of the tub, all pink cheeks and footy PJ's.

"No, silly. You aren't green and you don't live in a trash can." She giggled, referring to a Sesame Street character.

Jonah grabbed his daughter close and tickled her ribs. Hauling her over his shoulder, her shrieks ringing down the hallway, he carried her to her bedroom. He paused in the doorway of the room he had painted pale pink the very day the ultrasound revealed they were having a girl.

He pretended like he was going to set Lily down on the floor, but at the last second, dropped her onto the mattress. This was their nightly routine, and one would think she'd tire of it. Jonah grinned when she laughed breathlessly, and asked for more.

"It's late. Time for a quick story before I send you off to dreamland." He reached for the well-worn copy of *Goodnight Moon* in Lily's book basket.

"No, Daddy, read me the one about the fairies tonight. Please?" She pointed to a picture book with a group of brightly colored fairies on the front.

"Only because you're the cutest little girl I know."

He'd long ago memorized the words to *Goodnight Moon* when Paige had read it to Lily. It was a safe book. This one he had to make up on the spot, and that scared the hell out of him. He took a deep breath and prayed that he told it the same way he had the last time.

It wouldn't be long now. She was a smart kid. Heck, she was almost four already. Jonah couldn't bear to see the look on his precious daughter's face when she learned his secret. Daddies were supposed to know everything.

Lily snuggled under the covers, clutching her stuffed friends. Jonah kissed his daughter goodnight and smiled as she waved goodbye with her teddy bear's paw.

Jonah threw on an extra layer of dry clothes, still chilled after the soaking he'd gotten changing a tire for the woman stranded out on Rangeley Way. He couldn't get her out of his head.

She'd been driving the latest model BMW. Though evening had been setting in, he'd still been able to see that her outfit looked like something straight off a boutique store mannequin. A fitted wool jacket, tall leather boots (oh, yeah, he'd noticed how high those went!) and brand-new jeans that still had a crease down the middle.

She'd taken perfectly nice honey-blonde hair and had those professional highlights painted on to make it blonder. He couldn't understand why women did that to themselves. Waste of good money, if you asked him.

So why was it that she looked so "city" and still seemed "small-town" approachable? Unbidden, Jonah suddenly pictured her in one of his old plaid, flannel shirts and nothing else. She'd have her fancy hair all piled up on her head, and her bare toes painted some ultra-feminine shade of pink. *Whoa! Down boy!* It wasn't like him to react so physically to a stranger he happened to meet on the road.

Refocusing the direction of his thoughts, Jonah felt a pang of guilt. Lots of tourists missed the turnoff to the highway and ended up lost out on those back roads. He should have offered that woman directions. Wait, what was he thinking? He hadn't noticed it, but surely a fancy car like that would have state-of-the-art GPS. Frowning over how much time he was spending obsessing over soft brown eyes and lush curves, he shook the woman from his thoughts and headed down to his workshop.

He'd lived his whole life in this house and had learned woodworking beside his father as soon as he'd been old enough to safely wield the tools. They had started out making birdhouses and spice racks, the usual father/son woodworking stuff. Then as his skill set grew, his dad had taught him how to make furniture.

Jonah wished his dad were still alive. He'd love to be able to show him how he'd improved on some of the basic designs they had worked on together. He liked experimenting with the lathe, creating more and more intricate designs.

Tonight he had some sanding to do on a cradle he was making for the neighbors across the road. Ken and Thea were having their first baby in January. Thea had seen some of his previous work and gushed over the detailing. He hoped they hadn't bought a cradle yet, because this was going to be a gift from him and Lily.

Settling down on the cold cement floor, Jonah winced, thinking he should have brought down a nice, hot cup of coffee. He drew the cradle onto his lap as best he could, and gently began to buff the surface smooth. If he had a wife, she could sew a nice quilt to go inside. Now that would make a fine gift.

If he had a wife. He'd been thinking about that a lot lately. Not the wife part, really, but a mother for Lily. The older his daughter got, the more out of his element Jonah felt. Lily wasn't a baby anymore. Now she wanted her hair braided, she wanted to wear fairy costumes, girl things that he didn't have the first clue about. She needed a woman's influence.

But before he could convince someone to take them on and be a mother for Lily, he had to learn to read. Pure luck had allowed him to skate through life so far. The only person in his adult life that had figured out what he kept hidden from the world was his wife, Paige. She'd taken his secret to the grave.

CHAPTER 2

"Oh, it's you. I was just in the middle of cooking dinner."

"Thank you, I'd love to stay for a bit." Quinn spoke to her sister's back, as Kayla had already turned away from the door and headed back to the kitchen.

First the flat tire, now this. Clearly she had made a mistake in choosing to visit with Kayla before settling in at Nanny's house. Quinn set the cat kennel down and took off her dripping raincoat, hanging it on a coat rack to the right of the door. Grizzabella let her know she was fast losing patience being cooped up in her crate.

"Aunt Quinn!" Her nieces, Zoe and Crystal, met her at the door with far more enthusiasm than their mother had.

"Oh my goodness, who are these beautiful women in front of me and where are my precious little nieces?" Kayla could still hear, if the slamming of pots and pans in the kitchen was any indication.

"It's us, Aunt Quinn. Do we look all grown up?" Zoe preened, her smile huge as she tossed her long blonde hair over her shoulder.

"Here, let me take care of the fur ball." Quinn's brother-in-law, Jake, picked up the cat carrier and headed down the hall. "Hello, Quinn," he threw over his shoulder, almost as an afterthought.

She shrugged, figuring this was the best welcome she was going to get. Not that she deserved better. She hadn't been back for a visit since Crystal's second birthday. And that had been … four years ago. Some aunt she was. Quinn had her reasons, but that was a poor excuse.

The girls led her upstairs to show her their rooms. Oh, she'd been so out of touch. The last time she had been to this house, Zoe was into everything princess and Crystal was in love with

Minnie Mouse. They shared a room that was all frothy pink and tons of lace. Now they had separate rooms and very different personalities.

Crystal took her by the hand and danced into the first room on the right.

"Mommy let me pick out the colors. My favorite is purple and I didn't want anything else. So this is crocus and lavender. Those are both flowers." She swept her arms in opposite directions to indicate the different shades, nodding proudly.

"It's amazing, honey. You are one lucky kiddo to have this room all to yourself. So you like horses, huh?" Quinn referred to the scattering of posters covering the walls and the decals covering, well, everything.

"I started lessons last summer. Mommy says when I'm old enough I can help out at the stables, maybe earn enough to keep a horse there."

"That is so exciting!" Quinn smiled wide, as the little girl bounced in glee.

"My turn." Zoe interrupted. She waited in the doorway. "I'm across the hall. Come on."

This time Quinn was even more blown away. Her eldest niece definitely had her own vibrant style. She almost needed sunglasses to combat the glow of the nearly neon green on the walls.

Zoe flopped onto the zebra print comforter, hugging a sequin covered pillow to her chest and blew a kiss to a giant poster of Justin Bieber over her bed. Oh. My. Quinn was so out of touch with her nieces, it wasn't even funny.

"Last time you were here, I still liked pink." Zoe laughed. "How juvenile."

Eight years old, going on eighteen. Kayla had her hands full. Quinn thought of the cute pink sweater she'd just ordered online for Zoe's birthday. Maybe it wasn't too late to cancel it.

"Very chic." She breathed a sigh of relief when Zoe nodded in agreement. Thank God … she'd said the right thing. Maybe she had a chance of reconnecting with the girls after all.

Quinn slipped out of the room and headed down to the kitchen to offer some help with dinner. Kayla pretended she didn't see her at first, continuing to bang things around on the countertop. Quinn pressed forward, taking a stack of plates from the counter, and began to set the table.

"So I had a bit of an adventure a couple of miles from here." No response. "Had a flat tire."

"*You* changed a flat tire?" Kayla turned and looked down her nose.

"Hardly. I sat in my car with a dead cell phone and thought about walking the rest of the way in the rain."

Kayla huffed, nodding her head as though she expected exactly such a response from her sister. She turned back to the stove and stirred a delicious smelling Alfredo sauce simmering on the back burner. Quinn looked around for something else to do.

"Silverware is in the drawer by the sink. Not that I'd expect you to remember that."

Ouch. Score one for the Ice Queen. Quinn knew she deserved what she had coming, but that didn't make the barbs hurt any less. It was on the tip of her tongue to tell Kayla why, why it had been so hard, so painful to visit. But this wasn't the time or place. It could wait. She'd let Kayla blow off some of the steam that she knew had been building up for years.

"So this huge hulk of a guy showed up."

"Huh?"

"To change my tire."

"From AAA?"

"No, you're not listening. Some stranger. He lives near here, I'd guess. I doubt you get much traffic out this way."

Kayla finished draining the fettuccini and turned away from the sink, steam flushing her cheeks. She wiped her hands on the dishtowel tucked into the waistband of her too-snug jeans. This time she looked mildly interested, less standoffish.

"What'd he look like?"

"Well over six feet, hair as black as midnight, oh and his eyes, Kay. They were the lightest shade of blue I'd ever seen."

"He have a kid with him? A little girl?"

"I guess so, yeah, there was someone else in the truck I couldn't really see. You know him?"

"Jonah Goodwin. He lives out at the end of Tucker Pass, in his dad's old place."

"I don't remember him from school." Quinn's eyebrows squinched together as she tried to place seeing him at Scallop Shores High.

"He was homeschooled. His mom died when he was real little. Father raised him alone. Almost like history repeating itself. At least that's what's going around town. Jonah is raising his own little girl by himself now."

"How sad."

Kayla brought the bowl of wide noodles to the counter where she could see Quinn. She poured the sauce over them and stirred, watching her sister thoughtfully.

"Did he cheat?"

Quinn blinked at the abrupt leap to a new topic. She didn't appreciate the triumphant gleam in her sister's eyes, as though she took pleasure in knowing that Quinn's perfect life in the city had unraveled. She gritted her teeth and smiled politely. She took a moment to answer, breathing in the rich aromas of the sauce and the garlic bread browning in the oven.

"No, Andrew did not cheat. We just agreed that maybe we weren't as compatible as we thought." Quinn stumbled over the words, realizing they sounded weak, pathetic.

"But who filed for divorce?" Kayla was like a vulture, circling its prey, making sure the carcass was well and truly dead.

"Does it matter? Will it just make your day if I admit that Andrew filed for divorce?" Quinn hiccupped, trying to keep her tears at bay.

"You never said anything. I just wondered is all." She didn't look the least repentant.

"Yeah, well you never told me that Crystal loves horses or that Zoe hates pink." Quinn swiped at the tear that had slipped past her guard.

"Give and take, big sister. I didn't think you cared." Kayla's smile was smug. Her words delivered like a fist to the gut.

"Of course I care! I love them. I love all of you. Just because I didn't visit doesn't mean that I stopped caring."

"Sorry, but to my way of thinking, your fancy life in the big city was just too good for you to bother with the simple folk you left behind."

"You don't know me at all." Quinn had prepared herself for distance. It was what Kayla excelled at. But a full-on attack, on her first night in town? She didn't have the strength for this.

"I think it's best if I leave. Tell the girls I'm not feeling well. I'll see them soon."

Quinn knew her sister was biting her tongue. She had a lot more she could dish out, but she kept it to herself. For once, Quinn was grateful for the silent treatment as she took off in search of her cat.

If Kayla was waiting to unleash her anger at some other point, time would tell. But today had already been far too long and Quinn was done. She was back in town to stay and there would be plenty of time to mend relationships. And some sure needed a lot more mending than others.

• • •

Opening the front door with the key she'd found under the welcome mat, Quinn braced herself for the barrage of memories. It smelled the same. She couldn't even pull individual scents out, to be able to describe what she meant by that. It just smelled like home, like Nanny. A sob lodged in her throat, and her shoulders hunched with the weight of her sorrow.

She hadn't seen Nanny in four years. But they had talked all the time. She had revealed more to Nanny than to Kayla, though Nanny probably knew a lot more than Quinn realized. She knew how badly Quinn had wanted a baby, and how painful it was to visit with her young nieces, holding them and knowing she couldn't hold a baby of her own. Nanny understood. She had never made Quinn feel guilty for not coming home.

Nanny had been gone three months. Quinn hadn't attended the memorial service. She would have, but had come down with a nasty case of bronchitis the day before she was to leave for Maine. Kayla hadn't actually voiced her accusation, but let Quinn know she thought that was a rather convenient excuse. Quinn and Nanny had been on good terms before the old woman's unexpected heart attack. Nanny would have understood.

The rain had turned to a light drizzle as Quinn made a few trips out to the car to retrieve her belongings. Grizzabella darted off for destinations unknown once she had been allowed to leave her kitty prison. Quinn knew to expect her fur baby to come out of hiding in the night, and by morning she would find Grizzy curled behind her knees, her favorite spot to sleep.

Quinn wandered slowly through each room. Nothing had changed since the last time she had visited. In fact, nothing had really changed since she had lived here as a child, after her parents had died. The granny square afghan, with every color of yarn ever spun, lay over the back of the couch. Photos of Quinn and

Kayla as children sat beside newer ones of Zoe and Crystal on the fireplace mantle. There was room for more. Quinn touched the empty spot with her fingertips and came away with a layer of dusty smudge. Dust. Seemed fitting. It hurt to breathe through the pain in her chest.

Kayla had left the house alone, waiting for Quinn to come help her clean out all of Nanny's belongings and get it ready to sell. It was as though Nanny had only left to do a few errands. She'd be back soon. But she wouldn't be back. And Quinn couldn't go back either.

She had told her sister she'd come out to help get the house ready for sale. The truth was, she had nowhere to go. She could stay in her old room while they were cleaning and organizing, but after that, Quinn had no clue.

Andrew had moved out of their apartment in the West End the day he had asked for a divorce. But the apartment, just like all of their mutual possessions, had been sold and the profits divided between the two of them. Very civil, very amicable. He had given her a small settlement that would see Quinn through until she could get on her feet again.

She wasn't destitute. She just didn't know where her life was going. She knew she couldn't afford the life she'd lived in Manhattan. She'd had no choice but to come home to Scallop Shores. Now the only people she had left were the ones she had pushed away.

Longing to start fresh in the morning, Quinn turned off the downstairs lights and headed up to her old bedroom. The pumpkin orange walls made her head ache. She smiled to herself. Maybe she'd ask Zoe if she had any more Day-Glo green paint leftover from her room. Suddenly it wasn't looking so bad. What had she been thinking all those years ago?

Clearly they were going to need to make some improvements if they expected to sell this house. Quinn twisted the rod that would close the blinds on the window. The old plastic snapped in her hand. Yes, lots of improvements.

She dug a clean T-shirt from her suitcase and got dressed for bed. Switching on the bedside lamp, Quinn turned off the overhead light and rooted through her bag for the book she had just started. This one was on Norse mythology. Last month she'd read all she could find on old Irish myths.

Quinn had started a tradition a few years back. Andrew found it ridiculous. She didn't care. Every New Year's Eve she would write out on tiny pieces of paper one thing she wanted to learn more about. Then she'd throw them all in a hat, and at the stroke of midnight, draw one scrap of paper and that would be her focus for the year. And it didn't matter which one she chose, because they were all her interests and every paper had something wonderful on it.

She loved books, loved reading, but especially loved learning new things. To Quinn, books were the world's most amazing invention. So this year she was working her way through mythology from all over the world. In years past, reading had been a way to cope with the trouble she and Andrew were having conceiving. This year it had been a means of forgetting about her failed marriage. Next year it would be about expanding her horizons.

Quinn reached out to pull the comforter down. A plain white envelope slipped off the bed and fell into her suitcase. Curious, she grabbed for it. Her name, in Nanny's beautiful, looping penmanship, was scrawled across the front.

A letter from Nanny. How was this possible? Her heart attack had taken them all by surprise. When could she have written this, and how could she realize that Quinn would be back in her old room to find it? With shaking fingers, she drew out the paper inside.

My dearest Quinn,

I've never been one to be morbid, and I don't wish to start now. But I am getting on in years and I need to face facts. I haven't much time left. Don't ask me how I know. It's just a feeling, a bone deep feeling that refuses to go away. I need you to do something for me, dear heart. It will not be easy for you to comply, but I do believe you will come out of this a stronger and happier woman.

First of all, as your grandmother, I need to say this. Do not blame yourself for the dissolution of your marriage. Your Andrew was not the soul mate I know you are destined to find. Leave your heart open to love. He is out there and you will find each other.

Secondly, you need to take the time to learn more about yourself. You are an amazing young woman with incredible talents. But the world is missing out on you, dearest. You need to share yourself, share your gifts. There are so many people who could learn from you if you let them. Listen to me go on. I sound positively New Age.

Enough blathering on. This is where I must ask for your cooperation. I have been helping out a young father and his darling little girl. Lily is just a treasure, the sweetest and easiest little urchin to care for. Her father has no one to watch her while he works. They don't have much money, so I have asked him not to pay me. I do this because I can. Lily and her father have become like family to me and I do hope that you will consider that when you hear what I ask of you.

Lily needs you, Quinn. And I believe that you need her. I realize it is hard for you to be around little ones, knowing how desperately you crave your own. But Lily has no mother, and soon she will not have me. Please take over as her caregiver so her father can work unhindered. I know you will eventually need to find your own means of financial support, but until then, would you please care for Lily? It is my firm belief that you will come to love her as I do.

I will miss you, my dear heart. Know that I will be watching over you and Kayla. I will finally be reunited with your parents and I cannot wait to tell them what beautiful, strong women you have both become.

Until we meet again,
Your loving Nanny

Tears streaming down her face, Quinn set the letter on the nightstand, shut off the light, and slid beneath the covers. What Nanny
asked of her would test her emotional mettle. But Nanny had
never asked anything of Quinn before. Painful or not, she had no
choice.

CHAPTER 3

Jonah peered out from beneath Mr. Munson's kitchen sink. Lily sat at the older gentleman's dining room table, coloring quietly. Sighing, he smiled. He was so lucky. She never complained. Every day he dragged her from one odd job to the next. Every day she loaded up her little backpack, full of snacks, puzzles, things to keep her busy. It was his own childhood all over again. And Jonah didn't want that for his baby girl.

"You doing all right there, Cuteness?" He called around the bend in the U pipe.

"I'm drawing a picture for my fairy, Daddy. Maybe she'll like it so much, she'll let me see her." Lily turned the drawing around and proudly showed the crude stick person to her father.

He gave her a thumbs-up and slid back into place. He was almost done fixing the leak here. Then it was on to the Maguire place to repair their back porch railing, and the Petris to install their new front door. He was saving one for last. He'd gotten a call this morning from Nanny's granddaughter, Quinn Baker.

It was going to be hell going back into Nanny's house, now that she was gone. Jonah wasn't sure how Lily would react. His little girl still talked about the woman who had become the closest thing they had to family. But if this Quinn needed something done, then he had no choice but to go over there.

Property taxes were due soon. His dad's house may have been paid off, but the odd jobs Jonah did around town barely covered their groceries and bills. He tried to save as much as he could, but it was past time to rethink his business mantra.

His dad had started it, leaving the fancier jobs, the folks with more money, to the local contractor. Instead, he took on the people who couldn't afford to pay top dollar, senior citizens on pensions, neighbors on disability, anyone who needed work done but didn't always have the money to actually pay for it. Over the years they had been paid in vegetables from the garden, fresh eggs, a Christmas turkey (plucking that thing had been a real pain in the ass), whatever could be spared. When he'd been about four years old, one old neighbor had given him the pick of a new litter of puppies. Damn, he missed that dog.

What had started out as a noble work ethic by his dad had morphed into something else. He couldn't read. However illogical it seemed, he felt guilty charging an arm and a leg for simple handyman services that took more skill with tools than book smarts. He knew his rates were pretty low, but it just didn't seem fair to charge through the nose for fixing a stuck doorknob or building a simple cabinet.

Still, this scrimping and saving? Lily didn't deserve it.

Clearing out his workspace, Jonah hollered to Mr. Munson that he was finished. The old man shuffled into the room with his checkbook, pulling a pen from behind his big, floppy ear. He pointed it at Jonah as he moved to sit at the table to write.

"You could be a sight more professional, you know." He shook his head.

"I'm sorry, Mr. Munson. Have I done something to upset you?" Jonah snuck a glance at his daughter, who was gathering her toys back into her bag. Thank goodness she wasn't paying attention.

"A receipt. A bill. Some kind of paperwork that I can file away. Can't you write something like that up? Don't need to be fancy." The old man frowned as he leaned down close to see what he was writing.

"You're absolutely right, Mr. Munson. I should make up some simple forms. I'll get right on that." *As soon as I find someone to teach me how to read.* Jonah pasted on a bright smile.

Accepting the check from the old man's shaking hand, he and Lily said their goodbyes to Mr. Munson and headed for the old truck that had belonged to Jonah's father. Thank God his dad had at least taught him how to sign his name. Jonah may not have been able to read the fine print that came with a checking account, but he did know how to fill out a deposit slip and write checks.

Unfortunately, that had pretty much been the extent of the writing knowledge Caleb Goodwin figured his son needed. But Jonah refused to blame his father for his own lot in life. He squelched that kind of thinking the minute it tried to worm its way into his head. Besides, being able to write out numbers and copy names … Well, he guessed that made him only 95 percent illiterate.

"Daddy, do you think we could get another fairy book for bedtime? Nanny had a really good one on flower fairies," Lily asked as she was strapped into her secondhand booster seat.

"We'll see, kiddo." Jonah hated to tell her no, but they were really hurting for money, and the thought of making up a new story to go with new pictures was more stress than he needed right now.

They passed the library downtown, and Jonah frowned deeply. He felt as though going in that building and checking out a book would be like cheating somehow. Dishonest. Those books were meant for better people than him. He knew it was irrational, but he just couldn't help it. So many times he'd tried to get up the courage to ask someone that worked there if they knew of a program where he might learn to read for free. But he was too afraid of being judged.

The rest of the day's work was done and Jonah could no longer put off his last visit. If it proved to be too rough on Lily, he was out of there. He glanced over, nervously, as the truck bumped into the gravel driveway. Sure enough, his daughter bounced in her seat.

"We're at Nanny's house, Daddy! What are we doing here?"

"Nanny's granddaughter asked us to come by. You okay with this, Cuteness?"

"Yeah, Daddy." Lily wrinkled her pert little nose, looking confused. "It's Nanny's house."

"I know, baby girl, but Nanny isn't here anymore. You do understand that, don't you?"

"Yep. She's with Mommy and the other angels. She's up there." Lily gestured toward the sky, as Jonah helped her down from the double cab.

Jamming a hand through his hair and blowing out a deep breath, he jogged to catch up to his daughter, who had scrambled up the rickety porch steps and was knocking steadily at the door. They only stood there a moment before the door opened. Jonah blinked down at the woman he'd changed a tire for in the pouring rain only a couple of evenings ago.

Standing there in skin-tight black leggings and an oversized pink shirt that came all the way down to her knees, she looked like a sexy little pixie.

He'd have liked to see far less of her covered up like that. *Geez, where the heck did these random thoughts sneak in like that?* He gritted his teeth and nodded.

He had to wonder if she was struggling with her own inappropriate responses when she made no move to introduce herself or invite them into the house, but stood slack-jawed. Her neck craned to look up into Jonah's face. Since she wasn't shy about looking her fill, he felt justified in doing the same.

Quinn Baker had puppy dog eyes. He grinned at the thought, figuring no woman would consider that a compliment, even if he meant it as one. Her large brown eyes were warm and inviting. Loyal. Jonah wondered what made him think that. She had trusting eyes.

Her fancy blonde hair was stuffed up in a bun at the back of her head, held there by … Was that a pencil? Huh. And she had a smudge of dust across one cheekbone. Jonah had the strongest urge to wipe it away with his thumb. But, again, that was just inviting a slap.

"Hi, I'm Lily. This is my daddy, Jonah. And this is Nanny's house."

Jonah caught the brief flash of pain that crossed Quinn's face at the mention of her grandmother. She bent down to the little girl's level and held out a hand in greeting. Jonah watched Lily's face light up, thrilled to be treated like an adult.

"It's very nice to meet you, Lily. I believe we sort of met the other night. Your daddy is quite the champion tire-changer, did you know that?"

Lily nodded, sagely. "My daddy can do anything. He's the awesomest."

Shame wrapped around Jonah, hot and prickly. He only wished he could be the man his daughter thought he was.

• • •

"Come in, please." Quinn held the door for them as father and daughter crossed the threshold.

She tried to stop gawking, really she did, but the man was a mountain. Jonah Goodwin took the phrase "tall, dark, and handsome" to heights most men couldn't hope to compete with. And the fact that his constant companion was so tiny and vulnerable in comparison? Quinn imagined he had women swooning all over town.

"I have to apologize for the mess. I've been trying to figure out what to donate and what to sell." She lifted a half-filled cardboard box out of the way and set it in the corner where no one would trip over it.

"But this is Nanny's stuff. Not yours."

"Lily! You tell Miss Quinn sorry."

The child hung her head for the briefest of moments and mumbled an apology.

There it was again, though. This little girl, a stranger that she had only just met, calling *her* grandmother Nanny, a right and privilege that should have been hers and Kayla's alone. Quinn felt the biting sting of jealousy, knowing that this little girl had shared some of Nanny's last moments on Earth.

Lily went straight to Nanny's rocking chair, to a basket that sat beside it. Quinn expected to see Nanny's knitting supplies and was surprised to find the basket filled with children's books. The little girl seemed to be searching for one in particular.

Quinn watched her, tiny fingers plucking through books, sweet rosebud mouth pursed in concentration. Jealousy, a useless emotion anyway, began to fade; in its place, a warmth spread. She may not have been able to come home to be with her grandmother, but Nanny had not been alone.

"How about some cookies and milk?" Quinn offered up, when the silence between the adults became uncomfortable.

"Nanny used to give me gingersnaps." Lily led the way to the kitchen, carrying a large picture book with her.

"She sure feels comfortable around here." Quinn looked up, and up a little more. Good grief, the man was a skyscraper!

"Nanny … I'm sorry, your grandmother meant a lot to both of us. She was an incredibly kind woman. She asked us to call her that. It bothers you, though. I can tell Lily she needs to refer to her as Ms. Virginia, if you'd like." His smile was sad, understanding.

"No, of course not. She's so little, she wouldn't understand. I'm not bothered by it. I just … miss her." Quinn didn't dare look at him. She was too close to crying.

They joined Lily in the kitchen. The little girl had already seated herself at the table, swinging her legs in the large wooden chair. She looked so tiny sitting at the long butcher-block table that had been in Nanny's house at least fifty years.

Quinn got the plastic jug of milk from the fridge while Jonah retrieved two glasses and a little plastic cup. Quinn had to do a double take. That pink cup with tiny flowers on it hadn't been here the last time she'd visited. It looked like Miss Lily had really been a regular fixture here.

Opening a new box of gingersnaps that she'd picked up at the store yesterday, Quinn shook a pile out onto a plate. Gingersnaps had been her favorite, ever since she was Lily's age. Nanny used to buy them by the box, too. She wasn't the type of grandmother who wore an apron over a pretty flowered dress and baked all day. Nanny preferred her cakes and cookies premade, with none of the fuss.

"So what have you got there?" Quinn nodded to the book Lily was devouring with her eyes.

"It's about flower fairies. Nanny was teaching me all about fairies, before, you know … " Lily looked up at Quinn, her light blue eyes, so like her father's, filling with tears.

Quinn tore her gaze away from the sadness that mirrored her own pain. She focused on the picture book. Wow. Now that took her back.

"I remember this book! Nanny used to read to me about all the different kinds of fairies. Then we'd go out into the yard and build fairy gardens. We'd imagine them visiting us every spring and summer."

"She showed me!" Lily crowed. "There's a fairy ring around the big tree in the middle of the backyard."

"Is that still there?" Quinn flipped through the worn pages, smiling at Lily.

"They come back every year if you treat them nice." Lily nodded vigorously.

Quinn nibbled a gingersnap and finished her glass of milk. She snuck a look at the giant man sitting beside his little daughter. Love shone in his eyes as he split the last cookie in half and offered a piece to Lily. Giggling, she took it. Swinging his attention to Quinn, he held out the other half to her. Reaching out carefully, she plucked it from his large fingers and nodded a thank you.

"You all right if Miss Quinn and I go in the other room and talk business stuff?" Jonah stood up from the table and gave Lily's shoulder a little squeeze. She hunkered over her book and gave him a dismissive wave.

Quinn chuckled as they left the room. "How old is she? Sixteen?"

"She'll be four years old next month, but that kid sure can put me in my place sometimes."

Quinn found it amusing to see such a large man humbled by a wee sprite of a girl. He had the potential to be a really scary guy. Those incredibly light blue eyes could come off as menacing. The strength that lay coiled in those huge biceps and impossibly broad shoulders could terrify someone. Someone that hadn't seen him interact with Lily. Quinn realized she'd begun to ogle the poor man and hurried to the living room, where she doodled in the dust on Nanny's tall secretary.

"When you called you said you had a couple of things to discuss?" Jonah prompted.

"My sister, Kayla, said you are the resident handyman in town. We want to get this house fixed up so we can put it on the market. I've started a list of things that need to be fixed, or updated."

"I'd start with the front porch, myself. I promised Nanny I'd do it but it just kept getting pushed back. She always made me put my clients first." Jonah stared down at his scuffed work boots.

"That sounds exactly like Nanny. But my sister and I want to pay you for your time. This isn't a priority, though. We just ask that you do a little bit here, when you aren't busy with something else."

"I thought you wanted to get it ready to sell." He watched her curiously.

"Yes … and no." She turned away and busied herself with straightening the toss pillows on the old couch.

They walked through the downstairs, Quinn pointing out areas that needed repairs. Jonah checked on Lily, still swinging her legs at the kitchen table, as she poured over the fairy book. She gave him a thumbs-up and flashed the adults a big grin before returning her attention to the book. Quinn led the way upstairs, pointing out a couple of loose spindles in the railing.

"So, there is something else I wanted to bring up," Quinn said, sidling quickly out of the bathroom. Jonah took up nearly the whole room and she felt just a little too intimate, sharing that space with him.

"Something wrong?" He frowned, his face showing his concern.

"Nanny left me a letter. I guess you could call it a last request. I don't know."

Quinn turned and faced the hallway. Jonah joined her. He laid a large paw on her shoulder. The man should intimidate her. But instead, Quinn fought the urge to lean against him, to draw strength and security, to want him to wrap those long arms around her and draw her into a safe cocoon. At five foot one inch, to say she was vertically challenged was an understatement. But the more time she spent around Jonah, the tinier she felt. She took a step back and he dropped his hand as though he'd just been reprimanded.

"It's about Lily. Nanny wants me, wanted me … She said you had an arrangement. She watched Lily for you so you could work."

"Yeah, she was a lifesaver. Lily's a trooper now. She never complains about being dragged all over town so her old man can earn a living. But … "

"I know, and that's just it. I'm offering to watch Lily. It's what Nanny wanted. I realize I'm a stranger to you both, but I hope that a reference from Nanny counts for something."

"It's just that I couldn't pay her. I don't have the money for childcare. I barely earn enough to make ends meet. More often than not, we'd end up eating dinner here, with Nanny." Jonah looked miserable.

"Sure. I can do that too." Quinn's head bobbed as she agreed to more than what Nanny had asked for.

"No. I wasn't asking you to feed us. I didn't mean that." He was shaking his head, his hands shoved deep in his back pockets.

"I'll be honest with you, Jonah. I'm at a crossroads in my life. I don't know quite what I'm supposed to do. But Nanny knew me better than anyone else in the world. If Nanny thinks this is good for us, for all of us, then this is what I want to do."

Quinn held out a slim hand, her warm brown gaze holding his icy blue one. Jonah blew out a breath and grasped her hand, engulfing it in his. They broke eye contact quickly, but not before she noticed his jolt of surprise. Had he felt the same frisson of electricity that she had, when their hands touched?

CHAPTER 4

Macaroni and cheese, true culinary genius—and all he could afford. Well, that wasn't true. Jonah had snagged some hot dogs on sale for ninety-nine cents at Gifford's Grocery, in town. And the little cans of green beans had been two for a dollar. Yes, he and Lily were eating like royalty. He reined in his frustration, realizing how close he was to snapping the wooden spoon he used to stir the cheesy mixture.

Jonah heard a brief knock at the sliding glass door before his neighbor, Thea, poked her head in.

"Can I come in? It's your lucky day." She spoke in a singsong voice.

"Of course. How are you feeling?" Jonah snuck a look at her growing belly. It seemed like only yesterday when Paige had the very same bump. His breath hitched and he focused his attention on stirring the mac and cheese.

"This little one is a kicker. Ken is already picturing his son playing for the Patriots. And I'm envisioning our *daughter* as a Radio City Rockette." Thea chuckled.

"Still don't want to know, huh?"

"There just aren't enough true surprises in the world nowadays, Jonah." She patted his arm and held out a large Tupperware container.

"What's this?" He nearly groaned as the decadent scent of chocolate filled his nostrils. The dessert portion of this meal was now most definitely covered.

"Baby and I had a major chocolate craving today. I made several batches of brownies. I wasn't sure if Lily had any nut allergies, so I gave you the ones without."

"That was so kind of you, Thea. Lily will be thrilled. If she gets any before they're all gone." He held the plastic box possessively, licking his lips and waggling his eyebrows.

31

"You better share, Daddy. I'll be asking her later." Thea gave him a quick squeeze and waved on her way out the door.

Now there was someone who might have taught him to read, without judging his intelligence. Why couldn't he have gotten up the nerve to ask Thea before she and Ken had decided to start a family? No. They were close neighbors. They were friends. Admitting he didn't know how to read, asking for help ... It was a game changer. Thea (and Ken, because he couldn't exactly swear her to secrecy) would see him differently after that. It would destroy their friendship.

Immediately, his memory conjured a vision of sad brown eyes, messy blonde hair, and seductive curves, all wrapped in a tiny package. Quinn Baker. His body wanted him to consider Quinn for a different role altogether, but his practical brain had noticed all the books Quinn kept around. She could teach him to read.

"Daddy, I'm hungry." Lily bounced into the room, rising on tiptoe as she tried to see the stovetop and the counters, to gauge how soon dinner would be.

"If Your Majesty would take a seat, I will have dinner ready soon." Jonah frowned when he noticed Lily carrying a familiar book with her.

"Hey, Cuteness, where did you get that book?"

"Miz Quinn told me I could have it. She said I hafta be super careful with the pages 'cause then I can give it to my little girl someday."

"Well, I think we should give it back. That book belongs to Miss Quinn, and I'm sure she'd like to give it to her own daughter someday."

"She doesn't have a girl, Daddy. She's all by herself."

In the world of a three-year-old, possession was nine-tenths of the law. Now that the fairy book was in her hands, Lily was not going to give it up easily. Bile rose in Jonah's throat as he envisioned the first time she asked him to read it to her. Nanny had read this particular book to his daughter every day for a year. Lily knew exactly how it went. And he didn't.

Jonah concentrated on spooning mac and cheese onto two plates. He cut up Lily's hot dog into tiny bites. How could he distract her from wanting to read that book tonight? He normally didn't allow her to watch movies before bed, but maybe he'd make an exception tonight. Bah! That was just putting off the inevitable.

"Ketchup, Daddy!" Lily pointed to the refrigerator with her fork.

"Ketchup, please?" He spun on his heel and headed back to the fridge for her hotdog dipping sauce.

"Thank you, Daddy. I love you." Lily flashed him a grin that wrapped him right around her pinky. He would do anything in the world for her.

After dinner, and two brownies each, Jonah filled the sink with dish detergent and let Lily help with the dishes. She stood on a stool in front of him, mostly playing in the frothy bubbles. Dishwashing took a little longer than usual, but it was a lot more fun.

"I like her, Daddy."

"You like who, Cuteness?" Jonah carefully set the last glass in the dish strainer to dry.

"Miz Quinn. She says she can teach me to draw. I told her I draw fairies. She said when she was little she drew fairies a lot. But not in a long time."

"You know how Nanny used to watch you so Daddy could go to work and you wouldn't have to drag along? Well, Miss Quinn has offered to take care of you like her Nanny did. Do you think you'd like that?"

Lily whooped and leaped off her stool, jumping around and chanting "yayayayayay." Jonah shrugged. That would be a yes. She scooped her new fairy book up from a kitchen chair and darted from the room.

Jonah leaned against the counter and stared at the empty doorway Lily had just run through. He reached for the container of brownies and shoved another one in his mouth, whole. Quinn had asked him to trust her as he would have Nanny, in caring for his daughter. The thing of it was, she didn't have to ask. There was just something about her that made him want to trust her.

And he knew that trust would have him asking her to teach him to read. He wasn't sure when they would find the time, what with her watching Lily and him working. But in all these years, Quinn Baker was the first person he'd met that he was finally making concrete plans to ask for help. He was ready to put his doubts and fears aside for the sake of his daughter. That had to mean something.

The fact that she was also the first woman, since Paige, that he felt genuinely attracted to, was just something he'd have to ignore. Lily came first. Becoming the best dad he could be for her was his top priority.

Pushing off the counter, Jonah slapped at the light switch on his way out of the kitchen. He headed down the hall to start Lily's bath. He didn't deserve a woman. He'd already caused the death of one wife. If he were ever lucky enough to find a new mother for Lily, she'd be just that ... a maternal influence in his daughter's life. Any marriage to him would be in name only. It was safer that way.

• • •

"My first appointment shows up at one o'clock. I hope you plan on feeding me lunch. After that, I'm outta here for the day." Kayla breezed through the door without a backward glance at her sister.

"Good morning, so good to see you too. I picked up some coffee for both of us. Cady had some pumpkin spice muffins this morning." Quinn shut the front door, shaking her head when

Kayla didn't even say thank you before diving into the pastry bag from Logan's Bakery.

"So I stopped by Gifford's and asked for some empty boxes. Some young college kid filled my car with them. They've got plenty more if we need them."

"Anything we sell gets split down the middle. Whatever we don't sell, we donate. Nobody gets to keep anything for sentimental reasons." Kayla sent a harsh look at her sister, over her coffee cup.

"Okay, if that's how you feel. But I won't begrudge you anything. If you come across something special, you're more than welcome to take it home." Quinn refused to give her sister the fight she so desperately seemed to want.

"Always Nanny's good little girl, huh? Too bad she didn't see you for the selfish person you are." Kayla turned her back on Quinn, on their conversation.

Oh, it was good to be home. Quinn snatched up her coffee and the bag with the remaining muffin and trudged upstairs. The way this morning had started, it was best that they work in their own separate spaces for now.

Jonah would be dropping Lily off in an hour or so. Quinn hadn't had the opportunity to say anything to Kayla about this arrangement. She could only hope that Kayla's animosity was directed at her. Those two certainly didn't deserve her venom.

Quinn stepped into Nanny's bedroom. Windsong, that old perfume she swore only her grandmother ever bought, tickled her nose. It had never been one of Quinn's favorites, but she had restocked Nanny's supply every Christmas, just the same. She'd never be able to look at a bottle without thinking of her grandmother.

Feeling uncomfortable going through Nanny's unmentionables, Quinn started with the closet. She pulled out sweaters, blouses and dresses, wool dress coats, and a trench coat for the rainy season. Looking over each item for tears, stains, or too much wear, Quinn started three piles. The garbage pile lay on the floor, in the corner. The donation and consignment piles were each laid out neatly on Nanny's bed.

Grizzabella had staked out the very center of the large bed, stretching out languorously in an inviting patch of sunlight. She looked fast asleep but it was just a ruse. Whenever she sensed Quinn's hand was close enough for a pet, her little outboard motor would start right up, increasing in volume if she got a nice rub under her chin. She didn't know what she'd do if she didn't have her little fur baby.

"I want all of the pictures of my girls back—in their frames," Kayla hollered up the stairs.

"Duly noted, sister dear," Quinn sang back.

She held up a long plaid, wool skirt. The style looked to be from the '70s, given the yellows, reds, and oranges. Quite frankly, it hurt Quinn's eyes to look at it. But it was in good condition so she couldn't toss it. Maybe someone would buy it for a retro costume party. She shrugged. It could happen.

The closet wasn't overly stuffed and Quinn found that she'd emptied the rack a lot quicker than anticipated. She shook open a large garbage bag and began to stuff the clothes in that hadn't met passable criteria. This project left too much time to think. While she should be mourning her grandmother's passing, given her surroundings, Quinn found herself dwelling on Kayla's animosity.

Even her divorce proceedings with Andrew had been more civil than this. They had both agreed that what had been there at the beginning of their relationship, had fizzled. There was no "them." There hadn't been for a long time. Andrew, prompted by his mother no doubt, had tried to lay the blame at Quinn's feet.

He hadn't yelled at her. He probably thought he was being kind by pointing it out. But he had very calmly explained that she was broken. He suggested it was Quinn's fault that they couldn't have children. She brought nothing to the bedroom, as he put it. She didn't excite him. She was a failure at sex. Very calm, very civil, very over.

Now Kayla, on the other hand, she was going for the jugular. Quinn slumped down on the carpet, her back against the bed. She held the pastry bag in her lap and nibbled at the muffin. Communicating through email and text messages, she never picked up on the cues. If her sister had been snarky in her replies, the sarcasm just didn't translate electronically.

Quinn had tried calling, at first. But more and more often, their phone calls were punctuated with reprimands for the girls, screeches in the background, and a general sense of chaos. It was easier to keep in touch in other ways. And it wasn't like she'd ever missed a birthday, anniversary, or holiday.

What she couldn't wrap her mind around was that Kayla also seemed upset about the relationship Quinn and Nanny shared. Which didn't make sense at all. Quinn had left town. She couldn't pop over and visit with Nanny at any time, like her sister could. In essence, Kayla had Nanny all to herself. So what was her problem?

A knock on the front door signaled that more time had passed than Quinn realized. She scrambled up from the floor, brushed off her crumbs, and headed for the door. Kayla had beaten her to it, and Quinn reached the bottom of the stairs in time to hear her sister start to give Jonah the brush off. Oh no she didn't!

"Hey, there you are. Sorry I didn't get down here sooner. Kayla, you know Jonah and his daughter Lily, right?" Quinn wrestled the door away from her sister and held it wide, gesturing the newcomers inside.

"I know them, but why are they here? Did you hire him without discussing it with me first? There are other options, you know." Kayla looked suspiciously from Quinn to Jonah.

"Well, you know how Nanny used to watch Lily while Jonah went to work? Nanny left me a letter, asking that I take over. And here we are. Our first day hanging out together." Quinn's bright smile encompassed both father and daughter.

"What are you talking about? Nanny didn't babysit anyone." Kayla scowled.

"I don't mean to argue, but yes she did. Nanny watched Lily almost every day for a year, before … you know." Jonah's baritone held a hint of annoyance, not that Quinn could blame him.

"Nanny? That's *our* name for her! Did you tell them it was okay for them to call our grandmother Nanny?" Kayla's nostrils flared as she glared fiercely at her sister.

"She told us to. She told me she'd be my Nanny too. She said it was okay." Lily had pushed forward, her chin up, as she looked Kayla in the eye. "Are you mad at me?" She looked so brave, but Quinn could see the slight tremble in her shoulders that revealed how hard this was for her.

"Well, she never told me." Kayla tossed her hair over her shoulder and flounced back toward the kitchen.

Quinn watched her go, confusion scrunching her eyebrows together. Clearly Kayla and Nanny hadn't been as close as she'd always assumed. She turned and wrapped an arm around Lily's shoulders. Her heart tripped a beat as the small child sank against her. Briefly, Quinn closed her eyes against the stab of pain.

Her heart hurt from wanting a child so much. This, spending time with little ones, was why she had stayed away from Scallop Shores for so long. And yet it was such a good feeling too. Sensing the trust, the unconditional love that only a child can give. She looked up to find Jonah watching her curiously.

"Kayla. Not much of a morning person, is she?" Quinn sent an apologetic smile his way.

"Are you sure you want to do this? I can bring her with me to Old Man Feeney's. Lily loves his old Basset Hound." He ruffled his daughter's hair. "We're over there about once a week, it seems."

"Wow, Old Man Feeney is still kicking, huh? I bet he thinks things up for you, just for the company."

"I'd agree with you, if it wasn't for his sourpuss ways. Maybe we should send your sister over. I bet they'd get along great." Jonah ducked his head, like he was embarrassed for speaking out.

Quinn's laughter bubbled over. She nodded vigorously, since she couldn't speak. Lily looked from one adult to the other, their joke lost on her.

"Tell Mr. Feeney hi for me. Lily and I are just fine here. I think we may do some exploring in the attic, see if we can find some of my old toys from when I was a kid."

Jonah nodded, stooping down to envelop his daughter in a goodbye hug. Quinn swallowed hard against the lump in her throat. He kissed Lily on the cheek and Quinn felt oddly bereft when he didn't offer her one, as well. He opened the door and waved goodbye to them both. Lily blew him kisses until his truck was no longer in sight.

"She really did say I could call her Nanny. She really did."

"I know, sweetheart. You keep right on calling her that. I think she'd like that."

CHAPTER 5

There was something he wanted to ask her. Quinn had been watching Lily for a week now. Jonah would drop her off in the mornings and pick her up around five o'clock. Every morning when he handed Lily's backpack to Quinn he paused at the door, like he was about to say something. Then he'd shake his head just the tiniest bit, shrug, and wave goodbye. He did the same sort of thing on the other end of the day, as he and Lily were leaving.

Today she'd ask him outright. Sometimes people just needed a little push. Unless he intended to ask her out. Oh, God, what if that was what he was working up the nerve to ask? To know that he was already struggling with this, a rejection would crush him. Really, who would say no to someone as gorgeous as Jonah? Someone who didn't deserve to date a tall, dark and gorgeous man, that's who.

Quinn slid a pan of lasagna into the oven and set the timer. When Jonah stepped through the door to pick up Lily, the aroma of a home-cooked meal would convince him to stay and eat. Then she could put on a movie for Lily and offer Jonah some coffee. She couldn't offer wine. That would be setting the scene for a date. And Quinn wanted to discourage that. She'd put him at ease and then gently ask him if there was anything on his mind.

"Did you ever have a fairy visit you when you were growing up?" Lily sat at the kitchen table. Her head was cocked to the side, crayon poised in midair.

"Well, that sure was a long time ago. But now that you mention it, yes, I believe I had a fairy that used to visit me during the summer."

Quinn sat down across from Lily at the table. She peered down at the drawing of a pink fairy, with large purple wings and a golden tiara. Lily added pink slippers, the tip of her little tongue sticking out of her mouth as she concentrated on filling the color in.

"What was her name?" Lily set the crayon down and waited, expectantly.

"Um, well, I don't remember." Quinn grimaced.

"My fairy is named Misty Blossom. She watches me sleep. I made a bed for her in a shoebox, but I think she likes to be outside best."

"Yes, as I recall, fairies love nature. They probably feel a little trapped when they are inside."

Lily offered Quinn a piece of drawing paper from her tablet, making her realize, belatedly, that she should have brought her own sketch pad to the table. Grinning, Quinn picked up a pencil and began to create a fairy of her own. Drawing was her passion. A very old memory teased her brain, a voice she hadn't heard since she was ten years old.

"It's so important to have a passion, girls, have a passion and feed it. If you aren't doing what you truly love, you aren't truly living."

Manda Baker, Quinn's mother, had spoken those words every night for as long as Quinn could remember. Smiling wistfully, she thought back to when her mother was alive. She and Kayla would snuggle in their parent's bed for story time every night. Then after they read, if the girls were still awake, Manda would whisper to them about following their dreams. She'd tell them the story of how she and their father, James, had met. They had felt like the most-loved little girls in the world.

After their parents died, when Quinn was ten and Kayla was eight, Quinn took over the bedtime ritual. She read to Kayla from the very same book of flower fairies that Nanny had read to Lily. She used the same mantra, and urged her sister to follow her passion. Neither of them really understood what that meant, but they did know that it had been important to their mother. That made it important to them.

"Wow!" Lily gasped.

Shaken out of her reverie, Quinn focused on what the little girl was staring at. She'd been thinking and drawing at the same time. Her fairy had come out incredibly detailed, lifelike. She sat on the top of a toadstool, her tiny legs dangling over the edge. Gossamer wings folded out behind her; so delicate they were almost transparent. Her eyebrows angled up toward her cute, pointed ears. She wore a crown of daisies.

"Huh. Not too bad, is it?" Quinn slid the paper across the table for Lily to examine more closely.

"It's better than the pictures in Nanny's book!" Lily stated, emphatically.

"Thank you, that's very kind of you to say." Quinn chuckled at the little girl's enthusiasm.

A knock at the door had Lily scrambling from her chair. At the last second, she snatched up Quinn's drawing and raced with it to the front door.

"Daddy, Daddy, look at what Quinn drawed!"

Quinn opened the door and stepped back to let Jonah enter. He shook his head, gesturing at his paint-splattered clothes. Boldly, she took his hand and dragged him inside. The entryway was narrow and space was limited. Leaning back to meet Jonah's eyes, Quinn stopped herself before laying a hand on his chest for balance. What was it about him that just made her want to reach out and touch him?

"Daddy, lookit!" Lily squeezed in between the adults and shoved Quinn's sketch at her father.

"You drew this?" His deep voice rumbled, his eyebrows raised in surprise. "It's amazing."

Quinn could have sprouted her own fairy wings right then, and fluttered up to the ceiling. She tried not to let him see how much his compliment had affected her. She shrugged.

"Just having a little fun, is all."

"You ready to go, Cuteness?" Jonah winked at his daughter.

"Nope. She's not ready. And neither are you." Quinn stood in front of the door and folded her arms across her chest. "I've made a huge pan of lasagna and I'm afraid I'm going to need a lot of help eating it."

"Daddy can eat a lot of lasagna, can't you, Daddy?" Lily smiled wide.

"I suppose I could eat a serving … or two." Jonah blushed as his stomach rumbled so loud it was like it had a voice of its own.

The man blushes. Good Lord, could there be anything more charming? Quinn bit her lip and hurried from the entryway. She headed for the kitchen and began to take out vegetables for a salad. She could hear Lily's chattering to her father grow louder as they took their time following behind.

Jonah was also handy around the kitchen. As soon as he arrived on the scene, he washed his hands in the sink and then gently nudged Quinn out of the way as he took over chopping vegetables for the salad. Lily hadn't stopped talking since her father had arrived.

Quinn stepped back, taking in the cozy scene in front of her. This was the life she had always envisioned for herself. A frown dragged the corners of her mouth down.

"Hey, I'm sorry. I was just trying to earn my keep. Did you want to finish this up?" Jonah was watching her, his eyes full of concern.

"No, don't be silly. I was just zoning out for a second." Her hands fluttered nervously, looking for something to do. "You do the salad and I'll make up some garlic bread for the broiler."

Slathering butter onto a long slice of Italian bread, Quinn chastised herself. Her problems were none of their business. She'd do well to keep a lid on them. Sighing, she remembered Nanny's letter. This was supposed to be good for her, spending time with Lily and her father. She just wished it didn't hurt her heart so.

Lily filled in any gaps in the conversation at dinner. Gracious, that little girl could talk! Quinn met Jonah's eyes and they shared a smile. He reached for another slice of garlic bread, automatically breaking it in half and sharing with his daughter. Quinn enjoyed watching the dynamic between the two.

"Lily, you have been such a help to me all day, why don't I put a movie on for you and you can take the evening off. We'll put your dad to work instead." Quinn ruffled Lily's hair as they stood up to clear the dishes.

"Yay! Can I watch *The Little Mermaid*?" She raced on ahead, knowing where Nanny kept the DVDs.

"We aren't staying for the whole movie, kiddo. Just the beginning," Jonah hollered after her.

Quinn excused herself to go start the movie. Now that the time had come, she could see how difficult it was for Jonah. She was a bundle of nerves, trying to get him to ask his question. Oh, the whole thing was ridiculous! Smoothing down her hair, she took a cleansing breath and breezed back into the kitchen.

Jonah was standing at the sink with his back to Quinn. Or rather, with his backside to Quinn. She paused for a moment, enjoying the view. Until she realized that Jonah was looking at her reflection in the kitchen window. If she weren't so mortified, having been caught checking out the handyman's butt, she might have noticed the fact that he seemed to enjoy the attention.

Head down, she steered toward the coffeemaker in the corner. All thumbs with the filters, she finally managed to pluck a single one from the stack and stuff it into the filter basket. It wasn't until she had poured in the water and turned on the pot before she realized she'd forgotten to ask if Jonah even drank coffee.

"Um," she gestured at the gurgling coffeemaker.

"Yeah, I'd like some. Thanks." Jonah grinned.

He peeked in on Lily, who was curled up on the couch, wrapped in Nanny's crazy-colored afghan. They sat down at the table with their mugs. Quinn took a sip, trying to figure out what to say. She set her coffee down and tried to make eye contact. Jonah looked agitated.

"There's something I've been meaning to ask you," he blurted.

There it was. Her instincts were spot on. She nodded.

"I've been trying to come up with the right way to ask this." Jonah drummed his fingers on the tabletop, his expression sheepish.

Oh, God, he really was going to ask her out. She had to tell him no. She wasn't any good for anyone. But he was so good looking. And he was such a loving father. And he made her feel things she had no business feeling. Oh, what the hell—she'd go out with him. Just this once.

"Okay, here's the deal." He placed his palms on the table and leaned in close. "I was hoping that you would ... teach me to read."

Wow, it must have been the paint fumes coming off his speckled T-shirt, because Quinn could have sworn that Jonah just asked her to teach him to read.

• • •

Say something. Blink. Anything. Jonah frowned, waving a hand in front of Quinn's face. He'd expected a reaction, good or bad he couldn't be sure, but any reaction was better than this. Her face was slack and she looked like she didn't quite know where she was.

"Is that a no?" His face fell. It had taken him a week to work up the nerve to ask for Quinn's help.

"What? No. It's a yes. I mean, I guess so. I've never taught anyone to read before. Are you sure you want to ask me?" She looked completely bewildered.

"You seem really smart. And you have books, lots of books. I figure if you know how to read them then you could maybe teach me what you know." He couldn't look her in the eye.

"If you don't mind my asking, Jonah, how does someone get to be your age and still not know how to read? I'm not judging, mind you, just curious." She assured him.

He took a sip of coffee and sat back in his chair, wrapping both hands around the mug as he stared down into it contemplatively.

"My dad raised me by himself. He couldn't afford childcare so he just took me with him everywhere. By the time I was old enough to go to school and get out of his hair, he found that I was useful. He actually got more done with me around.

"When I got older, he had a free assistant. We got a lot more jobs that way. More take home pay. He told everyone that he was homeschooling me. I suppose he thought that, in a way, he was ... life experience and all." He shrugged.

"But you've gotten this far. Surely you have some skills. Lily tells me you read to her every night." Quinn's expression was sad. He didn't want her feeling bad for the little boy he no longer was.

"I look at the pictures and guess what's probably going on." He set down the coffee cup and leaned across the table, pressing his palms to the table surface. "Quinn, she's so clever. That's why I have to learn now. Before she catches on that her father doesn't know how to read. I can't let her find this out. I'm all she has and I have to be someone she can be proud of."

"She is very lucky to have you, Jonah."

They sat across from each other at the table. The sincerity in her stare made him squirm. Looking for something to do, Jonah got up and rinsed his mug in the sink. He hadn't quite thought this through. Being this close to Quinn was already hard enough on him.

He turned to see those beautiful brown eyes, always with just a touch of sadness, watching him. He wanted to sit back down, take her hands into his and get her to open up about what was bothering her. He wanted to comfort her, make her smile and laugh. Aw, hell, if he were being honest, he wanted to do a heckuva lot more with her.

She knew the truth about him and she hadn't run away. In fact, she had told him Lily was lucky to have him for a father. Quinn would have been the perfect choice for a new mother for Lily. But she was going to be his teacher. And he had to keep his distance. They had to keep their relationship at the student/teacher level. She deserved someone more intelligent and well-read. Maybe once he learned to read, he'd have the confidence to approach women in town. The only problem was that none of them were Quinn.

"You don't want Lily to know," Quinn said, her voice soft, so as not to alert the child in question. "How about we wait until she goes to bed at night?"

"You mean you'd come to our house?" Just thinking about spending time alone in a quiet house with Quinn made him hard.

"Well, unless you think that's inappropriate. She naps for about an hour in the afternoon. But your lunch hour should be relaxing, not rushing back and forth." She tapped her chin thoughtfully.

"No, you're right. It would be easier to do it at my house." Jonah forced an easy smile, trying to convince her he was fine with this.

"Um, okay then. I guess I should research some lesson plans, find out how the first grade teachers get their students to learn how to read." She clapped a hand over her mouth, her eyes wide.

"Wow—that was so insensitive! Please forgive me." Quinn stood and placed a hand on Jonah's arm.

They both froze, staring down at her hand together. He didn't move to knock it away and she didn't remove it. Jonah studied the top of Quinn's head. *Don't look up. You look up at me with those puppy dog eyes again, I am going to kiss you.* Slowly she took her hand away and they both began to breathe again.

"I need to get Lily home. It's late."

They headed for the living room and the sound of calypso music playing on the television. Lily was curled up in a ball, her head pillowed on her hand, snoring softly. Quinn put a hand to her heart and sighed. Seeing this, Jonah knew his little girl was in good hands when he couldn't be with her. He lifted Lily's sleeping form, shifting her to his shoulder where she snuggled against his neck, and headed for the door.

Quinn stuffed Lily's shoes in her backpack and then handed it off to Jonah as he walked by. She stopped him with a hand on his arm again, this time so she could lean up and drop a kiss on little Lily's soft cheek. She backed away before he could ask where his was. Opening the door, Jonah was grateful for the chill bite of the evening air. His traitorous body needed to cool the heck down.

CHAPTER 6

The bell jingled over the door as Jonah entered the hardware store. Mr. Pettridge, the owner, waved from behind the register and went back to reading his newspaper. Jonah liked that the man didn't hover over his customers. He knew if they couldn't find something they'd ask.

Browsing the aisles for new hardware for Quinn's kitchen cabinets, Jonah thought about their first lesson. It just sounded dirty. And she was coming over to his place after Lily was asleep. He set his jaw, gritting his teeth a little. If this was going to work, he had to stop thinking of her like that. Easier said than done.

There were bins full of drawer pulls at waist level. Jonah frowned, pulling out a few and holding them up to compare. Quinn and her sister wanted to sell the house. It hadn't seen changes in the last forty years, at least. He shrugged, choosing the style that wasn't too fancy and wasn't too plain. He found the matching cabinet handles and grabbed enough for the whole kitchen.

Would she leave again as soon as the house sold? The market sucked, but Nanny's house was close to the schools, downtown businesses, everything that made it a prime location. Jonah wouldn't be surprised if people were just waiting for it to go on the market. And if it happened quickly, what did that mean for his reading lessons? Or Lily's childcare?

Never mind the fact that Quinn was the first person he had ever had the guts to tell the truth to. That fact still had him reeling. He'd been married to Paige and kept his horrible secret to himself, until she'd found out quite accidentally. Oh, how she'd hated him then. Quinn wasn't anything like Paige, but he'd do himself a favor by remembering the past and not getting too close.

"That do it for ya?" Mr. Pettridge folded his newspaper and put it aside as Jonah set the hardware down on the counter.

"Probably be back tomorrow. You know how it is."

"Ayuh." He rang up the items, shook out a paper bag, and slipped them inside. "These yours or are you putting them on account?"

"I need to open a new account. Quinn Baker. She's fixing up her grandma's place to sell."

"Yep, heard she was back in town. Pretty surprising, that." The older man slid a contact sheet for new accounts across the counter at Jonah. And just like he always did, Jonah had a piece of paper already filled out by the client.

"So she stayed away a while?" He knew he shouldn't pry, but he convinced himself it was best to know all he could about the woman taking care of his little girl.

"Oh, yeah. Got herself into a fancy art school in New York City. Paid scholarship. Whole town knew that girl was going places. Then she up and married this hotshot Wall Street investor. About four years ago she just stopped coming to visit. Everyone in town figured it was because life was too exciting in the big city to bother coming back here."

"She's back now, though. Is she still married?" Geez, could he sound any more interested? This conversation was definitely going to make the gossip circuit.

"That sister of hers spread it around that Quinn is freshly divorced. Not sure on the details." The older man leaned in closer. "I don't think Kayla much cares for her sister. She sure seemed pretty happy about Quinn's marriage failing. Not very sister-like if you ask me."

"Yeah, I've met Kayla. She seems to have it in for Quinn." Or maybe she was just a miserable person who wasn't happy unless she was dragging everyone else down with her.

"Hey, while I have you here, Old Feeney ordered in a fireplace insert. It's pretty heavy and I can't see him coming to get it himself."

"He'd have probably asked me anyway. I've got plenty of room in the truck. You want me to come out back with you and get it?" Jonah offered.

"You don't mind, that'd be real helpful. 'Course if Ryan would see fit to come home and help out his old man, I wouldn't have to ask the customers for help."

Ryan Pettridge had left town on a football scholarship. Word was, he'd messed up his knee senior year. Scouts had dropped him like a hot potato. Too stubborn, or too embarrassed, Ryan refused to move back home. He still lived out in California, close to UCLA, where he'd gotten a business degree.

Jonah wondered if not having gone to school was actually better. It seemed that college held more disappointment than happily-ever-after. Folks leaving Scallop Shores and their families behind. At least it seemed like there were more hard-knock stories than successful ones. Maybe the successful ones just weren't as interesting to tell.

He needed to leave the gossiping to the old hens. He had work to do, and now an extra trip to make back to Old Man Feeney's. The bugger would act like Jonah had barged in and ruined a perfectly pleasant afternoon, like always. But now Jonah realized he really did crave human contact, like Quinn had insisted.

Jonah loaded the large cardboard box containing the fireplace insert into the back of his truck. As he drove off he wondered if he had enough time to head back home and clean up the kitchen and living room before it was time to go get Lily. Should he shave? Nah, that was just too obvious. It wasn't a date. Then why was he so nervous?

• • •

Quinn flipped on her high beams for the first time since she'd bought the high-end sedan. The light poles were few and far between on this stretch of road, headed away from town. Andrew Lloyd Webber's *Evita* blasted out of the speakers. Quinn sang along at the top of her lungs. She almost missed the strange looks she'd get sitting in traffic, belting out show tunes in Manhattan. Just the same, she turned down the volume as she approached Jonah's house.

In addition to her nightly mythology lesson, she had added books on curriculums and teaching reading. Jonah put a lot of faith in her abilities and she wanted to be the best teacher she could be. Quinn parked beside Jonah's old pickup truck and hauled out her tote bag, stuffed with lesson plans, books, paper, and pencils.

She smoothed the wrinkles out of her skirt and hoped her hair wasn't a crazy mess, having left it to flow around her shoulders. Jonah was used to seeing her in ripped jeans, dusty shirts, and her hair up, held there with pencils jabbed every which way. She didn't know why, but she felt like she should look presentable tonight. She'd look the part of a teacher.

Jonah answered the door looking as though he'd cleaned up too. His hair was damp from a shower. He had on clean jeans and a flannel shirt that looked so soft, Quinn wanted to nuzzle her cheek against it. He also had the sexiest five o'clock shadow going on. Clearly he didn't want to look like he'd tried too hard. Quinn shivered, wondering how it was possible to feel those bristling whiskers in places that were fully clothed and nowhere near Jonah's jaw.

"Come on in. You look … nice." His eyes traveled down her legs, over her toned calves and toward her trim ankles then back up again, before he gave a pained smile and turned to lead the way to the kitchen.

Quinn smelled coffee brewing and something else … bacon? They must have had BLTs for dinner or something. She hadn't been able to talk them into staying for dinner tonight. He'd wanted to get Lily home and ready for bed. And now here they were.

"Can I make you some coffee? I've got brownies, too. I didn't bake them. My neighbor brought them over. She's pregnant, baby is craving chocolate in a big way, I guess. This is the third time she's brought us baked goods this week." He trailed off.

He sounded nervous. What did he have to be nervous about? Quinn was just ... Quinn. Nothing special. Certainly not to men—Andrew had made sure she understood that clearly. Maybe he was just scared about learning to read. Well, hopefully she could put him at ease there.

"I'd love some coffee. I wouldn't say no to a brownie, either." She gestured at the things she'd brought with her. "Did you want to study at the table?"

"Yeah, that's fine. Thanks. Is there something I should have brought?" His eyes darted to her tote bag, like it was full of live snakes.

"Just yourself." She hoped her smile settled some of his nerves. Maybe it had been a mistake to dress the part of a teacher tonight. Jonah looked really distracted.

Quinn took out her books and materials and placed them on the table. She waited for Jonah to fix them each a cup of coffee and put some brownies on a plate. He set her mug down in front of her and then headed for the opposite side of the table.

"Oh, you should probably sit beside me. So we can share the book and I can see where you're having trouble." Quinn scooted her chair over.

"Right. That's a good idea," he said, looking like he meant anything but that.

Jonah moved his chair next to Quinn's and sat down hesitantly. Pretending not to notice his discomfort, she pushed the book toward him. She picked up her coffee and gave him a chance to settle in, take a peek at the materials. Nibbling absently at the brownie, Quinn groaned out loud.

"Oh my goodness! This is heaven." She sucked the chocolate off her fingertip and sighed, decadently.

Now Jonah wouldn't even look at her. He looked miserable. The poor guy. Was he having that hard a time getting up the nerve to learn to read? Quinn laid a hand on the soft flannel covering his large forearm.

"It's okay, you know." She offered, reassuringly.

"It is?" He still wouldn't look at her.

"We'll take this at your pace. Go as slow as you need." She squeezed his arm. He yanked it away.

"I need to move. I can't just sit here." Jonah scraped his chair back and stood up. "Can we do this downstairs? I need to keep my hands busy."

Apparently the question was rhetorical, as Jonah snagged the book off the table and headed for a door in the middle of the hallway. Quinn had to hurry to keep up. They were going to study in the basement? With the spiders and the dust and who knew what else? Now it was her turn to be uncomfortable. Clunking down the old wooden stairs in her high heels, she cursed her current clothing choice. Next time, jeans and sneakers.

She sneezed at the strong smell of sawdust. Sawdust? Expecting to see an old, dingy basement used as a storage dump, Quinn was surprised to find herself in a workshop. A very tidy workshop, with lots of machinery and tools she couldn't begin to name. This was quite the setup.

"I hope you don't mind. Being down here helps me think. I've got a couple of projects started. Maybe you could do your lesson while I work."

Quinn shrugged and hoisted herself up onto a stool, tugging her skirt down over her knees. Jonah's eyes lingered on her legs before he squeezed them shut, shook his head and then moved, putting the long workbench between them. He picked up a piece of sandpaper and began to sand down some dowels.

"Did you make those?" Quinn peered closer.

"The dowels? Yeah." He kept sanding, head down.

"Those are beautiful. So fancy. What are you making?" Quinn had slipped off the stool and come to stand directly on the other side of the workbench, facing him.

"You know the neighbor I mentioned? The pregnant one? I'm making a cradle for them, for the baby." In his element now, Jonah seemed more at ease than he had since Quinn walked through the door.

She liked seeing this side of him, the confidence, and the eagerness. He finally looked up, flashing her a grin.

"You want to see it? It's not done, but I can let you see how it's shaping up." He was like a little boy, so proud to show off his work.

He set down the dowel and the scrap of sandpaper and led the way to a sheet-covered lump in the corner. With a flourish, he whipped the sheet off and stood back. It was shaping up to be the most gorgeous cradle she'd ever seen. And knowing that it was handcrafted with love? Quinn burst into tears.

She covered her face in shame, backing up until she hit the workbench and could go no further. Years of pent up grief over her own childlessness spilled forth. She couldn't stop the wave of tears if she wanted to. And oh, did she want to!

"Hey, hey, it's all right. It's okay. We'll hide it under the sheet again. Like this, see? All gone." Jonah spoke to her like she was Lily's age, not a grown woman.

She shook her head, unable to speak, to explain her reaction. Her lungs burned and her ribs ached from the shaking she was giving herself. Her nose was running like a sieve and she had no choice but to wipe it on her sleeve. Charming, Quinn!

And then she was in his arms and it was getting easier and easier to breathe. His warmth surrounded her, calming, reassuring. He was whispering soft words into her hair, though she couldn't make out exactly what he was saying. It didn't matter a bit. She'd listen all night.

His flannel shirt really was as soft as she'd imagined. She laid her cheek against his chest, feeling tiny and frail against such a virile man. Emboldened by the oddly intoxicating mix of his soap and sawdust shavings, Quinn twined her arms up around Jonah's neck. She had to stretch up on her toes to reach.

This put her mouth up against his neck, mercifully flannel-free. He smelled so good. Surely he'd taste just as good? One little taste. The tip of Quinn's tongue darted out to make contact with the pulse that beat just below the surface. Her cozy cocoon got a little tighter as Jonah's arms turned to steel bands, locking her in his embrace.

Flattened fully against him and having nowhere else to go, Quinn continued her conquest of Jonah's neck. Soft little kisses, tiny licks. The man was delicious. The rumbling deep inside his chest alerted her that playtime was over. She glanced up, and then up some more, her gaze frozen by his pale eyes.

He waited until she made eye contact and then attacked, never taking his eyes off her as his lips plundered. His hands ran absently up and down her arms. His breathing was erratic. When he finally lowered his lids and moaned into her mouth, Quinn had to face the shocking truth that Jonah wanted her.

She had to stop this now! She couldn't let it go further. He'd find out that she was no good. A dud. That's what Andrew had called her. She was a dud in bed. No, Jonah was a good guy. He deserved someone special. Kissing her, wanting her, would be a very bad mistake. She shoved at the rock wall of his chest. Nothing.

He was too far-gone. Oh dear. Now he was kissing her neck like she'd done to him. It was so good. He was so good. Wait, that's right. He was so good that she couldn't saddle him with someone less than worthy. Unable to think of another way, Quinn brought her high heel down on his foot.

"Ow! What did you do that for?" Jonah backed away, staring at her like she was possessed.

"I'm sorry, but you weren't stopping. I tried to stop you. You didn't seem to notice." She cast a guilty gaze to the floor.

"Okay, maybe I didn't notice because I was too busy being seduced in the first place." He slapped a palm over his face and wiped it, like he was clearing away cobwebs.

Quinn scoffed. She wouldn't know the first thing about seducing a man. What was he talking about? Jonah looked wounded. Not his foot, he wasn't even paying attention to that. He looked like someone had given him the most amazing gift and then yanked it right back. Shame suffused her cheeks.

"I need to go." She turned, looking for the stairs. "I'm sorry. I'm sorry for crying and for falling all over you. You must think I'm a freak."

"I think," he said, a hand on her shoulder directing her where she wanted to go, "that there is a reason for everything you do, and you should never apologize for that. Go home, get some rest. I am going to take a very long, very cold shower."

CHAPTER 7

There was a hint of winter in the air as Quinn stepped out the front door of Nanny's house to walk into town. Wishing she'd brought her sketchbook, she settled for the camera on her phone, snapping shots of scenes she wanted to capture later. The trees were a riot of color, blazing reds, warm oranges, sunny yellows, and marbled variations of them all. She hadn't realized how much she missed autumn in Scallop Shores until this moment.

Nanny's old Cape was just off Main St. Driving through on errands, she didn't have the luxury of strolling slowly, reacquainting herself with old businesses and discovering new ones. She walked past the elementary school. She passed the library on one side and the Old Gaol and the colonial schoolhouse on the other, grateful that her little town set strict rules to maintain its rich historic past.

On her left Quinn noticed a building where the door and awning were painted in bright primary colors. Now that definitely stood out. Tumble Tots. Interesting way to mix in something uniquely modern with the colonial past. She paused, pressing her nose to the glass. Inside she could see slides, trampolines, mats, and foam climbing equipment. What a fun idea! She would have loved something like this when she was growing up. Had Jonah brought his daughter here? She frowned. He probably couldn't afford it. Well, if they had drop-in times, she was going to see if he'd let her bring Lily.

Lifting her hand in a salute to the Civil War soldier immortalized in the town square, Quinn continued on. She made a note to stop in at the antique store she spotted across the street. They might take some of Nanny's things on consignment. Or at the very least, they could tell her what was of value and what was junk.

She finally arrived at her destination, Logan's Bakery, run by Cady Eaton. It was the local hang out spot for old geezers like Mr. Feeney and his cronies. Quinn had also discovered that it was the only place in town that had an espresso machine. She couldn't miss her morning latte. There was also a delectable selection in the bakery case that she usually bypassed; but today was different. Today she was wallowing in miserable embarrassment. Today was a huge-sticky-bear-claw-warmed-up day.

"Hey, how's our resident artist doing?" Cady waved from one of the tables as Quinn stepped through the door.

"Oh, Cady. You can't call me an artist unless I'm ... *arting*." Quinn waved her hands in the air, letting Cady know she realized the word was made up on the spot.

Cady had been a few years behind Quinn in school, so they didn't know each other that well. But apparently she knew all about Quinn's scholarship to art school in New York. People in small towns tended to make a bigger deal about things than generally was warranted.

"Once an artist always an artist. You just need to find your spark again." Cady wiped her hands on her apron and rounded the counter to stand in front of her prized espresso machine.

"I know you're a vanilla latte, extra hot, person, but I thought it fair to let you know that I just got in pumpkin syrup. A little late, I know, but these guys aren't exactly beating down my door for pumpkin spice lattes." She hooked a thumb in the direction of the old men lined up on stools at the counter.

"Well, you know us citified folks, I'm just crazy enough to try one of your new-fangled pumpkin spice lattes." Quinn caught Cady's eye and winked. When Old Man Feeney let out a fussy snort, the women giggled in unison.

Quinn ordered a bear claw heated up and was about to turn and find an empty table when Cady gestured for her to lean closer.

"So you're newish in town and I know things aren't all that great with you and Kayla." The stern look she gave Quinn dared her to deny this. "Anyway, this is me playing matchmaker." She held up her hand before Quinn could say she wasn't interested.

"I'm not talking about a guy. I'm talking about a girlfriend. We all need girlfriends, honey. See that woman at the table by the window? That's Bree, the children's librarian. She is one of the sweetest people you'll meet. She's also painfully shy and therefore doesn't have many friends."

Quinn studied the woman sitting alone. She was young, a bit younger than her own thirty years. If she were that shy, Quinn guessed Bree would have been one of those kids that passed through school but no one could ever remember actually having seen her. Deciding they needed each other, Quinn nodded.

"You realize you are nosy as hell, getting into other people's business like this." She couldn't quite keep the grin from teasing the corner of her mouth.

"Welcome back to Scallop Shores, Quinn." Cady's smile was so big she showed all her pearly whites. "I'll bring your order to the table when it's ready. Have a nice chat."

"You're so not getting a tip."

"Story of my life, babe." Cady nodded toward the empty tip jar by the register.

Reaching inside for her best people skills, Quinn took a deep breath and headed for the woman sitting alone, her nose stuck in a book. Well, if that didn't say "buzz off, leave me alone" she didn't know what did. Okay, then.

"Bree, right? Hi. Quinn Baker. I was a couple of years ahead of you in school … I think."

"You painted the backdrops for the school production of *Camelot*. They were gorgeous." Bree smiled shyly from beneath her lashes.

"Wow, you remember that, huh? Cool." Quinn wasn't sure what else to add.

"It's all right. I preferred to remain in the background." She seemed to realize exactly what Quinn was struggling with.

"May I sit down? If I'm not disturbing you, that is."

"Not at all. I'm just used to sitting alone. I bring a book wherever I go." Bree set the paperback aside, stroking the cover like the cheek of a cherished lover.

Books. Now there was another passion that Quinn could get behind. She reminded herself to duck into the local bookstore, The Book Nook, before heading back home. She'd been relieved to find that her favorite place to spend her allowance and babysitting money was still around. Momentarily distracted by the thought of adding to her reading stash, she refocused on the conversation at hand.

"That's how I feel about my sketchbook. I can't believe I went out the door without it today. I feel like I'm missing a limb." Quinn chuckled.

"I would love to see what you're working on sometime." Bree finally met her gaze over the rim of her cup of tea.

"Oh, I'm not working on anything. Just doodles, stream of consciousness. I'm not … I mean, I'm not using my degree at the moment." Quinn looked down shamefully.

"What she means to say is, she's back in town to recharge and find that spark that had her all fired up when she left for college." Cady set Quinn's latte in front of her, adding the plated pastry and utensils.

"Does she do this to you too?" Quinn angled her head toward Bree.

"You mean like asking people to come up and talk to the poor woman sitting all alone, with only her book for company?" Bree arched a brow and sent a pointed stare at her old friend. "Yep. All the time. But I love her anyway."

"What can I say? I was meant to bring people together with coffee, good food, and conversation."

"Next she'll be hosting singles' parties after hours." Quinn shuddered at the thought.

"Ooh, I like that! Don't worry, I'll give you full credit for the idea." Cady patted her shoulder and bounced off to refill coffee mugs.

"I need to learn to keep my mouth shut."

"Eh, given enough time she would have eventually come up with it on her own." Bree smiled.

"So," Quinn took a sip of spicy pumpkin latte and licked the foam from her upper lip. "Catch me up on four years' worth of Scallop Shores' gossip. Did I miss anything really juicy?"

• • •

Octoberfaire had come to town. Jonah settled Lily in with the ladies on the committee. They put her to work setting out programs. He smiled to see his daughter so happy to be a part of the activities, and headed for his truck. He had a ton of tables and folding chairs to set up on the town hall's front lawn for all the vendors.

"Hey, let me help you with those. You don't want to throw your back out, do you?"

Jonah closed his eyes briefly, and gritted his teeth. Curtis Blaise nudged him aside and hauled down two tables at once. The man was a top-notch contractor, his building company currently working on a new housing development out by Perkins Pond. He'd been hounding Jonah to come work for him for years.

"Thanks. Appreciate it."

The two men got the truck emptied quickly, working silently. Jonah was grateful for the help and for the lack of conversation.

"The job up in Perkins Pond is going gangbusters," Curtis drawled in his Down East accent as he set the last stack of chairs down and clapped Jonah on the back.

"Congratulations. Your men do great work." *Please don't ask. Please don't ask.*

"Only the best work for me. That's why it sticks in my craw that you won't join my crew." *And here we go.*

"I'm happy with what I've got going around town. Keeps me busy. Keeps food on the table." Jonah glanced up to check on Lily's whereabouts. Still at the welcome table.

"I bet you'd just like to spoil that little girl of yours rotten. Surely you don't make the kind of money to do that with the odd jobs you've been working." Curtis followed his gaze to the little girl, a miniature version of her father.

"We're doing fine, Curtis. Thank you just the same." Jonah clenched his jaw.

"You're holding out for more money. Is that it? You know I'll give you anything you want. Your dad was great but your skills are a lot more impressive. Come on, tell me I'll see you at the job site on Monday."

"I've got a job I'm working on. Virginia Dansen's granddaughters are trying to get her house ready for sale. Probably keep me busy for a while." More like another couple of weeks, but Curtis didn't need to know that.

"I have never met anyone as mule-stubborn as you, Goodwin." Curtis shrugged, lifted his Red Sox cap off his salt and pepper hair, and tugged it back down again. "Why you wouldn't want to improve your lot in life is beyond me. Suit yourself then."

The older man waved and headed back to his own truck. Jonah blew out a frustrated sigh and started to carry a couple of tables to the vendor spaces. Of course he wanted to improve his lot in life. He wanted it more than anything. He flipped a table upside down, set the legs out and locked them in place before setting it back on the grass.

"Thanks, Jonah. I'll just need two folding chairs when you get a minute." Mrs. Bernard, one of Jonah's regular clients, draped a colorful cloth over the table.

Pumpkins, cornucopias, and multi-colored leaves set a festive tone for the day. He imagined she was going to sell her famous breads. This woman could bake! And Jonah was usually lucky enough to be one of her taste-testers when trying out a new recipe. His favorite was her cranberry-orange bread. Lily loved her blueberry-lemon bread. Too bad blueberries were no longer in season.

He continued to deliver tables to the rest of the vendors, stopping to help Sasha Winters, owner of Tumble Tots, who was struggling to set up a huge kettle for popcorn. She thanked him profusely, reminding him to stop by any time with Lily for a free class. He told her they'd visit soon. *If he ever got a spare minute.*

Still smarting over his encounter with Curtis Blaise, Jonah threw himself into finishing the set up. How could he work for the man? He couldn't fill out an application. He didn't have a diploma or GED. He wasn't entirely sure he could read a blueprint based on the drawings alone. He just couldn't pull it off.

Once Quinn taught him to read, he'd march over to Blaise's office and ask for that job. If it wasn't too late. If Quinn would ever actually get to the lessons, that is. Okay, last night was mostly his fault. At least he thought it was. Or she made him think it was. He pinched the bridge of his nose and wrinkled his brow.

Quinn Baker. The woman drove him nuts. She showed up for a study lesson wearing a dress and high heels. Did she think he was blind? Those heels accentuated the length of her toned legs.

And the way she'd worn her hair down, where he'd been able to see just how far it went down her back, all fluffy sex kitten? Oh, and that tight button-down blouse? After seeing her in oversized shirts and worn plaids, it gave new meaning to torture. A man can only take so much, and a man who had been alone since his wife died three years earlier was easy pickings.

Yet she didn't seem to notice how randy he'd been as soon as she walked in the door. She'd been focused on her books, her papers, her damned writing utensils. He couldn't concentrate on learning, not with the scent of her fruity shampoo luring him in.

Then he'd showed her the cradle. He'd been so proud. Yeah, he might not be able to read, but he could create something of beauty out of wood. Something that would last for generations. He'd wanted her approval. Instead, he'd made her cry.

Had she lost a baby? She'd wept like her heart was breaking. It had torn him apart. All he could think of was comforting her, making those awful sobs stop. At least until she'd started feasting on his neck. Not even a saint could have resisted those tentative licks, the shy kisses. Jonah grew hard at the memory.

"Hey, Jonah. I could use some help with the coffee urns." Stanley Gifford, owner of the only grocery store in town, threw cold water on Jonah's sizzling thoughts. Thank goodness.

The two men headed for the back of Stan's pick up to retrieve several industrial-sized urns. Jonah knew from experience that one of them would hold hot apple cider. His mouth watered just thinking about it. He and Lily would have to come back and enjoy some once the festival was in full swing.

Carrying one of the urns up the small grassy hill to the lawn outside town hall, Jonah spied the woman crowding his thoughts, coming toward him on the sidewalk. She wore a thick ivory sweater jacket, belted at the waist, with wickedly tall leather boots and painted-on jeans. The sun glinted off her sparkly dangling earrings.

Quinn lifted her arm and waggled her fingers at him. *Please forgive me.* He adjusted the heavy metal container against his shoulder, shielding his eyes, and pretended he hadn't seen her.

He could not afford Quinn's kind of distraction today. Out of the corner of his eye he saw her drop her hand. Her shoulders drooped. She hadn't bought it. He was a jerk.

By the time he'd finished helping out Stan, Quinn was nowhere in sight. He owed her an apology, both for hiding from her today and for forcing her to face some really difficult memories last night. Perusing the vendor tables, now full of homemade goodies, handcrafted items, and all kinds of treasures, Jonah tried to think of a gift. What did one buy their teacher/child care provider? Never mind that she was actually so much more than that.

The library had set out a table of old books. Some were leather bound and shiny gold on the outside of the pages. Jonah fingered one. It sure was beautiful. But for all he knew, he could end up buying Quinn a book about fly-fishing. Better leave the book buying to her. The sun glinted off something shiny on the next table over. Attracted, Jonah headed toward it.

The table was full of jewelry, baubles, earrings and such. Everything lay against a cloth of deep purple velvet. Heck, he wasn't even a woman and it had managed to draw him in. There, in the center, was a butterfly hair clip. True, he sure loved to see her wearing her hair down, but it seemed Quinn preferred to keep it out of her face. This was a lot prettier than those pencils she stuck in a bun.

The price tag took all but a dollar of the cash he'd stuffed in the pocket of his worn-out jeans. Looked like Lily would be getting the only cup of hot cider today. Smiling at the older woman who'd sold him the hair clip, Jonah took the small bag in a shaky hand and went to find his daughter. They had a delivery to make.

CHAPTER 8

They couldn't have asked for better weather for Octoberfaire. Quinn decided not to dwell on the fact that Jonah had brushed her off as she'd been walking home from the bakery. Turning her face to the sun, she smiled, happy to shirk her responsibilities, and leave all her adult worries behind.

She couldn't have found a better opportunity to reacquaint herself with everyone in town. Folks came out in droves to sample the goodies, get a jump-start on holiday shopping, and enjoy getting out in the crisp autumn weather. One last hurrah before they battened down the hatches for a harsh New England winter.

Given that Kayla was busy, she'd probably welcome the chance for the girls to get out and have some fun. Quinn couldn't wait to bond with her nieces. Were they into jewelry yet? Or should she steer them toward the handcrafted toys? Did Farmer Miller still offer pony rides? Crystal would be ecstatic.

Jake answered the door, his smile hesitant. He seemed almost nervous. Ushering her inside, he offered to take her jacket.

"Actually, I know Kayla is busy working today. I thought I might take the girls off your hands and head down to Octoberfaire. Think they'd enjoy it?"

"Oh, I'm sure they would." Jake turned his head, but not before he could hide a look of discomfort.

"Is it a bad idea? Too awkward? I know they barely know me." Quinn reached out a hand and forced her brother-in-law to meet her gaze.

"It's not the girls. They would love to spend time with you." He pressed his lips together tightly, as though it were an effort to bite his tongue.

"It's my wicked sister, isn't it? Oh, wait. She would have painted *me* as the wicked one. 'Quinn left us. Quinn thinks she's too good for us. I'm not going to let my girls spend time with an aunt who is just going to leave them when she gets bored.'"

Jake chuckled, implying that she'd been quite accurate in her assessment. But his laugh also let her know that he didn't agree with his wife. He looked more relaxed. She'd always liked Jake and it seemed he felt the same. Quinn knew she could count on her brother-in-law as an ally. It was sad that she even had to think in those terms.

"So I can take them to Octoberfaire?"

"If she asks, you snuck up on me, knocked me out, and stole the girls away for a day of decadence and ruin." He held his hands to his head, practicing the ferocious headache he'd have when he "came to."

"Thank you, Jake." Quinn threw her arms around him and gave him a loud kiss on the cheek. She hollered, "Girls? Grab your jackets, we're going to stuff ourselves silly at Octoberfaire."

Excited shouts preceded her nieces as they flew into the foyer. Jake tried to press a wad of bills into her hand and Quinn skipped out of reach. She dropped a kiss onto each little girl's head and opened the front door. Jake walked out and got the girls' booster seats from their minivan, transferring them to Quinn's BMW.

The short ride downtown was filled with girlish chatter. Quinn's smile was wide. She'd made the right choice, coming home. She had missed so much of their lives. And they were such animated, intelligent little girls. She couldn't wait to really get to know them.

"Hmm ... kettle corn or warm donuts? Oh! I see roasted nuts. How about those?"

"Crystal's allergic to nuts. If she eats them she'll die," Zoe announced dramatically.

Well, she could check off one thing she hadn't known about Crystal.

"Anything else either of you may be allergic to, before we figure out what to eat?"

"Nope. Not that we know about … yet." Zoe was reminding Quinn a lot of Kayla.

"Let's do the donuts. We can get something from the clam bake later."

They walked around with their warm donuts, exclaiming over the different displays. Billy Dale, a local musician, belted out covers of slightly outdated country tunes.

"Nanny used to take us here every year. There was a booth where kids could make their own Christmas ornaments. It was only October, but we always saw this festival as the kickoff to the holiday season." Quinn's eyes were shining as she took in the sights.

"Mommy never told us that." Crystal slipped her hand into Quinn's bigger one.

"I bet she never told you that every year we'd get our faces painted. I loved to get something new every year. And each year she'd get a red rose. I used to bug her about being so boring. She'd just turn up her nose and say she liked what she liked and that was that."

They continued to walk the village green, pausing to check out displays. The girls stopped to ooh and aah over a table full of baby things. Quinn stood behind them, swallowing hard as she watched Zoe fingering a delicate white blanket. She laid a shaky hand on the girl's shoulder.

"How come you don't have kids, Aunt Quinn," Crystal looked up at her aunt, curiously.

Before she could answer, Zoe piped up. "Mom says you couldn't be bothered with kids. That some women were born to be mothers and some women just wanted to have fun and no responsibilities."

Ouch. Both girls were watching her, so Quinn had no choice but to suppress her feelings. She felt as if Kayla had dug her talons in and ripped her heart from her chest. Acid churned in her stomach, slowly bubbling up her throat and she prayed she wouldn't embarrass herself by throwing up. Did her own sister hate her that much?

"I love kids. I love babies. I would have given anything to be a mother. But sometimes, we don't get what we want. Even when we want it more than anything else in the world." She smoothed a lock of hair away from Crystal's forehead.

"Well, maybe someday you'll have one. It just hasn't happened yet." Crystal said, hopefully.

"You have to be married to get babies, silly." Zoe spoke down to her sister. "And Aunt Quinn isn't married anymore."

"I'll put it in my prayers tonight that you get married again and have babies, okay, Aunt Quinn?" Crystal gave her aunt a quick squeeze.

Quinn couldn't even reply, for fear she'd burst into tears. She nodded and gestured for the girls to move along. They had spotted the pony rides and Quinn couldn't have been more relieved. She paid the high school kid who stood at the entrance and moved off to wait until the ride was over. Waving to the girls, she glanced at a nearby table of handcrafted items.

A husband and wife team had set up their display of stained glass night-lights. They were quite beautiful, and Quinn imagined they'd really look amazing when lit in a pitch-black room. She spied a horse one that might appeal to Crystal. But she had probably outgrown the night-light stage. Then her attention was drawn to one shaped like a fairy. The curved wings were opaque, the dress a pretty lavender. Her hair was dark ... just like Lily's. On impulse, she purchased the night-light and dropped the little paper bag into her purse. Lily had a birthday coming up next month. This would be perfect.

Zoe and Crystal were just heading for the pony ride exit when Quinn walked up. She bought them some hot chocolate at a nearby stand and led them to a patch of grass, out of the way. Crystal chattered on about what she wanted to see. Zoe nodded at a group of girls as they walked past. Conversation lulled, so Quinn tried to fill the silence.

"I bet you two are sad that Nanny is gone, huh?"

"I guess so." Zoe shrugged. "We never really saw her much."

"She lived right in town. What do you mean you didn't see her?" Quinn looked from one girl to the other.

"Daddy would come pick her up for Thanksgiving and Christmas. And we always parked at her house for the 4th of July parade," Crystal offered.

Nanny had kept Quinn informed on the happenings of her nieces when Kayla had been less than communicative. She'd just assumed this was because she saw them often. Why would Kayla keep her girls away from their great-grandmother? Especially when she was the only family in town? Quinn had a lot of questions for her sister.

"Quinn, Quinn!" Heading up the slope of the little hill they sat on was Lily. Her father was not far behind.

"Hey, cutie patootie! You enjoying Octoberfaire?" Quinn reached out and drew the little girl into her lap. She patted the ground beside her, hoping that Jonah would stop looming over them all, like a great silent giant.

"I got to help put out the programs. An' Daddy put all the tables 'n chairs out for everyone to put their stuff on. He's super strong." Lily flashed her dad a huge smile.

"Wow, so this all wouldn't have happened if it weren't for you two." Quinn grinned at the pride shining on Lily's face. "You must have met my nieces, Zoe and Crystal? Nanny was their great-grandmother." Quinn nodded at Lily and then the girls.

"I saw your pictures up on the fireplace. Nanny talked about you too." Lily smiled shyly.

"Nice to meet you. What's your name?" Zoe was visibly charmed by the tiny girl.

"I'm Lily an' this is my daddy. Nanny was our nanny too." Lily set her chin in a defensive expression, just in case she was called to battle over her rights to her surrogate grandmother.

"How did you know Nanny? Did she come to your house for dinner, sometimes, too?" Crystal asked Lily.

"Nanny watchded me so Daddy could work. I took naps at her house an' she made me lunch." Lily looked up into Quinn's face. "An' now Quinn does it."

Zoe collected the empty cups of cocoa and ran them down to a trash bin. Then she came back and asked if the girls could play tag under the big maple tree nearby. Distracted, Quinn waved them over. She looked up to find Jonah watching her.

"The more time I spend in this town, the more questions I have about my family. At first I thought Kayla hated just me. I have no idea why. But now it seems like Nanny was on her hit list too." She chewed her bottom lip, ignoring the impulse to scoot close enough to Jonah to lean against his broad chest.

"I couldn't afford to pay Nanny to watch Lily. I asked her not to go announcing it. It's stupid. I just like to keep a low profile around town. The less people know about our business the better."

The less people knew about him, the better chance he had of folks not uncovering his secret. Quinn got that. She had her own set of secrets she didn't want spread around town. She glanced over, suddenly remembering that things were supposed to be awkward between them.

"I'm sorry about last night," they spoke at the same time.

Reaching behind him, Jonah withdrew a small bag and held it out to her. He nodded at her to take it. Admittedly curious, Quinn accepted the bag, dived inside, and gasped with pleasure when she pulled out the beautiful butterfly hair clip.

"It's gorgeous, Jonah! But I don't understand. Why?" Withdrawing the ever-present sketch pencil from her hair, she twisted her long locks back into place and added her new clip. She turned her head to let him see.

"Call it a peace offering. An apology. You've got things you're dealing with and I seem to have made it worse." Jonah caught her eye and held her gaze. "But I'm not sorry about that kiss. I should be. We have a student/teacher relationship and I had no business messing with that." His light eyes darkened just a shade. "But we've got some kind of chemistry that I think is going to be pretty hard to ignore."

"Well, we have to find a way." Quinn turned away, unable to watch the pained expression on Jonah's face, as though she'd slapped him with her words. "It's for the best. Trust me. You're a good guy. You deserve someone who can make you happy."

"And you can't do that?"

"I ... I can't make you happy, no. I'm sorry." Her mind chose this most inappropriate moment to picture Jonah naked. Her cheeks bloomed a bright pink.

The girls shrieked and giggled a few feet away. The sun shone bright overhead. The sights, sounds, and smells that had filled her with joy just moments before, now seemed duller, shrouded in fog. Quinn closed her eyes, silently wishing for the bustling anonymity of life in the city. But even if she wanted to run back to the city, she had nothing left to run back to. It was time to start over.

• • •

"You had no right to take my girls out without asking me." Kayla had pushed her way through the front door and didn't stop until she was standing in the middle of Nanny's living room.

"Good Lord, this isn't a custody issue. I asked Jake and he said it was fine." Quinn shuddered to think about the fallout her brother-in-law had suffered because of her.

"Jake doesn't know you like I do." Kayla sneered.

"And I am some horribly bad influence who would do your children irreparable harm? Kay, do you realize how irrational that sounds?"

"They're my girls, my children. I raise them the way I see fit. If you had bothered to have any kind of contact with them, I might feel differently. But you didn't want them, just like you didn't want kids of your own."

"Okay, first of all, I have always kept up with your girls. When you stopped returning calls and emails, Nanny sent me pictures and updates. I always wanted to know about them.

"As far as having children of my own, that is my business and none of your concern. You don't get to judge me just because I have never given birth." Quinn kept the longing she felt out of her tone. Kayla didn't need any more ammunition.

"Just leave my girls alone. You're only here to pack up Nanny's house and then you'll be on to your next adventure. They are only going to get hurt if they become attached. I won't let that happen."

Quinn bounced down onto the couch and hugged a throw pillow to her chest. Where did this animosity come from? She closed her eyes and silently counted to ten before continuing. Opening her eyes, she was just in time to see Kayla pocket a tiny figurine on a side table by Nanny's rocking chair.

"Kay, I never meant to give you the impression that I was taking off again after we sell Nanny's house. If I made you think that, I am sorry."

"You're staying? You can't stay. You have nowhere to live." Kayla sounded like she was anxious to see her sister leave.

"I was thinking I could buy you out. You sell your half of Nanny's house to me. Then it would stay in the family. I could stay in Scallop Shores. I'd be a permanent part of the girls' lives."

Kayla wrinkled her nose like she'd just inhaled something unpleasant. Still standing, she turned and looked down at Quinn.

"You left us. You lost your chance. Nanny wouldn't want you to have her house. Just give it up. Move on. No one wants you here." Her triumphant smile told Quinn that she could see her words had hit their target.

"I went off to school. There were opportunities for me in the city. I wasn't deliberately abandoning you. Kay, I love you. I love the girls. I came back to start over, make amends. Why are you making that so hard?" Her sister's rigid stance meant a hug was out of the question.

"You'll leave again. It's best if you do it now. You said yourself, there are opportunities for you in the city. So go there. Be wildly successful. Marry another moneybags and drop us a postcard every once in a while."

"You're jealous? Is that what this is all about? Are you freaking kidding me?" Quinn threw the pillow aside and leapt up. "You're jealous of a sister who has done absolutely nothing with her art degree. A sister who has zero to show for a life in the city. A sister who has no job, no husband, and no kids.

"Kayla, you have it all. A loving husband, two beautiful children, a salon that you built from the ground up. If anyone should be jealous, it's me. And I'm not." All the bluster went out of her speech. Shoulders slumped, Quinn continued. "I'm happy for you. I'm proud of you. And I miss my baby sister. I just want to be part of your life again."

"That's sweet," Kayla said flippantly, "but I'm perfectly fine with the way things have been."

"I'm not going anywhere. You need to get used to that. I'm staying in Scallop Shores. I'll find my purpose. I may not know what it is yet, but I'll find it." Quinn stepped closer and forced Kayla to meet her gaze. "And I intend to get to know my nieces. They are beautiful, intelligent little girls and I can't wait to spend time with them."

Kayla tossed her hair back and swept regally from the room. She paused before opening the front door. "We'll see. I think you'll find that moving back to the city is in your best interest." Then she was gone.

Had that been a threat? Did Kayla intend to sabotage her chances of making a living in Scallop Shores? Could she do that? Quinn paused to study an old photo of her and Kayla, the year they had moved in with Nanny. When had her sister become such a bitter, unforgiving woman? Was it really all her fault? No. She'd made mistakes in her life, but she refused to take responsibility for the way Kayla turned out.

Heading into the kitchen, Quinn opened a can of cat food for Grizzabella, whose insistent yowling reminded her she was behind schedule. She opened the fridge and stared blindly, her mind on her conversation with Kayla, not on food. She needed a purpose. She needed a job.

Grabbing the jug of milk from the bottom shelf, she poured herself a glass and sat down at the table. She had a reason to stay—two reasons, Jonah and Lily. She'd made a promise to help him learn how to read. It was a noble request and she would do anything she could to help him improve himself. And Lily. The little princess had already wormed her way into her heart. She'd do anything for Jonah's daughter.

But neither one of those would pay the bills. If Quinn could convince Kayla to sell her half of Nanny's house, it would take up all of the settlement money that Andrew had paid her in the divorce. Depending on when that was settled, she'd need a job pretty quick. She'd need something that didn't interfere with the hours that Jonah needed her to watch Lily. And then she had to be around in the evenings to tutor Jonah in reading. What did that leave, the graveyard shift? Who needed sleep anyway?

Quinn rinsed out her milk glass and headed for her room. She'd take a long, hot shower and then she had a date with some Norse gods. Snapping off the light switch, she called for Grizzabella and trudged her way upstairs.

CHAPTER 9

Jonah left Lily and Quinn in the backyard of Nanny's house, raking leaves. They were laughing and squealing and having all sorts of fun. Fun that he'd love to join in but didn't have the time. He needed to get the stair railing and a couple of steps fixed inside. He needed to cut out a frame for the new window going in the attic, for Quinn's art studio. He needed to line up more jobs.

Hauling the planks he'd just cut through the back door, Jonah left them on his drop cloth and reached for his jug of water. He envied the girls. Lily didn't have a care in the world, her biggest problem being which flavor to choose for her cake, as her birthday was coming up in a couple of weeks. And Quinn had just decided to buy Nanny's house for herself. She was so excited to be putting down roots in her old hometown. She didn't have a job, yet she was buying a house. Oh, to have her kind of worries.

Jonah, on the other hand, was freaking out about property taxes coming due next month. Even if he lined up enough jobs, which would probably keep him working twenty-four seven for the foreseeable future, he wasn't sure everyone would be able to pay him right away. He couldn't be late with that tax money and risk accruing interest and penalties.

Setting a plank into place, Jonah stuffed a few nails between his lips for easy access. He drove the first nail home then grabbed another. Quinn's husky laughter rang out through the open back door. His finger slipped across the nail head just as he was swinging the hammer down. The string of curses that came flying out of his mouth, along with the extra nails, were not words that he was especially proud of his daughter hearing. But hear them she did, because two sets of footsteps thundered up the back steps.

"Daddy, Daddy! Are you okay?" Lily squirmed in Quinn's arms, trying to see around her caregiver.

"Is everything all right? Are you hurt?" Quinn looked squeamish, like she was trying to check for gushing blood but didn't want to see it, at the same time. She continued to shield the little girl until given the word that all was clear.

"I'm fine. I just hammered my stupid finger."

"That's a bad word, Daddy." Lily put her hands on her hips. "Well, that and a bunch of the others you just said."

Quinn glided to Jonah's side, kneeling on the step below. She took his hand and pulled it into her lap so she could see the injury better. Jonah held his breath and tried to resist leaning against her bosom as she played nursemaid. While she studied his swollen finger, he studied the lean column of her neck, the delicate shell of her ear, and the tiny diamond stud in her earlobe.

"This needs some ice, I believe. Nurse Lily, can you assist?" Quinn stood up, gripping Jonah's hand so that he understood he was to go with them. Lily bounced along behind.

Quinn let go of his hand so she could get the ice tray out of the freezer. Jonah stifled the groan that almost escaped over the sudden sense of loss. "*Get a grip, Goodwin,*" he mumbled under his breath. Lily threw her arms around his legs and hugged him tight. He patted her head with the hand that wasn't throbbing like a son of a gun.

"I have Strawberry Shortcake Band-Aids at home," Lily offered.

"It's not bad enough for a Band-Aid, Cuteness. But I sure do appreciate the offer." Jonah threw her a wink.

"Here we go, Mr. Butterfingers. We'll have you all fixed up in no time."

Quinn reached for the hand with the injured finger, set it inside her homemade icepack, and just before she wrapped the pack around the finger, she dropped a kiss onto the swollen tip. Jonah almost swallowed his tongue.

"I'm, uh … I'm … "

"Thankful for being doctored up by two of the most skilled nurses in Scallop Shores?" This time it was Quinn's turn to wink at Lily.

"I was going to say, I'm not a butterfingers. It was just an accident. Accidents happen." And if Quinn weren't around to distract him, they'd happen a heck of a lot less.

"Uh huh. You're welcome." To Lily she asked, "Is your dad always such a cranky patient?"

"Yep," was his daughter's simple answer. And she was right.

The girls returned to their leaf pile, and with the admonishment that he be more careful, Jonah returned to installing the new stairs and railing. He kept his mind on his work and whistled a tune to drown out the sounds of frivolity in the backyard. He only had nine more fingers, and he needed all of them in order to get his work done.

After the stairs were finished, he headed to the attic to frame out the new studio. Once the new window was installed, Quinn would have some amazing natural light to work by. But first she needed some real walls, not just insulation covered ones, and a safer floor. Jonah was framing it out so there would be a storage room for the things that were already up in the attic. She'd have a real retreat here, by the time he was done.

The day flew by and he was taping up the framing job for the new window that he would pick up tomorrow. Jonah cleaned up his work area and carried all his tools back out to his truck. Lily was waiting for him when he went back in to get her.

"Look what I did, Daddy!" She held out a piece of paper for him to see.

This word he could read. L-I-L-Y. She had written her name for the first time. Kneeling down in front of his daughter, he choked back tears of pride. His baby had written her first word, and she wasn't even four years old yet. She wasn't going to be like her daddy after all. This kid was going places.

"That's my girl. You show the world what you've got." He folded her into a hug and rested his cheek on top of her head.

Quinn stood off to the side, watching them, looking uncertain. Jonah caught her wary gaze and she mouthed, "I wasn't sure." He nodded his approval, giving her a thumbs-up and the biggest, most grateful grin he could muster.

"Go get your jacket on and meet me out at the truck, Ms. Cuteness." He stood up and swatted his daughter lightly on the bottom.

He and Quinn stood alone in the foyer. She still looked as though she had done something to step on his toes. He wanted to take her in his arms and assure her she'd done nothing wrong. He settled for squeezing her shoulder and whispering a quick "thank you" in her ear.

"You'll be by in a few hours then?"

"Wouldn't miss it." She grinned.

"I promise to focus more on my studies this time." His own grin was a tad devilish.

"No kissing."

"Well, I promise not to start anything, if you promise not to start anything." This time he chuckled as a blush spread from her cheeks to the edge of her hairline.

"Flirt." She gave him a shove out the front door.

"Later, Teach." He gave her a wink and headed for the truck.

His smile slowly faded as Jonah drove back to his own house. Yes, they had chemistry. He knew they'd be hot together. But that's all they had. If he were honest with himself, he had to admit that Quinn was too good for him. She would have made the perfect mom for Lily. The only thing ruining it was him.

He wasn't smart enough for a woman like Quinn. Sure, he'd been up front about his shortcomings. She knew his dirty little secret. She wasn't in for the horrible shock that sent Paige rushing off to her death. But in the end, it was Quinn who had taught Lily how to write her name. It would probably be Quinn who taught her a great deal more. That was too much to compete with in a relationship.

Quinn was great for a teacher and a caregiver for Lily. But that's all she could ever be. She deserved the kind of brainy guy who could hold up his end of a conversation when discussing literature or whatever new topic she had got it in her head to learn about. She deserved someone worthy of her.

Later that evening Lily dragged him back to the kitchen table, after he'd finished the dishes. "Daddy, let me show you how I write my name."

He was grateful. He was humbled. Thinking back to earlier that morning when Quinn kissed his finger, he was very, very frustrated.

• • •

"She thinks you hung the moon, you know."

"I don't know about that. After today, I'd say we were about tied."

Quinn sat at the battered kitchen table, waiting for Jonah to fix their coffee. He wore a different flannel shirt than earlier, and his dark hair was still damp. She might have liked to pick up where they had left off earlier, but the easygoing, flirtatious man who had left her house not so long ago was gone. The Jonah in front of her now was surly, trying too hard to be businesslike. But she wasn't stupid. She could sense the vulnerability that lay just beneath the surface.

"I thought you'd be happy. But I shouldn't have assumed. Lily is your daughter. It's your job to teach her these things."

"Well, she's got to wait for me to learn them first then, huh?" Jonah snapped back.

His shoulders slumped and he swore under his breath. Setting a mug of coffee in front of Quinn, he slid into the chair beside her and stared down at a knot in the heavy oak table. They were silent for a few moments. She sipped her coffee and waited. "It's rough, you know? Not knowing things I should have learned when I was a kid. Then trying to keep that a secret from Lily and the rest of the world. You're lucky. You are so smart, so confident. You decide you want something and the world just opens up for you." He peered sideways at her.

"Ha! Is that what you think? Oh, Jonah, you have it so wrong." Quinn's laughter had a hysterical edge to it. "There are so many things I want that I can't have. Even if I were the most intelligent, well-read woman in the world, I still couldn't have them."

His brows lifted and he parted his lips, like he wanted to ask. But he didn't. She raised her mug to her face, the hot steam relaxing the tension away. Of course he was curious. She took another sip, deciding to throw him a bone.

"I'm supposed to be this hotshot artist. I got a paid scholarship to a school in New York. Then I stayed. So the whole town thinks I'm some big deal. But I'm not. I'm just me. I'm a fraud."

"Why would you say that? You sound like you think you've got this obligation to the town, to make a name for yourself through your art. You don't owe anyone. You do what you need to do for you, no one else."

"You sound like Nanny." Quinn knocked her knee against his, yanking it back when the zing of awareness was almost too much to handle.

"Hey, you weren't the only one she lectured. I mean, talked to." Jonah covered his mouth with a fist, as he fake-coughed.

"How come you didn't ask her to teach you to read? You could have trusted her, you know."

"I was this close." He held his finger and thumb about an inch apart. "Guess I just waited too long." His smile was sad.

They worked on the lesson for a while. Jonah was a fast learner and Quinn tried to heap on the praise without sounding condescending. With progress came confidence and she felt a small thrill at being the one to bring that joyous smile to his beautiful eyes.

Quinn leaned back in her chair, working the kinks out of her neck as they took a break from reading.

"So Kayla is going to let you buy her out?"

"She didn't want to, but I offered to pay cash. I saw dollar signs in those mean little rat eyes of hers."

"Ouch. Is she really that awful?"

"It's mostly directed at me, or so it would seem. I wish I knew why. Something to do with my leaving town. She's being so childish. Doesn't want me spending time with her girls. Says I'm going to abandon them again."

"Are you?" He pierced her with those pale eyes and she realized he was thinking about himself and Lily.

"Of course not! I'm back in Scallop Shores to stay. Heck, I'm buying a house. If that doesn't scream 'putting down roots,' then I don't know what would."

Jonah nodded, tearing his eyes away and having the good grace to look chastised. Quinn softened her words with a smile. She fingered the corner of a page from the textbook they were using. She took a deep breath and sat up straighter.

"So I'm thinking I should get a job soon. Only … "

"Only you've got this non-paying babysitting gig that's really messing up your flexibility." He grimaced.

"I offered."

"Very graciously. Now we need to figure something else out." Jonah tapped out a staccato beat on the table with his pencil.

"What if it's something where I can bring her with me?"

"Sweetheart, I tried that. It's not the life I want for her."

"No, you don't understand. You've got a very specific skill set. Having a small child around power tools is dangerous." She leaned back in her chair, chewing her lower lip as she worked this over in her brain.

"You want to use your own skill set? Your art." She could see Jonah warming to her idea.

"I can paint." Quinn mused.

"Like houses? Getting on ladders?"

"No, silly. Like murals, or storefront window designs. Nurseries, kids' bedrooms." She grinned huge. She was liking this.

"What would you charge for something like that?" Jonah had refilled her coffee and set a fresh cup in front of her.

"I have no idea. But Lily could help! Oh, she'd love that." She was bouncing in her chair now. "Tomorrow we can hit the streets, see what kind of business we can drum up in town. Then we could figure out some sort of advertising. Lily loves challenging me with drawing projects." They both chuckled over this.

The evening's mood now energized, Quinn and Jonah went back to the reading lesson. She wasn't sure who started it, but they began to find excuses to touch. A quick meeting of knees, a brush of fingers when they both reached to turn a page at the same time. Quinn found she liked this. Something about Jonah dared her to be bolder, less panicked. She'd forgotten how good it was to touch, to be touched.

She thought about earlier that day. When he had hollered out in pain, she'd been so scared. She only calmed down once she saw there was no blood. Ice she could handle. She'd surprised herself when she kissed his finger before wrapping it in ice. It would appear she had surprised Jonah too. His eyes had become hooded and she thought she might have imagined him leaning closer.

A curious thrill had her wondering what might have happened, had Lily not been hovering at their knees. A wild thought came to mind. Could Jonah help her? Would he be willing to teach her ... how to please a man? Just as quickly, a different thought chilled her. What if it wasn't something that could be taught? What if you either had it or you didn't? Andrew was convinced she didn't have it. Quinn was suddenly determined to prove him wrong.

"Hey, where did you go?" Jonah nudged her shoulder.

"Hmm?" She blinked, owlishly, focusing on his amused face. Pink suffused her cheeks. Oh, if he only knew.

"It's getting late. You should get home and get some rest so you and Lily can go on your grand job searching adventure tomorrow."

Quinn searched out a clock, finding the digital reading on the microwave on the counter. Good grief, it was almost one in the morning! Where had the time gone? She scrambled up from the table, rinsing her cup in the sink and gathering her books.

"Hey, would it be okay if you left them here? I thought maybe I could practice. On my own ... " He looked unsure.

"Absolutely. I think that would be a great idea." Quinn lifted the books and placed them in his hands. "I'm sorry I kept you up so late. I think we did enough studying for two nights."

"Does that mean you won't be coming over tomorrow?" Her heart tripped as she detected disappointment in the tone of his voice.

"If the student wishes it ... " Her own voice was slightly husky as she considered the other student/teacher role she had in mind.

Jonah stared hard before shaking his head and turning away. He didn't meet her gaze as he walked her to the door. Embarrassed, Quinn felt like she'd been drinking wine instead of coffee, loosening her tongue and making her say completely inappropriate things.

Why did she always seem to walk calmly into Jonah's house, yet run out humiliated? She said a quick "goodnight" and willed her feet to take her slowly and steadily to her car. She would not run away again.

CHAPTER 10

She noticed the strange glow first, hovering just over the top of the trees. As Quinn drove closer to home, she caught glimpses of flashing lights, red and white, blinking from behind trees and houses. Her gut told her it was Nanny's house. Conflicted, she wanted to floor the gas pedal and hurry home, yet she also wanted to throw the car in reverse and get as far away from the horror she knew would be waiting.

Quinn had to park halfway down the street. The acrid smell of burning wood, plastic, who knew what, choked her lungs, stung her eyes, made her nose run. Her quaking legs took her half walking/half running up the street. Three different fire engines blocked Nanny's once-tidy driveway. Firemen in full turnout gear trampled the flowerbeds, their heavy hoses crushing Nanny's shrubs.

It was then she looked up and saw the entire house engulfed in flames. It wouldn't matter that the yard was destroyed. She wouldn't need a yard if she had no house to walk up to. Quinn staggered across the street to lean against a tall maple, tears distorting the flames that looked as though they were reaching for the moon.

Most of her things were still in storage in Manhattan. She didn't have anything of value here in Scallop Shores, nothing that couldn't be replaced. Her heart seized. Grizzabella! How could she have forgotten?

"Grizzy? Please, I have to get in there. I have to get my cat out." Quinn felt like she was in a football game, pushing against a wall of firemen who were determined not to let her get her hands on the ball.

"Miss? You need to stay here. Ma'am? It's not safe for you. We've got this."

"Then get her out! Get her out!" A sob choked off her screams. "Quinn?"

Someone gently shook her shoulder. She turned to inflict her wrath on this new interruption. Nanny's neighbor, Mrs. Newman, eighty years old if she was a day, stood shivering in her fuzzy pink bathrobe and slippers.

"Your cat, was it gray, really long haired?" The old woman shuffled closer, peering up at Quinn.

For the first time since she had entered this hell, a sliver of hope had Quinn nodding, one fat tear rolling slowly down her cheek.

"I saw it earlier. Fed it, actually. I was going to ask you about it in the morning."

"You saw Grizzy? She got out in time?"

"Well, I saw her earlier today. She took a nap on my rocking chair, on the back porch. She was still there at dinner, so I fed her some tuna."

Grizzabella must have snuck out when Jonah had the back door open, lugging the lumber in for the stairwell repair. Quinn had been so distracted with Lily that she hadn't noticed the poor cat was missing. Oh, these trucks, the flames—she must be terrified! But she was alive.

"Thank you, Mrs. Newman. Thank you so much!" Quinn threw her arms around the slight figure and sobbed tears of relief.

Turning back to the disaster that was to have been her new house, Quinn hugged herself tightly and watched her dreams go up in smoke … literally. She winced, hearing a window smash under the pressure from the fire hose. A scream slipped past her lips as the front porch collapsed. She knew, now, that there was no saving this house.

She and Kayla had moved out most of Nanny's belongings. They were just things, Nanny would have reminded her. Our memories live in our hearts. And Nanny had no need of memories now.

Though the house was a total loss, the fire was now under control. The neighbors could be certain it would no longer spread to their homes. They began to trickle away, back to their beds. Quinn stood alone, a safe distance from the flying ash and burning debris.

She'd have to call Kayla. Maybe someone already had, and she just didn't care enough to come out. She'd be happy. She hadn't really wanted Quinn to have Nanny's house. But she couldn't pass up the cash. She talked about expanding her salon.

Kayla would use this as an opportunity to push Quinn back to New York. All her things were still there. The job market was better. Everything she needed was in the big city. Quinn bit her lip hard enough to make it bleed. Kayla would benefit if Quinn no longer had a place to live in Scallop Shores. Kayla would get what she wanted—her sister gone. Eyes hard, breath coming out in furious pants, Quinn gritted her teeth and considered whether her sister was capable of arson.

"Ms. Baker? May I have a word?" The fire chief had removed his helmet and heavy gloves. He ducked his head as though he were showing respect for the bereaved. Well, in a way, she had lost a loved one tonight.

He cupped her elbow and guided her through the maze of hoses and firemen to a smaller truck, parked on the corner of her property. Quinn grimaced as she noticed Nanny's white picket fence had been knocked down in order to get the hoses through. Her tears ran in hot tracks, down her cheeks to drip off her chin.

"We can't save it, can we?" As if including herself would make her appear the least bit useful tonight.

"You'll be able to rebuild on this site. I imagine the foundation will remain intact."

If he found the fact that she giggled inappropriate, he didn't say a word.

"One of your neighbors called this in, about midnight. We think it started in the basement."

"How? What caused it? I'm not running the furnace yet. I didn't leave the dryer going."

"We'll have a team come through in the morning. Can you think of anyone who would want to see this house destroyed?"

Yes! The chief was watching her closely. He'd mysteriously pulled out a notebook and pen and was waiting for any scrap of information she could give him. Oh, she could give him plenty. But Kayla was her sister. Even if the woman was cruel enough to start a fire in order to get her to leave town, she was still her sister. She wouldn't rat her out, no matter her suspicions.

"I can't think of anyone." She faltered. "I was going to buy it myself."

His bushy white eyebrow arched, significantly. "And where were you tonight? A Monday night. Most people would have been home sleeping."

Was he accusing her? Did she need an alibi? And how would she explain the one she had? Scallop Shores was a small town. If she said she'd been with Jonah, everyone would assume they were having an affair. He didn't deserve that kind of attention.

"I was helping out a friend." She offered no more and he didn't press her.

"Well, tell this friend they may have just saved your life." He snapped his notebook shut and clipped the pen to the cover. "My suggestion would be to head back there and see if they can't put you up for what's left of the night."

"I will. Thank you."

The chief handed her off to a younger fireman. He ducked his head shyly, introducing himself as Tristan, as though it wouldn't be appropriate to grasp her by the hand, had she not, at least, known his first name. He helped her back over the hoses and around the huge puddles of mud and water.

"Are you okay to drive, ma'am?" He frowned, studying her face as though he expected her to faint at any moment. She gave him a curt nod and turned away, his hovering bringing her closer to another round of tears than she'd like.

Quinn stayed until every last flame was extinguished. She watched the hoses being coiled and put away. She stepped out of the way and let the fire engines rumble past. Standing for a few bleak moments, staring at the charred remains of the house Nanny and Grandpa Will had lived in from the day they got married to their dying days, Quinn let out a long shuddering sigh. Then she folded her bone-weary body into her car, laid the front seat back as far as it would go, and cried herself to sleep.

· · ·

He found her on the neighbor's back porch, rocking rhythmically back and forth in an old wicker chair. Her crazy-haired gray cat sat in her lap, glaring accusingly at Jonah. He took the steps slowly, keeping a close eye on Quinn's furry bodyguard.

"You should have come back last night. Or called me. I'd have come to get you." Nothing. She just kept rocking.

"Quinn, baby, it's time to go. Let's get you home."

"I have no home." Her words were spoken so softly he almost missed them.

Heading for the front of the house, he spoke with Quinn's neighbor, Mrs. Newman. He'd done a few odd jobs for her and knew her to be a kind old lady. She'd offered Quinn breakfast, coffee, tea, but she refused everything. Her cat, on the other hand, had welcomed the saucer of milk and diced chicken that Mrs. Newman left for her.

Jonah asked if she had anything that he could use to transport the cat to his house. He knew he was throwing himself to the gossip mill. She lifted her wispy white head until she could look him in the eye. It was clear she was waiting to be given more information, as though she'd earned the right by helping them out. He returned her stare for stare.

Jonah returned with an old pet carrier that used to belong to Mrs. Newman's late Pomeranian, Fifi. He braced himself for a fight. Whether from the cat or her owner, or both, he wasn't sure. He rounded the corner and crept gingerly up the steps.

"Grizza ... " What the hell was the cat's name? "Quinn, let's put her in here where she's safe." He set the pet carrier on the porch, opening the tiny door.

Sniffing the air, looking from her mistress to the carrier and then sparing a glare for the token male, the cat sprang lightly to her feet. Tail raised high in the air, she lifted her head in a regal pose and sauntered to the plastic crate. She looked back at Jonah as if to say, "You expect me to get in that thing? It smells like wet dog!"

He gave her the same stern look he gave Lily, when his daughter refused to do his bidding. He knew the cat was cussing him out in feline. With a hand under her belly, he helped her into the carrier. She growled deep in her throat but didn't scratch him. He knew she was saving her anger for later, when she'd pee in his shoes. Jonah shuddered. He'd always considered himself more of a dog man.

If he didn't already have the cat to carry, he would have gathered Quinn up as well. She looked so small, so defeated. He settled for pulling her up out of the rocking chair, drawing her into his arms, and willing his own strength into her vulnerable body. She didn't cry, but then he imagined she was probably all cried out. He bent to rest his chin on top of her head. He could smell smoke.

"Come on. You're coming home with me. I'm going to run you a bubble bath and Lily and I will make you the best French toast you've ever had."

"You need to get to work. Just drop us off at your house and I'll watch her so you can go." She spoke tonelessly.

She wasn't thinking clearly. Jonah's plans for the day were to work on her house.

He picked up the cat carrier and braced an arm around Quinn's shoulders, leading her down the porch stairs. He'd parked in Mrs. Newman's driveway, trying to shield Lily from the aftermath of the fire. Bless her, she was still sitting quietly in her car seat, playing with Barbies.

He helped Quinn up into the front of the cab and set the pet carrier on the back seat with Lily.

"Grizzy! Are you coming to my house? Wanna sleep in my room? My bed is big 'nuf for both of us." Lily was delighted to entertain the cat on the way back home.

True to his promise, Jonah ran a bath for Quinn, adding the only bubble bath he had on hand, Disney Princess. Somehow he doubted it was what she was used to. He knew a moment of panic and uncertainty as he led Quinn into the bathroom and waited to see if she snapped out of her funk long enough to know how to get undressed and into the tub. She gave him a shaky smile and gently pushed him toward the door. Thank God! So when the door shut, with him on the opposite side, why did he suddenly feel disappointed?

Lily declined to help him fix breakfast for Quinn, in favor of setting up her new furry friend in her bedroom. He should nix that while he could. Shaking his head as he began to get out the ingredients for French toast, he knew he was already too late. If he knew his daughter, she'd have that cat dressed in doll clothes and riding in a stroller before the morning was out.

He set to work cracking eggs and whisking them with milk, nutmeg, and cinnamon. He knew Quinn probably had no appetite after what she'd been through, but he hoped the delicious aroma wafting from the kitchen would remind her body that it needed to eat. She had looked so fragile, sitting in that chair. Nothing like the woman who had vibrated with excitement while discussing plans for finding work.

Just as he'd added the last piece of toast to the stack on the plate beside the stove, Quinn appeared in the doorway. She wore the longest T-shirt he could find, under an old flannel robe that he no longer used. Jonah was happy to see that the bath had returned color to her cheeks. Her blonde hair was hidden beneath a towel, wrapped like a fancy turban on top of her head. Not a bit of makeup. And, still, she was the sexiest woman he had ever seen.

"You ready for breakfast?" He cleared his throat when he realized his voice had come out several octaves higher than normal.

"I should eat." She shrugged, noncommittally.

Jonah fixed her a plate and threw a couple of slices onto his own plate, so she wouldn't feel weird eating alone. He set down a cup of coffee and a glass of orange juice.

"I wasn't sure which one you'd want." He ducked his head and slid into his chair.

Quinn murmured her thanks and poured a small helping of syrup onto her French toast. Jonah waited until she'd taken a bite and washed it down with juice. Satisfied that she'd behave herself and refuel, he tucked into his own food. He peered out into the hall for Lily, and when he didn't see her, voiced his question.

"Do they know how it started? I mean ... if you're okay talking about it."

"In the basement." She pressed her lips together tightly, shaking her head from side to side. "I just don't know how it could have happened."

Jonah thought hard. Could he have done something that would have started the fire? He always made it a point to clean up at the end of the day on every project. He hadn't been painting or working with chemicals. God, what if it had been him? What if he'd burned down Quinn's house, her future?

"I think I know who did it." Her voice was cold as she stabbed viciously at a forkful of soggy French toast.

"You do?" He tried not to choke on the huge lump that had formed in his throat.

"Kayla."

"Your sister? No. She's family. Family wouldn't do that to each other." Jonah reached out and grasped Quinn's hand across the table. Neither of them spoke for a few moments. He stroked his thumb over the soft skin.

"I can't stay here." Quinn tugged her hand away, staring at the spot where they had just been touching.

"Of course you can. You have nowhere else to go. Given what you're accusing Kayla of, would you really ask her to put you up? Even temporarily?" The way she rolled her eyes and blew out a snort told him his answer.

"But, I … "

"No buts. We owe you big time. You can stay in the spare bedroom. I'd say your cat could stay in there with you, but I think Lily has staked her claim."

She stared for a moment, without speaking. "Fine. But I'll do my fair share of cooking and cleaning. And it goes without saying that you go to work and I will stay home with Lily."

He wondered if she even realized how that sounded. The vision of domestic bliss. It was everything that he secretly wanted, yet realistically knew he did not deserve. Pouring more syrup on French toast that he no longer wanted, Jonah wondered what he'd just gotten himself into. He'd just finished convincing himself that Quinn was off limits. And, like an idiot, he invited temptation to move right into his house. He was nuts.

CHAPTER 11

This is exactly what she had been trying to avoid by staying away while her nieces were little. Quinn kneeled on the bathmat, dodged the occasional spray of bath water, and ignored the longing ache that filled her heart. Lily chattered endlessly, styling her Barbie's hair in the latest bubbly updo. She offered Quinn endless cups of tea, again topped high with frothy bubbles.

Had she been home ... correction, had she a home to go home to, she would have spent a quiet evening with her books. Ironically, things weren't any different when she had been married to Andrew. Sure, they had spent time together, but separate. He usually brought work home and spread out a little workstation surrounding his recliner. Quinn would spend the evening reading, with Grizzabella curled up on her toes.

For so many years she had longed for children to liven up the house. She dreamed of spending those quiet nights with an infant at her breast, her adoring husband gazing lovingly at the sight. She pictured bedtimes, longing for a daughter or two that she could slip into bed with, cuddle and dream about the future. Big dreams. She'd teach her children to reach for the stars, follow their passions.

But the children never came. And Andrew had become more and more withdrawn, less of a husband and more of a roommate. Wanting children had been a passion of Quinn's, and having lost that passion, it was easy to abandon another—her art. She threw herself into learning. It was all she had left.

Now she had the daughter she always wanted in Lily. But it was an illusion. Lily wasn't hers to love and cherish. She was hers to borrow, until someone better came along, someone worthy of Lily and her dad. Being here, living in their house, was far more tortuous than anything Kayla could have dreamed up. She had absolutely everything she could ever want, but it wasn't hers to take.

"Quinn? Will you read me a bedtime story?" Lily yawned.

"I'd be happy to." Happy and sad, at the same time. Quinn put on a bright smile. "You ready to dry off and brush those chompers?"

Jonah ducked his head in the doorway. "I'm done with the dishes. You want me to take over? You've done so much already."

"Hey, how often can you just sit down and put your feet up for a few minutes?" Quinn wrapped the little girl in a fuzzy towel and motioned for Jonah to go. "Shoo! We're having some girl time."

Lily liked this and giggled. She wrapped her warm, damp arms around Quinn's neck and hugged her tight. "I'm sad about Nanny's house. But I'm happy you came to live with us. You can be my mommy now. I love you, Quinn."

Quinn threw a panicked look over the child's head at Jonah, who stood frozen in the doorway. Neither of them said a word. She saw his Adam's apple work in his throat and he wiped his palms against his faded jeans. His jaw was rigid and she could plainly read the misery in his eyes. With a small shake of his head, he disappeared. Quinn rested a cheek against Lily's wet hair.

"I love you, too, sweetheart."

She finished Lily's bedtime routine, her heart aching the whole time. Jonah had looked just as lonely and bad off as she. And she wasn't the one to help him. Oh, how she'd have given anything to be the one. But he deserved a real woman in his life, in his bed.

And Lily. Lily deserved siblings, brothers and sisters that she could spoil with love and attention, teach them everything she had learned about life in her almost four years.

Jonah wasn't upstairs when she finally came out of Lily's room. She knew where to find him, though. Heading down to the basement, Quinn could hear the steady scritch-scratch of the sandpaper as Jonah worked on the baby cradle perched on top of his workbench. She slipped onto a stool on the opposite side of the bench and watched quietly. After a few minutes of silence, he spoke.

"You're good for her. I'm really happy that she has you for … girl time." He quirked his mouth in a sort of half-smile.

"But?" She knew there was more left unsaid than he was willing to put into words.

"I don't think we should encourage this 'mommy' angle. I mean, I want her to have a mother. She needs one."

"Just not me." Though she'd been about to say exactly the same thing, hearing it coming from Jonah wounded her.

"I'm not saying you wouldn't make a good mother. You'd make a great mom. Someday you'll make a great mom." He backpedaled, seeming desperate to say the right thing.

"Before you dig yourself any deeper, just stop." She smiled gently. "I won't be a mom. I can't be a mom." She reached out and ran her fingers over one of the spindles that had yet to be stained.

"You can't? Can't have kids?" Jonah frowned so hard he almost looked angry. He glanced down at the cradle and then at Quinn. "That's why you cried when I showed you the cradle. I was reminding you of what you can't have."

He threw the sandpaper down in disgust and swiped a hand over his face. "And now by offering you a place to stay, I've really shoved a bad situation in your face."

"No, you are helping me out. I was screwed, Jonah. I needed a place to stay. Kayla wouldn't put me up, even if I had asked. You did a friend a favor and I can't thank you enough."

"But then I tell you not to expect it to be permanent. I didn't mean … "

"It's okay. You're absolutely right. Lily needs a mom. But you need a wife, too. And that woman has to be a good fit for both of you." She drew her hand back and studied her fingernails, unable to meet his eyes.

"I'm not interested in a wife. I tried that. It didn't work out." His voice was gruff.

"I thought, I mean Kayla told me you lost your wife in a car accident."

She chanced a look at Jonah. His chest rose and fell rapidly. The icy fire in his eyes shot out sparks. He gripped the workbench with white knuckles.

"I did. Paige slid on a patch of black ice. She shouldn't have been out on a night like that." He offered no more.

Okay, she should give him his alone time. Quinn nodded and slid off the stool, smoothing out the new sweater she'd picked up on their shopping trip earlier in the day. She should go put away the rest of her new things. Jonah stepped around the workbench and grabbed her arm before she could go.

"I'm not trying to hurt you. I just want to make it clear that I need to find a mother for Lily. I'm not looking for a wife." He shook his head, clearly frustrated that he couldn't articulate this better.

"Well, since I'm not looking for either role, then we're fine. See? No feelings hurt." Quinn stared pointedly at Jonah's hand encircling her upper arm, his fingers searing her skin through the thick fabric of her sweater.

"Okay. We're good?" He didn't seem to realize he was still holding onto her arm.

She looked up to see him gazing intently at her face. Her eyes widened when his tongue came out to wet his lips. Oh, he may not think he needed a wife, but he needed something. Quinn tugged her arm out of his grasp, smiled a thin-lipped smile, and turned tail to run back upstairs to the safety of her borrowed bedroom.

How to keep from driving them both crazy while she was living here? She paced the confines of the small room. They were thrown together in close living quarters. He needed her to watch Lily during the day. He needed her to teach him to read at night. He needed a mother for Lily ... Quinn paused in the middle of the room. He needed a date.

She'd set him up on a date. Then he could find a mother for Lily and someone to help him ... scratch the itch that she could see building more and more each time they were alone together. That way he'd never learn how disappointing it would be to take her to bed. Problem solved. And the sooner she saw Jonah and his new lady love enjoying their new life together, the sooner she could put her own feelings for him to rest.

Scrapping happily-ever-after for something a little more cerebral, Quinn abandoned her pacing to curl up with a new book. Since her book on Norse mythology had burned in the fire, she decided to skip forward in her year of learning mythology to the next one in line: Ancient Egypt. Buried under the covers, she tried to concentrate on Ra, the Sun God. But she had put on Jonah's old T-shirt to sleep in and she could still smell him on the soft, worn fabric.

She closed the book and tossed it on the nightstand, turned off the light and gave her pillow a hearty punch. Reading, learning, soaking up facts had always worked before. Why was she so frustrated now? She groaned into the pillow when she really wanted to scream. It was going to be a long, sleepless night.

CHAPTER 12

He'd had to get away. Jonah made up a story about having to get to a worksite for a delivery of lumber by eight A.M. It wasn't true. But when he'd walked in on Quinn and Lily working on Lily's Halloween costume, some sort of fairy, the sight had stolen his breath. They were laughing and giggling, just like he'd witnessed the night before during bath time. It was ... perfect. And so he'd left.

He didn't really have anywhere to be until ten o'clock, when widow Apgar returned home from physical therapy. She didn't like the idea of anyone being in her house when she wasn't there. Hey, if the sound of hammering and sawing didn't bother her, who was he to say anything?

So here he was, in his truck, wipers slapping at the late October rain coming down in sheets. If this kept up, it was going to be a wet, muddy Halloween. Scallop Shores didn't offer indoor festivities, like some of the bigger towns. They still did the traditional trick-or-treating in their neighborhoods. The shops downtown offered goodies too. Not a social person, Jonah still couldn't help but wish they would open the doors to the high school gym and have some sort of party that got everyone out of the rain and cold.

Already cranky, his mood darkened when he couldn't find a parking space near Logan's Bakery. The place had barely opened for business. Where had everyone come from? Surely they didn't have reasons as important as his for lurking at a table for half the morning. He had to escape the most beautiful, intelligent woman he'd ever met. He had to hide from the look of pure joy on his daughter's face. He had to run from the urge to sweep them both into his arms and insist they become a family.

Jonah parked behind Logan's, in the dirt lot reserved for employees. Heaven help the person who tried to give him grief about it. He jumped from the cab of his truck, landing in a puddle that splashed his jeans with mud and chilly water. Awesome. Thankfully, his work boots were waterproof. He couldn't afford to catch a cold. And he certainly couldn't handle Quinn as a nursemaid—knowing she would insist on taking care of him.

Rounding the corner of the building, Jonah raised a brow at the stuffed dummy parked on the bench normally reserved for the old men in town. Someone, probably Cady Eaton, had thought it a cute idea to decorate with a scarecrow. He frowned. He was in too foul a temper to find it charming.

The bell jangled over the door as he stepped inside. He hung his coat up on the last remaining peg on the coat rack beside the door. Bypassing the counter, he headed straight for the smallest table, against the wall. Cady saw him enter and waved. She'd be by to take his order shortly.

Jonah stretched out his long legs and adjusted the ball cap on his head. God, he was beat! He hadn't slept a wink last night, thinking about Quinn and the cruel words he'd said to her. What the hell had he been thinking, inviting her to stay with them? This was all kinds of torture.

"Hey, handsome. I'm going to bet you'd like some coffee. You look exhausted." Cady sidled up to his table and leaned a hip against the edge.

"Yeah. Black. And keep it coming." He pinched the bridge of his nose with his forefinger and thumb.

"Anything sweet? I just iced up some cinnamon rolls. Still warm."

He'd skipped breakfast in favor of racing out of the house so he nodded. Closing his eyes, he was surprised when Cady returned so quickly, a mug of steaming coffee and a plate with his sweet roll in her hands.

"So how's that darling little girl of yours? Excited for Halloween?"

Ugh. Again, the scene in the kitchen came to mind. So domestic, so mother/daughter. Lily had looked adoringly at Quinn, like she was the most amazing woman on Earth. And when Quinn had enveloped his little girl in her arms, he could see his daughter had the woman wrapped around her little finger.

"She's great. They were working on her costume this morning. Gonna be a fairy." Crap! He had hoped to keep the fact that Quinn was staying with them, since the fire, under wraps.

"Oh, that's so precious. I hope you plan on swinging by here, at some point. I would love to see her all dressed up." Cady patted his shoulder and turned to go.

Whew, that was close. Maybe she hadn't picked up on his slip. Jonah took a bracing first sip of coffee and let out a long sigh.

"Hey, I just wanted to say, I think it's great that you stepped up and took Quinn in after she lost her house. That was so tragic. She's so lucky to have you." Her smile didn't indicate whether she thought they were more than just friends.

"Well, I think Lily would have had my head if I didn't offer. She's gotten rather fond of Quinn." Too fond, really.

The bell over the door saved him from conversing longer with Cady. She was a nice girl, but Cady was known for her matchmaking. And he did not want to be matched up. At least not with Quinn. Okay, dammit, he wanted to, but he couldn't do that to her. Someone like Quinn deserved a doctor or lawyer or … What had her ex-husband been? An investment banker? Something like that.

He stuffed his face with cinnamon roll, chewing being the only thing keeping the scowl off his face. Okay, Cady'd been right. It was still warm. Some of his bad humor melted away as he savored the spicy tang of cinnamon mixed with the sugary sweetness of the icing. Jonah wondered if he had enough cash in his pocket for a second one.

Licking the stickiness from his fingertips, he hunkered over his coffee, resting his elbows on the table. What was he going to do about Quinn? She'd offered to pay rent, which he hadn't wanted to accept, but he could really use the money right now. She was right there to take care of his little girl. She was also teaching him to read, and with that, giving him confidence that he'd never had before. He'd be eternally grateful. No, he couldn't take her money. But living together under one roof was getting too cozy.

He drummed his fingers on the Formica tabletop as he thought out his problem. Maybe he could ask around, see if anyone had an apartment, a room for rent. They'd still see each other when she came to watch Lily and give him reading lessons, but the temptation would be removed without the close quarters pushing them into each other's business. Right?

It would be for the best. Putting distance between them would also discourage Lily from thinking about Quinn as prospective mother material.

Quinn might even find an apartment with neighbors more like her. Maybe she'd find herself living next door to that doctor or lawyer he envisioned for her. They'd fall in love and get married. Then they'd have enough money to adopt. She could be the mother she'd always dreamed about.

Wow. Wishing for Quinn's happiness really had the opposite effect on his. This sucked. Someone cleared their throat, dragging Jonah from his melancholy.

"Is this seat taken?" Quinn's sister, Kayla, stood smiling down at him.

"Uh, no, please sit down." Hesitantly, he pushed the chair out for her to join him.

Kayla set her paper coffee cup down and settled into the chair he'd offered. She perched on the edge, not removing her coat.

"I apologize that you lost a significant source of income with the destruction of our grandmother's house." She was offering condolences to him? Interesting.

"I'm sorry you and Quinn lost the house. It was a beautiful old thing." Where was this conversation going?

"Yes, well, if you like that sort of thing." She waved a hand in the air. "So now you're saddled with my sister. Do I understand that correctly?"

"No. I'm not saddled with her. I offered her a place to stay. She didn't have anywhere else to go." He waited to see if his barb found its mark.

"Sure she does. She can go back to New York. Very simple." She took a sip of coffee and set the cup back down. "You know all her things are still in storage there."

"I think she may have mentioned that."

"I'm going to be frank with you, Jonah. My sister doesn't stay in Scallop Shores. She comes out for brief visits and then she leaves when she gets bored.

"She's a free spirit. I think it's the artist in her. She's so much more suited to a big city, don't you think? Imagine the adventures someone like her can experience in the Big Apple. Quite exciting."

"I imagine if she agreed with you, she'd still be there. My understanding was that she was home to stay, to reconnect with her loved ones."

"Oh, I know she thinks that now. But wait until winter sets in. Nothing to do. Everything closed up early. The short days, the long nights. She'll get restless."

"So what you're *not* saying," Jonah growled through gritted teeth, "is that you'd like me to convince your sister to leave town." He leveled a look on her that he would have given a cockroach crawling toward him on the floor.

"Oh, be realistic, Jonah. You don't make enough to support an extra mouth to feed. You can barely support your own daughter.

Quinn doesn't have a job. I don't see her pounding the pavement in search of one. Which can only lead me to believe that she doesn't intend to stay long enough to get one. Do yourself a favor and kick her out now. She's just using you."

Jonah closed his eyes and counted silently to ten. Upon opening his eyes, he saw that Kayla was still there. Still looking as though she were offering him a way out of an unpleasant situation. He scraped his chair back and stood up abruptly, wincing when he drew the attention of nearly every customer in the bakery.

"I happen to enjoy our arrangement. We're all happy. Quinn deserves to be happy. Just like she deserves to have family. And if we're all she has, then Lily and I are going to be the best family that we can be." He took away some satisfaction at having rendered Quinn's viper of a sister speechless.

Slapping a ten-dollar bill on the counter by the register, Jonah caught Cady's eye. He nearly lost it when she winked and gave him two thumbs up. People had already started whispering while he shrugged into his coat. He'd given these small-town gossips enough fodder to last till the holidays, at least.

The rain was still coming down steadily as Jonah trudged back out to his truck. He'd have to sit in widow Apgar's driveway for a while and wait until she got home. He started the engine, backed out of his space, and headed for Main St. His conversation with Kayla replaying over and over in his head, he gripped the steering wheel tight, his frown deep.

Whatever issues he had with Quinn paled in comparison to the crap her sister was putting her through. They only had each other. Why wouldn't Kayla welcome her sister home in any capacity? Jonah couldn't wrap his mind around it.

He'd meant what he said. If Kayla was unwilling to step up and be the family that Quinn needed her to be, then he and Lily would fill in. He'd be like a big brother to her. Big brothers protected their sisters from guys that they didn't think were suitable. He would just protect her from himself. Problem solved.

• • •

"I don't date, Quinn. I just don't have the time." Bree's look was apologetic as she quickly glanced away.

"He's a super nice guy. And you can see how adorable his daughter is." Quinn pleaded her case.

"I'm sure he is. Jonah is certainly easy on the eyes. He's also got that sad thing going on. You know, the one that makes you want to comfort him?" Bree blushed. "But I really don't date. When I'm not here I'm helping my mom. I've got three young half-sisters. She's got her hands full with that bunch."

Quinn let out a long sigh and looked up to make sure Lily was still occupied. She shared a huge beanbag chair with three little red-haired kids. Good grief! Were those … triplets? Bree caught the direction of her gaze and chuckled.

"Speaking of having your hands full. Those are Shannon Fitzgerald's triplets." She gestured at the young woman perusing the children's DVDs.

"Wow." Feast or famine. She couldn't have even one child and this other woman was gifted three at once. Quinn smiled through the bitter sting of jealousy.

She returned to the drawing notebook in front of her. The day had dawned drizzling and cold. Lily had been antsy. She couldn't blame her. Now that she was staying at their house, Lily never got a change of scenery. Having already figured out she was going to try to set up Bree with Jonah, Quinn decided to pack up her notebook and bring Lily out for a little socialization at the library.

"May I?" Bree was peering curiously at the sketchpad.

"This is just something silly I've been working on. Lily claims she has this fairy. It visits her. So I started drawing pictures to go with the different stories she tells me."

Quinn turned the sketchpad around and slid it across the table to Bree. The other woman snatched it eagerly, starting at the beginning and turning the pages slowly. Her smile got bigger with each drawing. Her expression grew enchanted, really drawn in. Surely they weren't that good, were they?

"Oh, this is magical," she breathed. Bree traced a finger lightly over the pencil sketches.

"You really think so? I mean, Lily likes them, but she's three." Quinn shrugged, self-consciously.

"The detail. I feel like they could just flutter off the page." Bree's grin was huge. "And books, illustrations, are my life. I know something magical when I see it."

Lily giggled from the other side of the room, and Quinn looked up to check on her again. One of the little boys was tickling her ribs. His mom crossed the room and sat down on the floor in front of the small group. She held up a book. *Llama Llama.* The kids settled down eagerly for a story.

"Her birthday is next month. I was thinking of making up a little book for her. You know, add some color to the drawings, and write up some descriptions, maybe a little dialogue."

"That's perfect. She's going to love it."

"I had bought her a fairy night-light. It was stained glass. So precious. At Octoberfaire" Her lips pulled down in a frown. "Then the fire ... "

"Oh my gosh! I haven't even asked you about that. I knew you were staying with Jonah and Lily. I am so sorry. Did they ever find out what happened?"

"It's under investigation. They know it started in the basement. But with the house a complete loss, it's impossible to find out if there was any sign of forced entry." Quinn shook her head. "I can't even remember the last time I was in the basement, to be honest. I'm not sure if I could tell if something was a fire hazard or not."

Kayla had called her to come sign some insurance papers that had been delivered to her house. Quinn couldn't determine if she'd had anything to do with the fire. She wasn't acting guilty, but she didn't seem at all upset over the loss of Nanny's house, which really got under Quinn's skin. That had been their home for over ten years.

"Well, I'm just glad that you weren't hurt." Bree's declaration pulled her back into the moment.

"So, a handmade book? You think she'll like it?" Quinn took back the sketchpad and flipped idly through the pages.

"I think you don't give yourself enough credit. You are an amazing artist and you need to share your talent with the world."

"Well, let's start with one little girl and see how that goes." She giggled.

But Bree's statement made her think of the bedtime rituals with Kayla and their mom. "Follow your passions," she had told them. She loved sketching. It was a release mechanism for her, a stress reliever. She could get lost in a drawing. Adding a little shading here, more depth there, it could go on indefinitely. And she loved it.

There was something about drawing for someone else that gave it all new meaning. To make a whole world come to life for a child was fascinating. It was heady, powerful. Quinn hadn't felt like this since art school. No, this trumped art school. She had been creating for herself and her instructors then. She wondered if other little girls might find the world of fairies as thrilling as Lily did. Would they like her drawings as well?

"So what are you going to do about Jonah?" Bree asked.

"Hmm?" She'd forgotten about that particular mission.

"I don't know. He has been so kind to take me in. I just want to repay him." Quinn looked down quickly, focusing her attention on adding petals to the rose bush she had drawn.

"I don't get it. He's hot. He's super nice. He's hot." Bree repeated for emphasis. "Why don't you date him?"

Quinn could feel her new friend's gaze upon her, but she refused to make eye contact. *Let's see if that one acting course in college paid off.*

"Yeah, he's a great guy, just not my type." She tried a careless shrug.

"Tall, dark, and extremely handsome? What is your type then?"

"I dunno. I've always preferred blond men. You know, that Nordic look." Good grief, she was so bad at this!

"Ah. Like Thor. I get that." Bree nodded. Wow. She'd bought it.

"Consider it a favor? Have dinner with him. Enjoy each other's company. I'm not asking you to marry the guy. Just show him he doesn't have to play the widower anymore. Sometimes I think he forgets."

Okay, that was a lie. By the looks he'd been giving her lately, the kiss they'd shared, he was definitely ready to shed the role of grieving widower. And as much as she'd like to be the one on the receiving end, she just couldn't be what he needed. Better that she find someone for him, someone she liked and trusted. Before he went out and found someone on his own. And what if Jonah and Bree really hit it off? She lifted her gaze and flashed her friend a hopeful smile, all the while wanting to thunk her head against the tiny table they were scrunched at.

"Okay, I'll go. But just the one time. I'm not looking for a relationship. I'm doing it for you." Bree shook her head like she couldn't quite believe what she'd gotten herself into.

"It will be fun. You'll see." *And I'll try not to stay home and rave like the jealous lunatic I am turning out to be,* thought Quinn.

CHAPTER 13

"I'm sorry, Quinn. I just rented out that last studio apartment. I was holding it for you, figuring you'd need it after the fire, but Kayla said you were heading back to the city."

"Thank you, Mr. Hodgkin. I'm afraid my sister was misinformed. You have a nice day." Quinn held her smile in place until she and Lily got back to her car.

She'd been having the same conversation all day. Armed with a list of available apartments and possible job prospects, Quinn had started the day full of optimism. Now, the only reason she was still smiling had to do with the impressionable young girl tagging along with her. The last thing she needed was for Lily to bring home a new supply of colorful phrases that a preschooler should not be allowed to repeat.

But, really? Kayla had certainly been a busy little beaver, chatting up everyone she could think of who might help out her big sister. Quinn had even gotten the stink eye from one particularly prickly landlady, who had not-so-subtly suggested that she'd set fire to her own house to be rid of it, and Scallop Shores, that much sooner. Oh, Kayla was good!

She hadn't realized just how good until she'd given up on finding an apartment and instead tried to find a business that could use her talents as an artist. It appeared Kayla had thought of everything. The two major preschools in town turned her down because they needed someone reliable, someone they knew would be there long-term. Dave Gifford, the owner of Gifford's Grocery, waved Quinn off the minute he saw her approaching.

"Kayla already told me your rates, Quinn. I think you're better off taking your business plan to the big city … where they can afford you."

"But I haven't even come up with what I'd charge yet. Kay was mistaken, Mr. Gifford. If you'd just listen to me, instead of my sister ... "

"Good luck with your life in the city, Quinn. You're just too fancy for us small-town folk." Gifford handed a lollipop to Lily, patted her on the head, and headed for his office in the back of the store.

"Quinn?" Lily's voice wavered. The little girl tossed the sucker into the nearest garbage can on her way out of the store.

"Yeah, sweetie?"

"You aren't really moving back to the city are you?" She tugged on Quinn's hand until Quinn crouched down at her level and gave the child her full attention.

"No, Lily. The city and I are done with each other. We just weren't a good fit."

"Daddy and I will take care of you. Nanny would have liked that." Boy, this kid was wise beyond her years.

"I believe you've got that right." Although it was supposed to be the other way around.

It was nearing lunchtime so Quinn drove them to Mona's Cafe. Mona's was a new addition for Quinn, having sprung up and become a huge success while she'd been living in New York. She remembered Mona as the head lunch lady in the high school cafeteria. She was pleased to see that Mona had really made a name for herself. She deserved it. She was such a hard worker.

The restaurant's namesake was working the hostess stand. She gave Quinn a big smile and Lily an even bigger one.

"Well, you'll be wanting to sit with your family then." She gestured toward a table by the window.

Quinn's brother-in-law, Jake, and his girls sat perusing their menus. Mona led them over and asked if Jake wouldn't mind a couple more diners at his table. Though his smile was genuine, Quinn thought she detected a flash of guilt.

"Hey, do you suppose it's quiet enough that the girls could have their own table? It might make them feel more grown up," Jake asked Mona.

"Not a problem." She set the girls up in the middle of the room where Jake and Quinn could easily see them, while keeping their own conversation to themselves.

Quinn considered slipping a few little toys from her purse to keep Lily occupied, but found the little girl already chattering away with her newest friends. Shrugging, she slid back into her chair and leveled her gaze on Jake. To his credit, he maintained eye contact.

"I'm sorry." He sighed.

"Yeah? And what did you do to be sorry about?"

"Not me. Kay. I'm not even sure what she did, to be honest. All I know is she came home quite pleased with herself yesterday afternoon."

"Bitch." She spat out the word that had been trapped on the tip of her tongue all morning. It felt good to get that out.

"Where was she that night, Jake?" She didn't have to elaborate. He knew exactly what she meant.

"She was home, with me. She couldn't have done it, Quinn. Even if she'd had the opportunity, I don't think she could go through with it. She's got it in for you. I'll give you that. But she's not psychotic."

They stared each other down until the waitress came to take Quinn's drink order.

"She's been running all over town, telling everyone who will listen that I am moving back to the city." Quinn shook her head in disgust. "All of a sudden, no one will rent an apartment to me."

"I had a feeling it was something like that." Jake frowned.

The waitress served the girls first, grilled cheese sandwiches and French fries all around. Lily's eyes were wide with delight. Quinn wondered if the child had ever been out to eat before. It would have required Jonah ordering from a menu. Somehow she didn't think he would have found the challenge worth it. Watching Lily having such a great time with Zoe and Crystal took the sting out of the bad day she'd been having.

"Hey, so what brings you guys out on a weekday, anyway?" She suddenly realized it was a school day.

"The girls had a dentist appointment this morning and I decided to just let them play hooky the rest of the day."

"Ah, so you're one of the cool dads," Quinn teased.

"I sure like to think so."

They dug into their burgers, Quinn swiping the pickle spear off Jake's plate when he turned to check on the kids. He feigned outrage when he noticed it missing. Zoe cut Lily's sandwich into quarters, to help make it more manageable for her. How sweet was that? Quinn was proud of her nieces.

"You going to stay at Goodwin's?" Jake asked, swallowing a French fry whole.

"Doesn't seem like I have much of a choice. I offered to pay him rent but he won't take it."

"He's a good guy. Damned hard to get to know, he keeps to himself so much. But Nanny liked him. So if he's okay in her book, he's okay in mine."

"Jake, why didn't Kayla spend more time with Nanny?"

"Wish I knew. You'd think with her being the only family she had in town, that Kay would have made more of an effort."

"I had no idea. I just assumed you guys saw each other regularly."

"I tried," he said. "I thought having her over for Sunday dinners would be good for the girls. Kay said Nanny wouldn't go for it. I figured she'd asked her already, so I dropped it."

"I missed so much, living in the city. I miss Nanny. I miss Kayla. The way she used to be." Quinn ducked her head, playing with the straw in her tall glass of iced tea.

"We see her. I don't know why she puts up this front with you."
Jake harrumphed. "I wish we could lock you two in a room, force
you to get everything out in the open—and settled."

"Name the time and place and I'll be there." She quirked a
brow.

Quinn settled back in her chair, watching the girls sharing
their fries and blowing bubbles in their milk. She'd denied herself
moments like this for far too long. And no matter what obstacles
Kayla threw her way, she would never regret coming home. *Bring
it on, Kay! You show me how bad you want me gone and I'll show you
how even more determined I am to stay.*

• • •

Time's up! You failed! How's it feel … chump? These words and more
taunted Jonah throughout his day. Property taxes were due tomorrow and he hadn't managed to scrape the entire amount together.
He was shy just over five hundred dollars.

Jonah carried another load of clothes up from the dryer for his
client. She hadn't asked him, but Mrs. Oswald was older, frail. She
shouldn't be navigating those stairs. Better he do it than risk her
getting hurt.

He headed back to the living room and took a swig of water
from the bottle he always carried. His real job here (God, had
he really been reduced to this?) was to create a play area for Ms.
Oswald's four cats. She envisioned ramps and tunnels attached to
the walls, over the doorway, you name it. She had no family, no
children, or grandchildren. Who was Jonah to say what she did
with her money. As long as he was being paid.

The problem was, he wasn't being paid enough. He needed
a real job, steady work, a reliable paycheck. He needed to tell
Blaise that he'd work for him. But not yet. Not until he could get
his GED and hope to hell that the man didn't look at the date

on it. He'd assume Jonah had earned it back when his dad had supposedly been homeschooling him, right?

Setting down his water, he got back to work. He and Ms. Oswald had worked on the design together. It was Disneyland for cats. He bet even Quinn's fur ball would like it. He climbed back up on his ladder and nailed a board to the supports he'd drilled into the wall earlier. A couple of Ms. Oswald's cats were heavy enough to be mistaken for small dogs. Better to be safe than sorry.

At five o'clock, Jonah cleaned up his work and headed home. He still had a couple of hours before this project would be finished, but he had set a strict schedule long ago. Too little of his day was spent with Lily, as it was. So when five o'clock came, he stopped what he was doing and hurried home to his favorite girl. The fact that Quinn would also be there, likely with something delicious simmering on the stove, was just a big, fat bonus.

Throwing his toolbox in the back of his truck, Jonah hauled himself into the front seat and headed for the house. All his doubts came flooding back. Driving made him think, and thinking was bad. He'd brought this all on himself. He could have paid the taxes if he had taken Quinn up on her offer to pay rent while she was staying with them.

He knew she was using her own money to buy their groceries and cook the elaborate meals he'd been coming home to. It was his house, he should be the provider. What did that say about him, when someone who didn't even have a job was helping him pay for the food on his table? It rankled.

Flexing his fingers on the steering wheel and cracking his neck from side to side, Jonah had worked himself into a real temper by the time he pulled into the driveway. Soft light from the house, spilling out onto the lawn, did nothing to sooth his jangled nerves. However unfairly, he'd put Quinn at the center of his problems. They'd managed just fine until she came along. Now Quinn was parenting better than him. She cooked a damned sight better than he did too.

Stomping his boots on the mat by the door, Jonah caught the scent of clam chowder and fresh baked bread hanging heavily in the warm air. His stomach rumbled loudly. *Oh, shut up!* He threw his coat toward the hook attached to the wall and glared as it slid to the floor. It could stay there for all he cared!

"Hey, you're home. Dinner is almost ready. I have something to show you. I'm so excited. I can't wait to see what you think." Quinn met him at the door like an eager puppy.

"Where's Lily?" He snapped out. Jonah didn't care if he sounded irritable. Damn it, he *was* irritable!

If Quinn noticed his mood, she chose to ignore it. "She's watching a video in the living room." Bouncing like a spring on the balls of her feet, Quinn gestured impatiently. "Come on. We'll be back before the video is over. I promise."

She dragged him down to his workshop. That should have set warning bells off right there. This was *his* space. Skipping past the workbench, Quinn headed for the corner where he had set the cradle. The cradle that he had just finished building last night. Jonah's steps slowed. He knew he did not want to see what she had to show him.

"See? I finished it for you." With a flourish worthy of Vanna White, Quinn stood back and swept an arm out to show Jonah what she'd done.

He had finished sanding the cradle last night but had yet to stain it. His intention was to coat it in a nice mahogany finish, something rich and glossy. His beautiful cradle, his pet project for the last few months, was now white. And not only that, Quinn had hand painted zoo animals in a random pattern.

Jonah felt his blood begin to boil. His eyes narrowed as he stared down at the detailed little giraffes and elephants. A monkey swung from a vine. A freakin' monkey … on his cradle. He could swear he was taking off layers of enamel as he ground his teeth to keep from screaming.

"I was talking with Thea. She told me she'd just bought the bedding set for the baby's room. It's this adorable animal print, and I thought how perfect it would be to have the cradle match their nursery theme."

"This was *my* gift to them." He rumbled.

"I know, and it's gorgeous. I just had some time while Lily was napping. I got restless and wanted something to do. I wanted to help." She sounded nervous. Things were finally sinking in.

"It was my cradle and you ruined it," he snarled, turning to face a very pale Quinn.

"That wasn't my intention." She was shaking her head vigorously. "I wanted to give back. I wanted to help." Her lower lip began to tremble and tears made her eyes shimmer.

"Oh, I think you've done quite enough, thank you very much." He spun on his heel. A clear dismissal. "All that hard work. All the nights I stayed up late. And for what? It's gone." He raked his hands through his hair, leaving deep furrows.

"Okay, hang on." Quinn stepped in front of him, forcing him to see her. She swiped at her cheeks with the back of a hand. "I painted your precious cradle, yes. I did not take an ax to it. If you would just cut the drama queen routine, you'd see that you have an incredible piece of handmade furniture to give your neighbors. They are going to love it."

"It was my cradle. You didn't ask me if you could paint it. You just went ahead and did it. You ruined it. It's not what I had in mind at all. But you couldn't leave well enough alone, could you?"

"I'm sorry. I'm sorry I ruined your precious cradle. I'm sorry that you're in a pissy mood and taking it out on me. I'm sorry I wanted to help be a part of such an amazing piece of craftsmanship." Her tears had returned in earnest, and with them his guilt.

But before he could say anything, take back his hurtful accusations, Quinn had run upstairs. He heard a soft murmur exchanged and then the sound of the spare bedroom door shutting. Damn.

Dragging himself up the steps, Jonah was met at the doorway by his daughter. She smiled brightly, having blessedly missed the exchange in the basement. She hugged him around the waist and held a finger to her lips.

"Shh … Quinn has a headache. She went to bed. She said eat without her."

His appetite had deserted him. But Jonah dutifully spooned up chowder into two bowls and cut them each a generous slice of sourdough bread. He found a salad chilling in the fridge when he went to dig out the butter. Somehow the sight of it made him feel ten times the heel he already was.

He set the food on the table and joined Lily. She took a bite of the thick soup and swallowed before swinging her gaze to her dad.

"Did you see the cradle? Wasn't it so cute? Quinn worked for a really long time on it. She was practicin' her animals on paper so she'd get 'em just perfect. I think she got 'em perfect. Don't you?"

The mouthful of chowder he'd been about to swallow turned sour on his tongue. He deserved to choke on it.

CHAPTER 14

"The End."

Quinn set down her pen and blew on the ink to dry it before shutting the book. She'd bought a blank book at the huge warehouse craft store a couple towns over. Sturdily bound, it would hold up when leafed through several times a day. Well, at least it was her hope that Lily loved the book so much she looked through it often.

Lily had been telling Quinn stories about Misty Blossom from the first day they read Nanny's book on flower fairies together. Misty was Lily's fairy. She visited often, having her own spot in Lily's bedroom. But her friends lived in the garden and she missed them terribly if she spent too much time inside the house.

So Quinn had taken snippets from all of Lily's anecdotes and compiled a storybook, complete with detailed drawings of Misty Blossom's adventures. The more she drew, the more she wanted to draw. And now that the book was finished, her fingers itched to get started on the next one.

She glanced at the closed door to her bedroom. She was hungry. She'd heard Jonah put Lily to bed a while ago. With any luck, he had sequestered himself in his own room. Or more likely, he was downstairs stripping her paint job from his damned cradle, trying to salvage his precious baby. Quinn's heart squeezed painfully. She'd wanted to help make it special. But he was right. It was his gift to Thea and Ken. She should have asked.

A soft tap at her door had her scrambling off the bed. Her hands went automatically to her hair, smoothing down the flyaway strands. Her eyes went to her bare legs and she then frantically searched for the jeans she'd removed earlier.

"Just a minute." There. Hanging from the bedpost. Hurriedly, she shimmied back into them, took a deep breath and opened her door.

Jonah stood in the hall, a wooden tray in his hands. A steaming bowl of chowder, side salad, and a stack of bread slices weighed it down. Ooh, there was even a tall glass of chocolate milk. Quinn's mouth watered as she reached for the tray. Instead of handing it over, Jonah nudged his way through the door.

He placed the tray on the bed, and though it was sturdy enough, Quinn was scared of what might happen to her book if anything spilled. She started to snatch it up, but he'd spotted it and looked intrigued.

"May I?" He lifted the book and paused, glancing at her with an arched brow.

"Be my guest." Quinn was more interested in feeding her stomach than fighting with Jonah. She left him to the book, climbed up onto the bed and tucked into the chowder she'd really been looking forward to since that afternoon.

"Misty Blossom was a flower fairy," Jonah read aloud.

His words were drawn out and hesitant, but he was reading. Pride welled in her chest. She didn't want him to stop, so she pretended to focus on her dinner, all the while listening intently. He was doing it.

"This is incredible, Quinn. You took Lily's imagination and brought it to life." He held the book reverently, looking at her with astonishment and awe.

"I guess we both have our talents." Uncomfortable with the way he gazed at her, she returned her focus to her food tray.

"I'm sorry." His voice was gruff. "It's not how I envisioned the cradle." He paused a beat. "It's better. You made it better than I could think of."

Quinn glanced up, her spoon halfway to her mouth. She didn't think that was true, but it was kind of him to say.

"So what's really bothering you?" She asked quietly.

Jonah frowned, looking up as though he'd been caught in a lie. Did he really think she wouldn't see through his mood? Something was bothering him. A big something.

"I'm just in a bit of a snag. It will work out. I've just got to figure it out." He'd gone off somewhere. She watched him staring into space.

"Can I help?" She knew it killed him to even have her ask, but she also sensed that this was something he wasn't going to be able to handle alone.

Looking around the room, Jonah set the fairy book on the dresser. She watched him struggling. He clenched and unclenched his hands. He gripped the dresser, grimacing into the attached mirror. Then he paced to the bed and ran his hand along the wooden foot rail, bouncing his palm on the round knob at the end. Quinn remained silent.

"Property taxes are due. It's the first time I've ever … " His voice trailed off and he stared at the floor. He looked so ashamed that Quinn wanted to cry.

"It's the first time you haven't been able to pay," she finished for him. "Well, and for good reason. Your water bill has gone up from all the showers I'm taking. I'm running your washing machine and dryer, and turning on extra lights. I'm a mooch." She put down her soup bowl and stood up. They both knew a higher water bill wouldn't really make that kind of difference. She was being kind. And he let her.

Jonah was shaking his head and seemed genuinely surprised when he looked up and realized how close Quinn had gotten without his noticing. Whatever he'd been about to say seemed to have been forgotten. She pushed her advantage.

"You turned me down once and that was very kind but unnecessary. Now it's biting you in the butt." She held his eyes with hers, daring him to deny it. He squirmed.

Neither of them spoke for a moment. And this suddenly made Quinn very aware of her surroundings. Jonah was in her bedroom. Lily was asleep, down the hall. Very tall, very virile Jonah was in her bedroom and they were very much alone.

Gazes locked, Quinn could pinpoint the exact millisecond that Jonah realized the same thing. His eyelids became heavier and his eyes left hers to focus on her mouth. As though it were summoned, her tongue made an appearance, slipping out to wet her lips before disappearing again. Jonah's nostrils flared and his chest rose and fell with increased rhythm. He started to lean in closer, a man on a mission.

"Hey, I've got an idea!" Quinn backed up, though it took all the willpower she had and then some. He blinked, like he'd just been awakened by a hypnotist. "Let me help you pay the taxes. And in exchange, you could help me out with a favor."

"What kind of favor?" He drawled out the question.

The way he was looking at her made Quinn feel as though she were a piece of chocolate, one that he intended to savor, letting the flavor melt slowly on his tongue. She shuddered. Damned if he didn't make her want to give in, give up her secret. But she couldn't, wouldn't be able to look him in the eye after, see his disappointment.

"I have this friend," she began. His eyes narrowed. "Maybe you've met Bree. She's the children's librarian in town. She's incredibly sweet."

"And just happens to be single?" Jonah turned toward the darkened window.

"Look, it's just a date. Take her out to dinner tomorrow night, get to know each other. This could be the start of something amazing."

"Until she finds out I can't read. She's a librarian, Quinn. I think that's probably up there in her top three wish list for a date. Must be well-read."

"You can read. You read to me tonight. You didn't even realize it. You may not be reading college level stuff yet, but you are getting there. Don't deny yourself happiness because you think you don't deserve it." She stood her ground, her fingers twitching as she ached to go to him, reach out and stroke that strong back.

He kept himself turned away from her, as he appeared to ponder her conditions. Quinn watched him lift a hand and could tell he was pinching the bridge of his nose. She'd seen him do this when he was concentrating. He spun around and threw his hands up in surrender.

"Okay. You've got me. I'll go out with Bree—on one date—if you pay what I'm short on the taxes."

"And going forward, you let me pay rent like I should have in the first place."

"Fine, but I'm buying the damned groceries from now on," Jonah growled.

"Fine."

He stalked to the door like a great dark panther. Quinn clamped a hand over her mouth to keep from calling him back, begging him to take her to bed. She ached in places that had never felt this alive when she'd been married to Andrew. Frustrated and nearly out of her mind with need, she rushed to shut the door behind him. Locking it, she slid to the floor and hugged her knees as tightly as she could. She cursed her traitorous body, trying to remind herself that she was doing both of them a favor by setting up this date.

• • •

This was all wrong. Jonah worked a finger between his buttoned up collar and his Adam's apple. He'd decided against a tie. Ties were for weddings and funerals, as far as he was concerned. But he still felt like he was choking.

"How is your steak?" Bree asked him from across the table.

"Just the way I like it." He looked up at her and forced his lips into a smile.

He had left Quinn's room last night cranky. Okay, hot and bothered, with a big emphasis on hot. Fine. She wanted him to go out on a date with her friend, he would. And because he was in a mood, Jonah had chosen the Italian restaurant by the water. He'd show Quinn what she was missing. He would lay on the romance tonight.

Or so he had thought. Bree was all dolled up. He wasn't sure he'd ever seen her in makeup but she sure did clean up nice. Her hair was piled up fancy on top of her head, so he could see the pretty earrings she wore. She even had on a little black dress, not a shapeless flowery skirt like she wore to the library every day. Which told him she had really been looking forward to this date.

Jonah felt like a jerk for taking her somewhere special when his heart wasn't even in it. Quinn was right, damn it! They weren't good for each other. It was in his own best interest to date around, find someone suitable for him and for Lily. He *should* be on this date. He just didn't want to be.

Paige's parents had called, out of the blue, to ask if Lily could visit for the weekend. She'd been thrilled to have a sleepover at her grandparents' house. But that left Quinn all alone on a Saturday night. He shouldn't care. She was a big girl, she could keep herself busy for one evening.

"What do you say we skip dessert and coffee?" Bree's question took a moment to penetrate his brain and then Jonah became alarmed.

"Um … " He didn't want to hurt her feelings, but clearly Bree thought this date was going a heck of a lot better than he did.

"I know you're anxious to get back to her. It's okay." She reached out and patted his hand.

"No, Lily is at her grandparents out on Cape Cod for the weekend."

"All the more reason to hurry home." Her smile was knowing … approving.

"But I thought … " He wasn't even sure how to finish that sentence.

"That Quinn set us up so that she wouldn't have to face the fact that she had feelings for you?" Bree pushed her plate away and nodded at the approaching waiter. "Don't get me wrong, Jonah. You are a very handsome man. But I did this as a favor to Quinn, and I suspect you did the same." She stared him down until he nodded.

The waiter brought the check and Bree tried to give Jonah money for her dinner. He pushed her hand away and counted out enough cash for the total. Not used to dining out and unsure what a customary tip should be, he threw an extra twenty down and stood up. He scowled at the young waiter, who's lascivious look showed exactly why he thought they were rushing off without ordering dessert.

Jonah dropped Bree off at her house exactly an hour and a half after he'd picked her up. He couldn't even look at her as she undid her seatbelt. He was pond scum. They had both agreed to do Quinn this one simple favor. Bree went to a lot of trouble to hold up her end of the bargain. Jonah, not so much. So he was startled when she leaned across the seat of the pickup to give him a quick kiss on the cheek.

"You two belong together. Stop all this nonsense and just let it happen."

She slipped out of the truck and shut the door. He felt as though he'd just been reprimanded. Given that she worked with children all day, he probably had. He waited until she let herself into the house and backed out of the driveway. The part of his evening he'd been waiting for since before he'd agreed to this cursed date was here—going home to Quinn.

He broke speed limits to get there. He didn't care. He tore up gravel spinning into the driveway. He didn't notice. He started to get out of the truck and realized the flowers he'd bought for Bree were still in Lily's booster seat. He snatched them up and carried them inside, to Quinn.

"Hello?" He hollered from the doorway, flinging his coat and missing, again.

"I'm in here. Everything okay? You haven't been gone long."

He found her in the living room, sitting cross-legged on the floor with her back against the couch. Her sketchbook was on her lap and drawings of fairies were scattered all around. She'd been using charcoal, judging by the smudge on her cheek and her grubby blackened fingertips. Her hair was held up with a pencil, as usual, and she was wearing his T-shirt. Quinn looked so much better in his clothes than he did.

When she didn't get up, he joined her on the floor. His long legs looking awkward in this small space. She didn't move the sketchpad, seeming to use it as more of a shield than a drawing tablet. She refused to look at him. He watched emotions flicker across her face, one never staying long before another took its place. Nervousness, relief, frustration, anger, pleasure. What would she settle on? Jonah felt like he'd put his last dollar in a slot machine and was crossing his fingers for a winner.

"We had dinner. Didn't feel like dessert. End of date." He shrugged.

"Yeah, what'd you have?" She still wouldn't look at him.

"I ordered the steak and she had the shrimp scampi."

"You went to Luigi's!" Her lips pulled down in a pout and she shot him a glare.

Jonah grinned triumphantly. Caught reacting, Quinn quickly returned her focus to the drawing pad. But it was too late. He set the bouquet of flowers on top of the notebook. She tried, and failed, to hide her gasp of pleasure.

"What, Bree didn't want them?" She couldn't conceal the delight in her voice.

"I didn't want to give them to her. I would much rather give them to you."

This time he took matters into his own hands, lifting her chin with one finger and forcing her to meet his eyes. She'd wedged her bottom lip between her teeth and he couldn't tell if it was from nerves or if she wanted to cry. He smoothed his thumb over her lip so that she'd release it. He had her full attention now.

"I did you a favor, like you asked. I went through that sham of a date. Now it's over and I'm home—where I wanted to be all along."

"Oh, Jonah," she breathed.

He wasn't sure if he moved in closer, or if it was Quinn, or a little of both. But no sooner had she uttered his name than they were mashing noses and scraping teeth. He pulled back enough to gain control, this time claiming her mouth slowly, seductively. He wanted to take his time. Need clawed at him, trying to take over. Quinn's fingers in his hair, stroking his scalp set his blood to boiling.

Hungrily, he feasted on her lips, her tongue, licking the corners of her mouth. The tiny mewls purring from Quinn's throat were enough to push him over the edge. He ran his hand down her back, stopping when he reached the hem of her shirt. Then he headed back up, with his hand on her skin instead. So soft. So warm. She felt like rose petals. His hand glided up her ribcage. When he reached the creamy satin of her bra, Quinn squealed, pushing at his hand and scooting away.

"Oh my God—we can't!" She panted.

"Why not?" He growled, frustration plucking away at his self-control.

"I can't." She was shutting him out, refusing to meet his eyes again.

"Tell me. Make me understand." His lungs burned as he drew in breath once again. He hadn't even realized he'd been holding it.

"I'm … no good at this." Her face was bright red. She looked miserably embarrassed.

"Uh, I was having a pretty good time there myself." He raked a hand through his hair and tried to make sense of what she was telling him.

"It wouldn't have lasted."

What the hell had her looking so ashamed?

"Baby, if you're trying to tell me that you aren't sexy, that you don't know how to please a man, you are very much mistaken."

"I am trying to tell you that! And I'm not mistaken. I have been told that. Time and time again." She'd drawn her knees up tight and thrust her chin out.

"Your ex-husband?" His voice was gentle.

"Andrew said I was a dud in bed. He said I couldn't please him, that it was my fault. I tried. I tried everything I could think of." Her face flamed red at whatever memories that admission stirred up.

Knowing Quinn and how she liked her research, Jonah imagined she really had done her best to please her husband. And knowing how he, himself, felt about her—before she even tried to please him—he knew without doubt that the fault lay with the fool she'd married, and not with Quinn.

"I'm here to tell you, Quinn, that you are perfect. You are sexy. You have me tearing my hair out just to be with you."

She shook her head, starting to speak, but he reached out and covered her mouth with a finger.

"Don't say a word. Just let me prove it. Please. I need to make love to you more than I need to breath." He stared deeply into her eyes, waiting, willing her to want this as much as he did. After a few agonizing moments she gave him a shaky nod. Thank the Lord!

CHAPTER 15

Her heart hammered so loudly in her chest that Quinn was afraid she wouldn't be able to hear anything Jonah had to say. Fortunately for her, he wasn't talking. He stood up, reaching down for her hand and drew her up against him. He never stopped touching her, as though she'd become a lifeline for him. Quinn tried to stay in the moment but it was all so surreal, very different from the way things had been with Andrew.

Then he lifted her into his arms and carried her down the hall to his bedroom. Snapped back to reality, she watched his face for any sign of fatigue or pain. Men really did this? She thought the whole sweeping the woman off her feet thing was something romance authors made up. Jonah's jaw was rigid and he breathed harder than normal, but one look in his eyes and she understood that it wasn't from carrying a hundred-twenty pound woman; it was from hunger, need. His raw strength and virility had her trembling.

He laid her down on top of his worn patchwork quilt. Quinn scooted to the side so he could lie down beside her, only he didn't. He just stood there, staring down at her as though she were a gift he was about to unwrap. She tried not to squirm under the scrutiny. Andrew had always insisted on making love in the dark. She'd assumed he found her body unattractive.

Jonah had flipped the light switch on as they'd entered the room. He made no attempt to turn it off now. Panic zigzagged through Quinn's body, causing all her old doubts and fears to rise to the surface. Why didn't he turn out the light?

"You are so beautiful." His voice was low, gravelly.

"I ... you haven't seen me without my clothes on." She licked her lips nervously.

"It can only get better." With each word he drew closer and closer until he was hovering over her. "Have I told you how good you look in my shirt?"

"I'm sorry, I shouldn't have ... " She plucked at the neckline, her fingers needing something to do.

"I think I need to institute a rule here." He narrowed his eyes and placed a huge palm over her mouth. "No apologizing. No excuses. No negative words about your body, or anything you do with your body."

He leaned down, their chests finally touching, their lungs working to achieve syncopation.

"Feel free to shout my name as loud as you'd like. Praise God, cuss, or talk dirty. But do not doubt yourself and your ability to please me. Do you understand?"

Quinn nodded, only half hearing what he had to say. His chest was so broad. His shirt strained at the seams. He was a mountain, and he was, however briefly, hers. She would agree to anything he asked, as long as he kept touching her.

Jonah reached for the hem of her T-shirt and this time she kept quiet as he lifted it up and over her head. He tossed it over his shoulder, again stopping to look his fill. Quinn bit her lip. He couldn't take his eyes off her. The more reverently he looked, the more her heart swelled. It would be so easy to fall in love with this man.

And then his mouth was on her, kissing and licking every inch of uncovered skin. He even laved her nipples through the white satin bra she wore. That was a new experience for her. She watched his nostrils flare as the darker color showed through the white fabric. Then with a groan, he exposed one creamy globe and feasted. Before he could ask, she reached behind her back and undid the clasp. This time it was Quinn who threw the article of clothing over Jonah's shoulder to join the growing pile on the floor.

"Please." Her breathing was ragged and her voice sounded like it belonged to someone else.

"Please what?" He was grinning at her like the devil himself.

"I need to see you. I want to touch you." Unaccustomed to boldness, she found she liked it.

Jonah sat up, nearly popping buttons in his haste to remove his shirt. Quinn settled back against the pillows, content to watch the show. She'd been right to think of him as a mountain. The man was chiseled. His skin was still a light tan from summer. Quinn nearly swooned, imagining him working sans shirt. His chest was smooth, not a whorl of chest hair to be found. She'd never been a fan of hirsute men.

"Keep going." She propped her arms behind her head and gave him a saucy grin.

"As you wish." Jonah wiggled his brows.

He undid his belt and shucked off his pants, revealing form-fitting boxer briefs. Definitely a pleasant surprise. He hooked his thumbs under the elastic waistband and looked to Quinn for a signal. She swallowed hard and nodded vigorously. Off came the underwear and Jonah stood there, tall and proud.

"No more games. I need you, Quinn." His voice was a purr, promising pleasure.

He dragged her to the edge of the bed and made short work of the rest of her clothes. Together, they hauled the covers down and fell in the center of the big bed. Vulnerability had her desperate to cover herself beneath the overhead light. *Trust him. Let go.* Quinn took a deep breath and focused on him.

She slid her foot up and down Jonah's coarse calves. She breathed deep the spicy soap he used in the shower. She tasted the salty tang of his skin. She marveled at the power she seemed to have to draw moans and gasps from deep within his chest.

"Enough," he rumbled, flipping her to her back and nudging her legs apart with his knee.

"You do this to me, Quinn. Only you." He looked deeply into her eyes, his own so serious, so sincere.

She could feel him there, touching her, ready for her. It was a night of new experiences and she was loving it. Greedy for more, she lifted her hips, desperate to take him in. With a look that bordered on agony, he gripped her hips and drove deep. They gasped as one. Quinn grabbed madly for Jonah's shoulders, her hands scrabbling their way down his back. Their movements choreographed, it was like they were made for each other.

Her name was on his lips as they finished together. She didn't feel clumsy, awkward, or … lacking. The perfect end to a perfect experience. Their limbs entwined as Jonah lay on his back and drew Quinn up on his chest. She rested her head for a moment, listening to the thrum of his heartbeat slowly return to normal. She no longer felt like apologizing. She had nothing to apologize for.

"Now do you believe me?" He whispered against her hair, stroking her back with long, tapered fingers.

"I do." Through a pleasure induced fog, Quinn tried to make sense of her sex life with Andrew. He had been her first lover, and quite frankly, the only man she had to compare to Jonah. And this, wow, this was no comparison. Whatever had been wrong in their relationship had to do with Andrew.

She snuggled closer, breathing in their mingled scent.

"Stay with me. We've got all night. Who knows when we'll have another chance like this?" Jonah tightened his arms possessively around her.

It felt too good, being in his arms. She couldn't argue even if she wanted to. Quinn felt as though she were slowly melting down into the mattress.

"Do me a favor." It wasn't a question.

"Um?" She'd nearly been asleep.

"Don't set me up on any more dates." Jonah kissed her forehead and drew the covers over them, slapping off the light before finally settling in for the night.

• • •

Chaos reigned the day Lily Goodwin turned four. Children raced down the hallway of the small house, shrieking and laughing as they went. Quinn finished placing the candles on the cake she had designed, licking frosting from the tip of her finger and smiling at the results. The pain that she'd gotten used to carrying around whenever children were present was dim, more a memory than the squeezing hurt that made it difficult to breath.

Jonah was setting up a game of pin the tail on the donkey, but he'd have to catch the partygoers first. Only a couple of rooms away, still she missed him. They were keeping their relationship to themselves, though she figured only a fool would miss the knowing looks they exchanged whenever they were together. A smile spread across her face. She just couldn't turn it off.

"Someone is quite pleased with themselves." Kayla stood in the doorway, her arms crossed over her chest.

"It's a happy day." Quinn refused to apologize for her good humor.

She would repair her relationship with her sister if it killed her. And the way things were going, it just might. She knew Kayla had wanted to tell her to go fly a kite when she invited her and the girls to Lily's birthday party. But she had accepted. And Quinn figured it was better not to question her sister's motives. But that didn't mean Kay couldn't sneak in a few barbs when no one was listening.

"I would have thought you'd go for someone with more money, someone else who could support you. But I guess you made enough from your last marriage to float you for a while."

Target acquired.

"Kay, can we get through one afternoon without spitting venom? I know you have your issues with me. I'm charmed by your perceptions of the type of person you seem to think I am, but this isn't the time or place."

Jonah slipped through the doorway just then, looking from one sister to the other.

"Girls, are we playing nice?" His eyes narrowed as he looked to Quinn for any excuse to throw her sister out of his house.

"Kayla was just offering to help me carry the cake out to the banquet table."

Jonah swung his gaze toward Kayla, who moved into the kitchen and took up her position beside Quinn. He nodded, picking up a stack of plates and napkins. He snatched up the cake knife before either of the women could reach for it. Quinn smirked. She wouldn't need that. She was going to kill her sister with kindness.

Lily squealed with delight over her fairy themed birthday cake. Quinn had managed to hide it from her until it was time to blow out the candles. Even the adults oohed and aahed over the detail. Quinn was just happy that she could do this for her. She would give this little girl anything, if it meant seeing the joy on her face like she did right now.

Everyone sang happy birthday and Lily blew out her candles, with a little help from her dad. He pulled her into his arms and gave her a big kiss. It was all Quinn could do not to join in. It stunned her to realize just how important these two people had become to her. Watching them together, she realized that if things between her and Kayla never resolved themselves, it wouldn't be the end of the world. She had Jonah and Lily now.

Jonah cut the cake and passed out slices to the party guests. Quinn knew it was the first time a lot of these folks had ever been inside his house. It had taken some convincing to get Jonah to step out of his comfort zone enough to host a birthday party for Lily. He'd explained that they had always done something low-key at home. She found that sad and unfair for this exuberant little girl who just loved people. So she'd pushed for a party. To look at him now, no one would ever be able to tell that the idea had originally terrified him.

Quinn accepted a plate, her cheeks flushing warmly as their fingers tangled, however briefly. She looked around the group assembled, hoping no one had noticed the exchange. Kayla was wiping frosting from Zoe's nose. Thea and Ken had eyes only for each other. Shannon was smiling down at her triplets, Lily's newest friends. Bree had brought her three younger half-sisters, who were each around Lily's age. All of them busily stuffing their faces with cake.

And then there was Cady, who had supplied the frosted cake, leaving the decorating to Quinn, as requested. Cady who didn't miss a thing. Cady who now winked at Quinn. Feeling the warmth seep down below her neckline, Quinn wrinkled her nose and stuck her tongue out at her friend. They both chuckled softly to themselves.

The women made short work of clean up, once everyone had had their fill of cake and ice cream. Lily sat at the head of the long banquet table, proudly wearing her birthday tiara. Her eyes went wide with excitement as Jonah carried in the pile of gifts that had arrived with the party guests. She bounced in her seat. Quinn doubted the little girl had ever seen so many presents at once.

She opened up puzzles and board games, stuffed animals, and books. Someone had given her a Barbie with pink hair and sparkly fairy wings. Lily had ripped open the box and held her like a precious gem. She'd been especially pleased with her father's gift—a jewelry box filled with all sorts of treasures she could dress up in. She draped a strand of sparkly beads around her neck and slipped several rings onto her tiny fingers before reaching for Quinn's gift-wrapped package.

She seemed to know, without asking, who the present was from and fixed Quinn with a solemn smile. Theirs was a close bond, forged quickly but fiercely. Lily knew Quinn could see inside her, where she kept all her dreams and wishes. Lily knew that Quinn could be counted on to give her a gift so perfect that she wouldn't have even realized how much she wanted it.

Quinn stood to the side, waiting for Lily to unwrap her present. She was foolishly nervous. The child was four, for goodness sake. She'd be happy with anything Quinn gave her. But still, she chewed on a knuckle, watching the child pluck delicately at the wrappings.

The gasp that followed was music to her ears. Quinn smiled as Lily turned the pages of the book she'd written and illustrated. Lily's stubby fingers caressed each drawing and her face was a study in delight as she turned the pages ever so slowly. Unable to see what the fuss was about, everyone started crowding in close. Quinn backed away from the table to give them room. Jonah dropped a hand to her shoulder and squeezed.

"She is so lucky to have you in her life," he whispered.

"I'm the lucky one." Quinn reached up and patted his hand.

She caught Kayla's calculating look and stepped away from Jonah. Her sister skirted the table to get a better look at the book she'd created. Quinn braced herself for whatever criticism Kay could dish. Therefore, what Kayla said next completely floored her.

"This is really good, Quinn. I mean, this is published author good. Have you ever thought of taking it to one of the publishing houses in New York? Do you have any connections back there? I bet someone would jump through hoops to get their hands on this."

The other adults were nodding in agreement. Kayla looked pleased that she had been the one to suggest it. Quinn immediately questioned her sister's motives, seeing this as an opportunity for Kayla to push her into moving back to the city. But she smiled and accepted the praise.

Kay was right. Living in Manhattan, she had befriended some people in the publishing industry. The wheels started to turn and Quinn contemplated a possible visit to see if her work really was decent enough to be published. She turned to Jonah and was met with an unreadable expression. She wasn't sure why, but she sensed he didn't approve of her making a career out of her artwork. The idea stung.

CHAPTER 16

Lily's furniture had been pushed to the center of the room and covered with a large plastic sheet. The same plastic covered the floor. Lily, herself, sported shades of purple, pink, and green on her shirt, her hair, and even her cute button nose. Quinn stood on a ladder, working on a more detailed portion of the wall. Having his daughter in the room was the only thing keeping Jonah's eyes, and hands, off Quinn's perfect little behind.

As an extended birthday present, Quinn had designed a fairy mural for Lily's bedroom wall. Jonah had seen the sketches, but now that they were actually on the wall, with color being added, he was blown away. Lily's bedroom was being transformed into a fairy wonderland. Thinking back to Quinn's idea of making her murals into a business, he had to admit it made sense. He could see parents paying an arm and a leg for one of these murals.

Quinn was an artist, a damned good one. She wasn't the starving art school grad, fresh from college with a diploma and no prospects. She was going places. Why, for the life of him, she chose to stay in Scallop Shores, Jonah couldn't understand. Maybe Kayla was right. Quinn would be better off in the city. She had opportunities there.

She could find her Mr. Right. Jonah frowned as he stuck another small paintbrush into the thinning solvent and worked it through the bristles. Quinn deserved so much more than a handyman and his daughter. He wanted her to have the chance to mother her own children. Even if he secured a full-time, steady job working for Blaise, Jonah would never make enough to adopt a child for her. And he sure as hell wouldn't let her use her own money she'd earned through her art.

They'd been so good together. She smiled down at him from her perch on high and he remembered how her hair looked fanned out across his pillow. Her lips had been swollen from their kissing, her eyes heavy and hooded.

And she thought she was no good in bed. She was more than good. She was fiery and passionate, giving everything she had and not afraid to ask for what she needed. She was everything Jonah could have asked for in a lover. And as much as it killed him, he could never touch her again. Not and keep his sanity, anyway.

"Hey, slacker, I need to switch out some of these brushes." Quinn held a fistful of smaller brushes.

He'd been sitting foolishly on the floor, holding up a bunch of brushes and staring at the woman who had stolen his heart. *Crap! This was not supposed to happen.* Jonah scrambled to his feet and maneuvered his way through an obstacle course of open paint cans, piles of drop cloths, and buckets full of supplies. It was a miracle nothing had spilled yet.

A different kind of awareness skittered through his veins as he got closer to Quinn. He didn't just want her in his bed, easing an ache, scratching an itch. He wanted to wake up beside her and know that whatever the day held, hardships or happiness, they were in it together.

No, no, no! Imagining a life with Quinn at his side was about as believable as one of Lily's fairy stories. It just couldn't happen and he needed to shove all these useless feelings aside.

"Mommy, Daddy, look! I drawed us," Lily announced proudly, turning to reveal a trio of stick figures, all holding hands. A family.

Jonah stumbled blindly into a cluster of paint cans, the colors mixing into a pastel rainbow on the plastic drop cloth. At the same time, Quinn dropped the bundle of paintbrushes, some heading straight for the bottom of a paint can, some bouncing to the floor. She stared at him, her wide eyes huge in her suddenly pale face.

"Did you … "

"I didn't … "

Lily looked from one adult to the other, seemingly unaware of her slip of the tongue.

"I need some air." He pivoted on his heel, without another word, and stalked from the room.

"Jonah!" she screeched, and it was all the reminder he needed to slip his sneakers off before he tracked paint out into the hallway.

He kept going, out through the back door, across the deck and onto the back lawn. The chilly sod was damp and quickly soaked through his socks. Muttering a few of his favorite curse words, Jonah made for the Adirondack chair he'd placed on the edge of the lawn. It should have been stored weeks ago—he was lucky he'd been lazy about preparing the yard for winter.

There was one hell of a mess in Lily's room right now, and he was a jerk for skipping out on it. Lily would be confused, maybe a little scared at his behavior. He'd all but accused Quinn of putting the words in his daughter's mouth. He knew she hadn't. Caught off guard, he'd said the first thing that came out of his mouth. Coming on the heels of his sudden revelation, it was too much to handle.

Jonah leaned back in the chair, resting his head against the hard wooden surface. Paige had wanted him to build a fire pit out here. She'd talked about the parties they'd throw, the friends they would invite. It was something they butted heads over often. Jonah didn't have friends, didn't socialize. The more people got to know him, the bigger the chance of their finding out that he couldn't read. It was a shameful secret, and one that he hadn't even shared with his wife.

Now that Quinn was teaching him to read, he felt his confidence growing. Soon, he'd be able to ask Blaise for that job. But how to explain to an entire town why he'd kept to himself for so long? Folks knew who he was. He wasn't a complete hermit. Work had taken him all over Scallop Shores and even into a couple of the surrounding towns. That's how he'd met Paige.

To Paige, Jonah had been a handsome stranger. He was tall, dark, and mysterious. She had no clue he'd been raised by a single dad who put more stock in learning a trade than in learning to read. She didn't know that other kids his age thought there was something wrong with him. He couldn't have made friends if he had wanted. No one else in Scallop Shores was homeschooled. That made him weird.

He hadn't realized just how much he had hungered for another person to talk to, someone to spend time with, until he met Paige. They rushed into marriage and it was too late to change his mind before Jonah realized that hiding such a huge part of his life from her would be a full-time responsibility. It wasn't long before the name calling started: he was cold, closed-off, and uptight. He wanted to think she was too prying, nosy, but he knew she had every right.

Gripping the arms of the chair and digging his sodden heels into the muddy grass, Jonah frowned at the line of trees separating his property from his neighbors'. He had been a horrible husband, right from the start. And it was Paige who had paid, first with a lonely existence away from family and friends, and finally with her life. And he wanted to do this again? No, he didn't deserve the love of a good woman. He had a penance to pay for his first marriage. A penance he would probably be working off for the rest of his life.

Pity party for one, please! Jonah shook his head, pinching the bridge of his nose.

Movement at the edge of his vision had him swiveling his head to the side, in time to see a large buck step out of the woods onto the lawn. He held his breath and watched to see if it would come any closer. This big guy was brave, roaming the woods during hunting season. Jonah hadn't made a sound, but the deer seemed to have known he was there all along. He turned his big rack toward the Adirondack chair and the two males stared each other down.

Obviously, he didn't deem Jonah to be much of a threat because he continued to amble around the edge of the lawn, stopping to nibble at the grass a couple of times before meandering back into the trees.

Something about that encounter with one of nature's creatures humbled him. Jonah was reminded that there was so much more to life than his petty problems. He could grouse about it later. Right now he had a room full of spilled paint to clean up. He headed back for the house, searching for another glimpse of the deer but it was gone.

"Saw a deer on the lawn," he threw over his shoulder as he spied Lily at the kitchen table. He shucked off his wet socks and threw them on the doormat.

"No way! Awesome," she squealed, after swallowing a bite of a PB & J sandwich. Quinn was nowhere to be seen.

"Where's Quinn?" Cleaning up his mess, no doubt.

"She made me lunch and went back to my room."

Guilt made his limbs feel heavier, his ears and face hot. She should have left it for him. It wasn't her fault he'd freaked out. Shamefully, he padded on bare feet to Lily's bedroom, where he found Quinn. Up on the ladder, working on her mural.

"You aren't cleaning up." He blinked.

"Of course not. It wasn't my mess to clean up." She threw over her shoulder.

"I know that. I just thought ... "

"Yeah, maybe you ought to do a little less thinking today." She fixed him with a stare, arching a brow.

She could have turned this into something. But she was letting it go. He could even see the barest hint of a smile at the corners of her mouth. Unbidden, and completely against his will, came the thought, "I am head over heels in love with this woman."

So this was how God intended to punish him for cutting Paige's life short. Stick the most beautiful, perfect woman in front of him.

Have him fall hopelessly in love. And remove all hope of a happily ever after. Good move, God. Good move.

• • •

It was raining, cold, steely drops that were just this side of freezing. Quinn stood at the back door, watching as the rivulets chased each other down the glass. She'd spent all morning chopping vegetables for a beef stew. Now she was rewarded with the delicious smell of simmering juices as the crock-pot worked its magic.

She stayed away from the living room. That particular scene was just a little too cozy for her to handle right now. Jonah lay on the couch, Lily sprawled across his chest, both napping a lazy afternoon away. Quinn had already been in for a peek. It was so tempting to think that this could be hers. But the quiet domestic scene had only reminded her of what she couldn't offer.

It was high time she look for other living arrangements. She'd gotten too comfortable here. She and Jonah had only made love the one time, okay, several times that one night. Once Lily returned from her grandparents' house, Jonah had kept his distance.

But she'd caught glimpses, moments when he watched and didn't think she noticed. She did her own fair share of ogling too. Not that she would do anything about it. Even if he had convinced her that her marriage had been a sham—and that it wasn't her fault.

She would always be grateful to him for that. Jonah showed her that she hadn't failed as a wife. Andrew's issues were his own. Touching the cold glass door with her fingertips, Quinn wondered if Andrew would ever find true happiness. She hoped so.

She couldn't begrudge him trying to pin all the blame of a ruined marriage on her. He was under a lot of pressure from a domineering mother. The woman was old-fashioned and had a very specific vision of what she expected her son's life to include.

Turning away from the back door, Quinn headed for the spare bedroom she'd been using. She had made a second copy of Lily's fairy book and it was ready for submission. Well, ready as it would ever be. The idea of trying to sell it to a New York publishing house was both terrifying and thrilling. What's the worst they could say? No? Fine. She had created it for Lily, anyway.

Snatching up the envelope, her keys, and purse, Quinn slipped from her room and headed for the front door. She didn't bother to leave a note. She'd be back before they even woke up. Shutting the front door quietly behind her, she ducked her head and braced her shoulders against the bitter preview of winter. Note to self: buy a thicker jacket!

The trip to the post office was uneventful. Not many people were braving the roads today. Twilight was making it hard to see as she navigated the backcountry road home. With the dark, the temperature would be dropping. Quinn knew enough about New England weather to be especially mindful of black ice patches. She drove carefully and was surprised to see every light on in the house as she drove up.

She wasn't even clear of the car when the front door opened and Jonah ran out, barefoot, and wearing a thin Henley shirt with no coat. Heedless of the weather, he rushed up, gripping her shoulders painfully.

"Do you know how dangerous those roads are? You didn't leave a note! I could have driven you. Why did you have to go and do something so foolish?"

Quinn's mouth opened and closed, like a fish out of water. She had no idea what she was supposed to say. Jonah's eyes were round with fear, genuine fear. He was shaking, but she had the feeling it had nothing to do with the freezing rain that had now turned to icy pellets as the sun went down. He pulled her close, wrapping her in those big strong arms and mumbling against her hair.

"What would I have done if I lost you? If Lily lost you? We need you, Quinn!" His body shook, and she couldn't be certain but she thought he might be crying. What on earth?

"I just went to the post office," she offered, lamely.

If he heard her, he didn't acknowledge it. He continued to whisper into her hair, his words softer, indistinguishable. His shaking subsided. He held her away from him, staring deeply into her eyes. He looked so sad, troubled. Quinn reached up and placed a palm to his cheek. He nuzzled against it.

"Why? Why did I have to fall in love with you?" he asked, miserably.

Then his lips were on hers, claiming her, possessing her. His kiss was a shelter from the rain, the cold no longer penetrating. Quinn reached up, standing on her toes to be able to loop her arms around his neck and kiss him back the way he should be kissed, the way he needed to be kissed. His feelings lay out in the open, raw and vulnerable. Kissing meant there were no words, no way to ruin the moment with whatever awkward tripe she could jumble together.

Jonah pushed her up against the car, his body shielding her from view. She gasped into his mouth as his cold fingers made quick work of the many layers of clothing she wore, searching for warm skin. His hands shook, whether from fear or need, Quinn couldn't tell. But if he kept it up, she was going to become a mewling mess out here.

"Daddy? Is Quinn okay?" Lily stood in the open doorway, peering through the gathering darkness.

"She's fine, Cuteness. She's just perfect."

Jonah touched his forehead to hers, his breathing ragged. Quinn held his face in her hands, using the last of the daylight to study his eyes, question his actions. She had scared him, really scared him.

"We need to talk about this." It wasn't a question.

"I know. I promise. Later, after Lily is asleep." Jonah closed his eyes and shook his head. "I'm sorry. You must think I'm crazy."

"Traumatized by something huge, yes. But crazy? Nah." Quinn kissed him softly before releasing him.

"Daddy, I'm hungry," Lily whined from the doorway.

"Me, too. Whatcha makin' for dinner, kiddo?"

He took great pains to appear back to normal, but Quinn could see he'd been really shaken. She followed behind him, using his large frame for cover as she dealt with her own reactions to his kiss, and his admission that he loved her. Her head swam and she felt like she was in a fog as she entered the warm house. She'd gotten too close. Now it was too late. Because Jonah wasn't the only one in love. She had fallen for, not just Jonah, but his precious daughter as well. And there was no way this could end well.

CHAPTER 17

The foolish man had gone and gotten himself sick. Quinn had sent him straight in for a hot shower after running outside in bare feet. She'd practically spoon-fed him the hearty beef stew that had been simmering all day. She set him up on the couch with every extra blanket and quilt she could find.

She'd put Lily to bed herself. Even his four-year-old knew "Daddy should have worn shoes in the rain. It was slushy." She slipped into bed, shaking her head like a tiny adult. Quinn bit her lip to keep from laughing. Sometimes Lily was far too mature for her own good. She was going to give them a run for their money someday. Well, not them. Just Jonah. It was too damned easy to think of a future with them.

By the time Quinn had headed back out to the living room, Jonah had a raging fever. Maybe he'd already caught something and a jaunt through a November storm just encouraged it to come on like a freight train. In typical male fashion, he moaned, gripping her hand like a lifeline. Why men always treated illness as though they were truly dying, she'd never understand.

And so they never had that talk. Was this about Paige and how she'd died? Could it be his way of letting her know he still had feelings for his late wife? But he'd professed to love *her*. Though she was hurt and confused, Quinn let it go.

It wasn't like he could get too far away from her. She knew where he lived. She could corner him in the middle of the night, in his bed, if she really wanted to talk. Though talking wouldn't be her first choice if she had Jonah cornered in his bed in the middle of the night.

"Earth to Quinn. Come in, Quinn." Cady's voice broke through her troubled thoughts.

They sat in the bakery, at a back table. Cady had just closed up for the day, but invited Quinn and Lily to stay while she cleaned up. Quinn sent Lily to a table in the opposite corner, breaking out a new Barbie and fresh coloring book that she'd been saving for just such a moment. They had a few uninterrupted minutes.

"You aren't even touching your brownie. You want it warmed up?"

"Sorry, I'm just distracted today. I'm worried about Jonah." Quinn plucked a napkin from the dispenser on the table and began to twist it.

"He's just got a cold. He'll be fine. And as soon as he's fine, you and Lily will catch it." Cady reached out and swiped a corner of the brownie, slipping it into her mouth with a wink.

"That's not it. I went out the other day, mailed my book to an editor friend in NY." She shushed her friend, who had let out a squeal before clamping a hand over her mouth and waving at a curious Lily.

"It was rainy and cold, and by the time I got home it was getting a little icy too. I know how to drive in this stuff, been doing it all my life, practically." Quinn looked down and noted, with surprise, that the napkin lay shredded before her. She pulled out another and started over.

"He was waiting for me to get home. He came running for the car with no shoes and no coat, crazy-like. He pulled me into a hug and it was like I had terrified him. I swear he even cried." Quinn blinked to see that Cady, herself, was a little misty.

"Oh my God, he loves you." She grabbed the napkin from Quinn, while there was still some substance to it, and dabbed her eyes.

"Well, he kinda mentioned that too, in among his crazy ranting." This time Quinn tore off a piece of moist brownie and licked it off her finger. She closed her eyes and smiled.

"Ah … Because of how his wife died." Cady leaned forward and lowered her voice. "She'd been driving on a bad night, really bad. Ice was unavoidable. They said she'd been speeding too. Her car hit a patch of ice, she lost control and went over the side of the ridge, not too far from their house. Paige was dead before anyone arrived on scene."

"He'd mentioned it. No details or anything. It must still be so hard to talk about." Quinn's eyes flew to the precious little girl coloring by herself. "Was she his soul mate?"

"I don't know." Cady shrugged. "No one knew much about either of them. Jonah's lived here all his life, but no one really knows him."

She should have realized that. Jonah had a huge secret to keep. How lonely that must have been for him, for all of them. Paige must have really loved her husband to live out there in the woods and cut herself off from town life.

"Ever since you came into town, he's stopping in more, being friendly. Folks knew him from the odd jobs he did around their houses, but he'd never stopped in town to socialize." Cady let the implication hang.

"What can I say? I dragged him out of his shell." She smirked.

"You brought Bree out of her shell too. She's talking more, hiding behind her books less."

"Well, I'd say you had a lot to do with my involvement in Bree's life." Quinn patted Cady's hand and gave her friend a genuine smile. "I really need to thank you for making my transition to Scallop Shores an easier one. I didn't expect so much opposition." She looked out the window and groaned.

Cady turned to see. "Well, speak of the devil's spawn." She giggled, looking only mildly repentant.

"There is another mystery I don't know if I'll ever be able to crack." Quinn watched her sister saunter down the sidewalk with her girls; girls that she did not want Quinn getting to know.

"Thanksgiving is coming up soon. You two celebrating together?"

Quinn let out a bark of laughter that had Lily turning in her seat. She gave the child an indulgent smile and turned back to the conversation.

"If she's planning something, I was not invited."

"She came to Lily's birthday party," Cady supplied.

"Yeah, and that's still blowing my mind. I think she was just looking for a way to humiliate me in public."

"Ah, so since Thanksgiving isn't a public forum, she doesn't have any reason to invite you and make you feel miserable?"

"Something like that."

"I wish I could tell you why she seems to have it in for you. Truth is, Kayla didn't start badmouthing you until you got to town. I guess she considers Scallop Shores hers."

"She always did have a hard time sharing." Both women chuckled.

"So make the first move. Invite yourself and tell her you're bringing ... whatever she can't resist. Just make sure you ask if Jonah and Lily can come too."

"I'm so sick of making the first move. It shouldn't be this hard to try to have a relationship with your own sister." Quinn watched Kayla cross the street, dropping a kiss on Zoe's head as they walked. Would it really kill her to show her own sister that kind of love and affection?

"You two need to sort this all out, just the two of you." Cady's eyes got huge and she clapped her hands excitedly. "I've got it! Invite her to the city for a day. Go get spa treatments, go shopping, and take her to all the places you loved when you were living there. Show her you aren't afraid to share your city with her and maybe she'll open up to you."

Quinn considered. It wasn't a bad idea. They needed to talk, and they needed to do it away from the gossips in town. Jake would watch the girls. If they went on a weekend, Jonah would be home to stay with Lily. She nodded. They could take her car, that way they would have four hours each way of nothing to do but talk. If she could even convince Kayla to spend that much time alone with her to begin with.

• • •

Winter arrived early in Scallop Shores, dropping nearly five inches of wet snow. Jonah knew from experience that he'd be cursing the white stuff by January, but there was just something magical about the first snow of the season. Just the day before everything looked tired and depressing. With a blanket of snow, it looked fresh, invigorated.

The snow had actually started falling the night before, so they knew they'd have something to look forward to in the morning. Lily had woken him up, bouncing on his bed and chattering about how Santa had brought the snow. He tried to reason that one out, but it would take some coffee and a peek into the four-year-old psyche. Way too early for that.

Quinn stood in his doorway, excitement in her eyes as she held out two mugs of coffee. He beckoned her in and they drank their first cup of coffee together in his bedroom, Quinn perched on the end of his bed.

Jonah pictured a different scene, with Lily coming in to wake both of them, climbing under the warm covers to snuggle as a family. Instead, they watched her dance in front of the window, chattering about all the different things she was going to do in the snow that day.

They all got dressed quickly, layering on turtlenecks and sweaters and doubling up on their socks. Jonah was dismayed to see that Lily had outgrown her snowsuit over the past year. He wasn't so much bothered about the added expense, it certainly came with raising a daughter. But it was proof that his little girl was growing up. It wouldn't be long before a snow day meant an excuse to sleep in, then spend the day chatting on the phone with her girlfriends … and boyfriends. He shuddered.

"Daddy, I want a snow fort. Can we make one?" Lily held up the plastic brick maker they had bought last year.

"You don't want to make a snowman?" Jonah tried to hide his disappointment.

"'Nother time. Come on." Lily jumped off the deck, a safe enough feat on a day like this.

"She's a take charge kinda gal, isn't she?" Quinn winked. "I picture her as a CEO of her own firm someday."

Jonah remembered the last words Paige had hurled at him as she'd tossed clothes in an overnight bag to leave for her parents' house. She had a different future pictured for their daughter, a much bleaker idea than the one Quinn had laid out. He started at the hand gripping his arm.

"We're overdue for that talk, you know." Her voice was gentle, but insistent.

"It's not pleasant, Quinn. I'm just trying to protect you." He watched his daughter romp across the back lawn, stopping to make a snow angel every so often.

"I'm tough. I can handle it." She turned him to face her. "And nothing you say is going to change anything between us."

She hadn't said she loved him. Maybe it would have been easier to spill his guts if she'd told him she loved him. *Stop it! Can't think like that.* He didn't have a future with Quinn, and the sooner he accepted that, the better off they'd all be.

"I'll come find you tonight."

His body hardened at her words, his reply sucked right out of his lungs. Did she know what she was doing to him? Even in an ugly green knit cap, her nose bright red with cold, Quinn was gorgeous. Her brown eyes focused on his mouth and Jonah had the brief satisfaction of realizing that her thoughts were going down a similar path. Good.

They all worked together, building a snow fort worthy of a princess. When it was done, Lily kicked the adults out. She insisted that if they stayed, her fairy would be too shy to make an appearance. He asked if it might not be too cold for a fairy to be out and about. Lily shook her head and told him that her fairy loved her and would stay with her no matter the weather.

Quinn had that sparkle in her eye, the one that said she was already plotting out her next illustrated book about fairies. A frisson of fear gripped Jonah's heart and gave it a quick squeeze. Sometime soon she would be moving out of their house, finding a place of her own. Sure, it may be in Scallop Shores, but it wouldn't be with them.

He couldn't expect Quinn to stay with them forever. The fairy tale life they'd been living, with two parents and a perfect little girl, had been just that, a fairy tale. It wasn't real.

"I'm going to get started on the driveway." He needed a break from this Hallmark moment.

"Grab me an extra shovel and I'll do the deck here," Quinn offered.

She followed him toward the side of the house and the entrance to the basement. Jonah hurried inside, anxious to grab the shovels and head back out before Quinn could follow him. He didn't know whether he'd be able to keep his hands off her if they found themselves alone. When she remained in the doorway, making no move to enter the basement, Jonah felt a pang of disappointment. *Can't win for losing.*

"What do you do when we get really dumped on? Say a foot or more?" Quinn questioned him as he joined her in the bracing cold.

He wanted to kiss the bright red tip of her nose.

"I've got a plow for the front of my truck." He handed Quinn a shovel. "It's another way to make ends meet in the winter."

"What an awesome job!"

He turned to scowl at her, assuming she was being sarcastic, and was surprised to see the enthusiasm on her face was genuine. He frowned, unable to see things from her angle.

"How so? I have to get up about four A.M., bundle a sleeping kid in the truck and get driveways and parking lots clear so the people who run this town can do their jobs." He shook his head, already picturing the nightmarishly long winter ahead of him.

"You get to see it first. You see the roads, the driveways, and parking lots all pristine and unmarred. You get to step out into that absolute quiet, that calm that comes after a big snowstorm. It must be so relaxing."

"I can take you with me someday ... if you want." He didn't know why he offered. It had just slipped out.

"I'd love that." Quinn stretched up and kissed his whiskered cheek. Her lips were warm.

She turned on a booted heel and headed for the backyard again. Jonah could still feel the imprint of her lips on his cheek. The woman drove him crazy. It was getting harder and harder to remember a life that didn't include her. But was it Quinn, or was it just that he had been so lonely that he latched onto the first single woman he'd met since he came out of his self-imposed shell?

He made short work of the snow on the front porch. The physical activity a welcome distraction to the turmoil that had his thoughts jumbled and his body buzzing like a live wire. Tossing a thin layer of rock salt over the stairs, Jonah continued on to the driveway. Working up a sweat, he abandoned his coat on the porch railing. He pulled his flannel shirt out of the waistband of his jeans and rolled the sleeves up, exposing the thermal shirt beneath.

It wasn't a true blizzard until the sky dropped at least a foot of the white stuff. He could probably get away with not shoveling the driveway, letting the wheels of his pick up carve out their own ruts on his way in and out. But if they got a cold snap, everything would turn to ice. Then he'd have a skating rink for a driveway. His truck could probably manage it, but he wouldn't let Quinn and her fancy Beamer risk it.

An hour later, bone-weary and hungry, he turned to survey his work. The driveway was clear, if a bit narrow for his taste. He had cleared off both vehicles. Standing the shovel upright, in a pile of snow, Jonah turned toward the house.

His mother's row of yellow rose bushes were just lumps of white butting up against the front porch. Lily's ladybug sandbox was hidden beneath the snow. The storage shed on the side of the house looked ignored, lonely. Jonah frowned. It *had* been ignored. Damn shame.

His dad had meant for it to be a workshop. He'd rigged it up for electricity. But after Paige died, Jonah decided it was too far away to keep an ear out for Lily. So the shed had become a dumping ground for off-season items and enough junk to fill out a garage sale or two.

It would make a damn decent studio, though. There was plenty of light and he could put in a drafting bench or whatever Quinn needed. It wasn't insulated for year round use, but that was an easy fix. He could see her fixing it up with curtains and rugs. Flowers too, probably. A working art studio. Right here, where she wouldn't have to leave.

"What are you staring at?"

Jonah jumped aside, swiping a hand across his face as his cheeks warmed, having been caught woolgathering.

"Just trying to figure out what to do with that sorry shed on the side of the house." He accepted the thermos of coffee that Quinn handed him.

"Ooh! That would make the cutest little playhouse for Lily. Don't you see it?" She waved a gloved hand to encompass the shed. "Little gingham curtains, some cozy rugs, tiny furniture.

Oh, she'd love a little book nook. And you'd have to put in a little table and chairs. She could color out there, have tea parties."

"You've got vision, I'll give you that." He swallowed hard. "And would you be there, helping me get all this set up?"

"I don't know, Jonah." She pressed her lips together and cast her eyes to the snowy ground.

"What if I told you I wanted you there, in that vision?"

She glanced up, tucking her bottom lip between her teeth. He thought he read hope in those soulful eyes. Maybe he just wanted it too bad to think it could be anything less.

"I wish I could be what you needed me to be. You don't know how badly I want it too. But we've talked about this. Lily needs a mother, but she deserves brothers and sisters too."

"We'll get a dog. Two dogs. She'll never be lonely."

"Do you know what Lily is doing right now, Jonah?" Quinn looked toward the house, moisture brimming in her eyes. "She's making out a list for Santa. She asked me how to spell mommy and baby brother."

"Aw, crap."

"Yeah." She took a deep breath. "I really do wish I could be what you both need. But I'm not that person." With one last anguished look in his direction, Quinn hurried back to the house.

The magic of the first snowfall of the season was gone, and with it, the hope of a future that included Quinn. Jonah snatched up his shovel and headed for the basement. This time he cursed the steely gray sky, as it began to spit more frozen precipitation.

CHAPTER 18

She should have been cozy and relaxed. A fire crackled in the fireplace, giving off plenty of warmth and creating shadows as the flames danced in the grate. Quinn had fixed a pot of hot chocolate to go with the cookies she and Lily had baked that afternoon. Lily tended to have a heavy hand when it came to frosting, so they had stuck to plain old chocolate chip this time.

Quinn's nerves were on edge. All she wanted to do was cry. She kept thinking back to that moment in the kitchen, Lily surrounded by crayons and paper. The first of the season's snow had brought with it thoughts of Christmas. Lily had been working on a wish list for Santa. Quinn had expected to hear her ask for toys, something fairy related. But she said that Santa could bring *her* toys to the kids who might not have any. She wanted a mother and a baby, a brother if Santa wouldn't mind if she chose.

Quinn had been rendered speechless. How did one respond to a plea like that? It wasn't her place, anyway. She simply helped the child spell out her words and put her letter to Santa in an envelope, addressed to the North Pole. She'd give it to Jonah later.

Squirming on the couch, she took a sip of her cocoa and tried to get comfortable. She wasn't feeling well. Even her chocolate tasted off. Maybe she was getting Jonah's cold, a little late. She tossed an afghan over her legs and waited for Jonah to come back from tucking his daughter in.

"You got any more of that?" He stood in the doorway, gesturing to her tray on the coffee table.

"The hot chocolate or the cookies?"

"Both." He licked his lips and she squirmed for an entirely different reason.

"There's an extra mug on the counter. I left the plate of cookies there too. Bring me another one, would you?" They might taste a little weird to her, but she was suddenly famished. Starve a cold, feed a fever … how did that go?

Jonah returned with a mug and filled it from the pot on the coffee table. He'd brought the entire plate of cookies. Bless him! Quinn expected him to head for his ratty "man chair," a little closer to the fire. So she was surprised when he put a pillow behind his back and sat facing her from the other end of the couch, their legs tangling as he adjusted the blanket over both of them. Quinn raised an eyebrow but didn't say a thing.

For a moment, they ate their cookies and drank their cocoa in silence. The only sound in the room was the crackle and snap of the logs settling in the fireplace.

But Quinn was still tense, worried for Jonah, upset about Lily's letter. She couldn't be lulled into relaxing by the fire on a quiet evening. Setting her mug down on the tray with a louder-than-necessary thud, she held her agitation in check. She wanted to scream at Jonah to talk, already.

"You okay?"

"Of course. I don't know what you're talking about." She was too defensive. She worked at evening her breath. There, that was better.

"I've scared you. And you've probably asked around and no one has any answers for you. The mysterious Jonah Goodwin who lost his wife under shady circumstances." His voice was teasing, but he wasn't smiling.

"I'm concerned for you, not for myself." Quinn ran a stocking clad foot over his hard shin. "I've just had an emotional day. I'm strung out. If you thought it was because I'm scared of what you have to tell me, you're wrong."

He sipped at his cocoa, staring into the flames. He looked so sad. It had to have been an emotional day for him, as well. That was a lot of pressure to put on a single dad who wanted to give his daughter the world. He wanted to give Lily a mother. Quinn was sure he wanted to give her that little brother too. But how to explain to a young child that things like this took time, and careful planning?

"I hid the fact that I couldn't read from Paige. Not the best way to start a marriage, but I felt like I didn't have any choice." His large fingers gripped the mug tightly as his story started to unravel. "She didn't understand why I kept us so isolated out here. I didn't have any friends in town. She wasn't from here, so all her friends were a couple towns away. She was lonely."

Quinn watched his face, remorse and guilt fighting for dominance. He set his jaw and met her eyes, an attempted smile falling flat. She gave him one of her own instead, pouring as much warmth and encouragement into it as she could. He reached down and squeezed her knee in silent acknowledgement.

"I'm not even sure how I was able to keep her in the dark for so long. I just used my coping mechanisms on her, same as I'd been using to get by since my dad passed."

"You made it seem like it was her idea to read things aloud? You had her fill out paperwork?"

"Yeah, I'd pretend I was reading it all wrong, when I really didn't have a clue what it said. She'd laugh and correct me. But then she started asking questions, putting things together."

Jonah paused to take a few sips of hot chocolate. He reached for the last cookie on the plate and gave Quinn a wry grin that said he knew he hadn't been the one to empty the plate so fast. She shrugged, a small smile tugging at the corners of her mouth. Chivalrously, he split the cookie in half and handed a piece to her. She nodded, encouraging him to go on with his tale.

"Her ten year reunion was coming up. She was so excited. Started asking me about my high school experiences. Paige had pegged me for a jock." His laugh was short and bitter. "I think I might have liked that." He stared into the flickering flames, like he'd gotten lost in old memories.

"She didn't buy that you were homeschooled?" Quinn had the strangest urge to defend Jonah from his late wife.

"She did ... at first." His face took on a sour look and his light eyes became hard, cold. "Then she started snooping around for my paperwork. She was like a damned private investigator, couldn't leave things well enough alone.

"She wanted to know what contractor I worked for, since I'd led her to believe that I wasn't just a handyman but a real construction worker. I told her it was none of her business. That went over well."

Jonah set his mug down on the coffee table and adjusted the pillow behind his back. Then, restless, he swung his legs out from under the afghan and sat with his back against the back of the couch. He raked his hands through his hair, his tight muscles standing out like cords on his arms.

"This is too hard on you. Please. You don't have to finish." Quinn had pulled her knees up to her chin and hugged them tightly. She shook her head back and forth.

"No. I've got to say it. Hiding things is what caused all this to happen. I can't hide the truth anymore. I'm the reason Paige died. I killed her."

• • •

Way to scare the hell out of her, Goodwin! Jonah stared miserably at Quinn, cowering at her end of the couch, pulled up into a tight ball, like she was afraid he was going to do her in next. He'd only meant to say that he took full blame for what had happened that night.

"That didn't come out right." He looked down, ashamed.

"Just go on," she whispered, peering at him over the tops of her bony knees.

"It was just … we were fighting." Did Quinn shrink even further into the couch, or was that just the way his guilty imagination was reading things?

"Paige hadn't turned up any record of homeschooling, any records that I had ever filled out, even. She asked if I knew how to write. I think she'd meant it half-jokingly, but I couldn't hide the look on my face. She'd blown my secret right out of the water."

Quinn watched him closely. Maybe she wasn't as scared as he'd first assumed. She looked like she was sad for him. Jonah wiped his hands nervously on his jeans, the denim rough beneath his fingertips. He bit his lip and turned his attention back to the fire.

"We were in the kitchen. She pulls out a cookbook, slams it open in front of me, and points to a page. 'Read it,' she yelled. I couldn't. God, you don't know how bad I wish I could have." He dropped his face in his hands, his whole body quaking as he relived the most painful night of his life.

"I tried to apologize for lying, well, for not telling her my secret, my truth. And you know what? That isn't the part that bothered her."

Jonah turned a grief stricken face to Quinn, reaching out for a hand, a touch, anything to keep him grounded in this moment, this reality. She was up on her knees, grasping both his hands in hers, tears streaming down her cheeks.

"She told me that I sickened her. She said she was disgusted that she could have ever thought herself in love with an illiterate. Then she went to our room and started packing a bag.

"My first thought was Lily. She was going to take the one thing, the only thing I'd ever done right in this world." This time, the terror that he knew filled his eyes was mirrored in Quinn's as she leaned in close, hanging on his every word.

"I ran in and begged her not to go, not to take Lily. I promised to go to school, take lessons, whatever she wanted me to do." He licked his lips and continued. "She laughed at me. She packed up her bag, gave me the cruelest look and told me she had no daughter. That there was no way she was going to raise a child with a stupid gene, like her father." He winced, repeating the words that had beaten him worse than fists ever could.

Taking in huge gulps of air, shaking uncontrollably, Jonah found that he just couldn't finish. His mind replayed that last moment, that look of contempt on Paige's face, over and over again. After a long while, he finally became aware of a hand rubbing his back, feather light kisses being pressed to his brow.

"I think I can fill in the rest. It was dark and cold out, raining to the point of freezing. No one in their right mind would have gone out in it. But Paige wasn't thinking clearly. She only wanted to get away." Quinn didn't wait for confirmation.

"She hit a patch of black ice, lost control of her car and went off the embankment, hitting a tree."

"She died at the scene." He searched her gaze, looking for what, salvation, perhaps?

"She did. You, on the other hand, were at home, taking care of your baby girl." She left the rest unsaid, but her expression dared him to try to pin Paige's death on himself.

Jonah closed his eyes, giving himself over to sensation, the feel of Quinn's hands stroking his back. If he were a child, he'd curl up in her lap, be lulled to sleep. He had half a mind to do it anyway.

"You said it. You got it out. And I'm still here. You didn't scare me away. Paige was wrong." She waited until he looked up to finish. "Illiteracy isn't a disease. And it doesn't mean you're stupid."

She pushed him back against the couch cushions and frowned.

"And why are we having this discussion anyway? You have mastered reading, my friend. There is nothing more I can teach you that you can't teach yourself by diving in and devouring as many books as possible."

Jonah hauled Quinn onto his lap and settled his hands on her hips.

"Do I have to hand in my man card now? I think I might have been crying for a bit there."

"Are you kidding me? Don't you know sensitivity is a huge turn-on for women?" She punctuated her point with a little wiggle that had his eyes rolling back in his head.

"Well then, it seems our thoughts might be headed down the same path." He tugged on her belt loops, causing her to fall forward.

When she squealed in pain rather than excitement, Jonah grasped her shoulders and gave her some breathing room.

"Did I hurt you?"

"No, I don't know what's wrong. My boobs hit your chest and I felt like they were going to explode." Unconsciously she rubbed them. "I think I must be starting my period soon," she said.

Warning bells jangled in Jonah's head. Snatches of memory nagged at his brain, trying to get him to remember. Paige hadn't complained about her boobs hurting during a normal menstrual cycle. But he remembered her bursting into tears over the pain just before they found out she was pregnant.

"Is it possible that you could be pregnant?" He asked, his voice thick with emotion.

"Jonah, you know that's not possible. I can't have children. Andrew and I tried for years."

"Were you ever tested? Was he? Do you know for a fact that when you made love he … you know … finished?" He felt uncomfortable asking, but he needed to know.

"I didn't want to actually hear the news from a doctor. I guess I thought that if I never got diagnosed, that I could still hold out hope."

"I think we should pick up a test."

"A fertility test? Don't I have to make an appointment with a doctor?" For such an intelligent woman, Quinn was adorably clueless right now.

"A pregnancy test, sweetheart. I don't want to get your hopes up, but something about this situation is bringing back all kinds of memories about Paige finding out she was pregnant with Lily."

"Pregnant? A baby?" Her mouth opened and closed like a fish gasping for air. "Jonah, you know if it turns out you're wrong I'll be worse than crushed."

"Think about it. Has anything else been off? Foods taste different? Just not feeling yourself but you don't know why?" He could tell by the look on her face that she was, in fact, experiencing just those things.

"A baby." Quinn's stunned look slowly gave way to joy. "I get to pee on a stick!" She slapped his leg as she chortled.

He *had* told her he didn't want to get her hopes up, right? Well, she'd gone straight from clueless to giddy in thirty seconds. He wasn't one hundred percent certain. But the possibility was there. This certainly was an emotional roller coaster ride of an evening. Reliving the most painful night of his life and now a second chance at love and a whole family? Maybe Lily would get her Christmas wish after all.

CHAPTER 19

Quinn huddled inside her ski jacket, stuffing her gloved hands into the pockets. Her breath came out in white puffs. She hurried along the sidewalk, rock salt crunching beneath her boots. She wasn't late for her appointment with the insurance agent, she just found herself vibrating with excess energy. Nerves, more like.

She and Jonah had stayed up late the night before, talking. For the first time since she'd moved back to Scallop Shores, she cursed the inconvenience of small-town life. In the city, she could have darted out at midnight and found any number of pharmacies open twenty-four hours. She could have bought a pregnancy test last night and had the results in only a few minutes.

Instead she had to get through this appointment with Kayla before she could swing by the drug store and pick one up. And since she was going to see her anyway, Quinn decided to follow through with Cady's idea and ask her sister on a girls' day out. Multiply those nerves times a million. She wouldn't even think about Thanksgiving yet. Better to see how things went, or didn't go, in Manhattan.

She had almost reached the insurance agent's small office, located between Terry's Fluff & Fold and Petal Pushers, the florist shop, when her eye was drawn to a window across the street. Luckily the street was empty, because Quinn stepped from the curb and just kept walking, seeing nothing but Tiny Treasures' precious window display.

Pressing her gloves to the glass and trying not to fog up the window with her breath, Quinn gazed longingly at the baby mannequins sporting the tiniest little sweaters she'd ever seen. Pink and blue, yellow and mint green, even the plain white ones were too adorable for words. And the blankets—oh, and the itty-bitty shoes. She turned away before she started bawling like a lunatic. Pressing a hand to her belly, she silently prayed that Jonah's suspicions were right. She prayed for a miracle. Taking a deep breath, she forced herself to march back across the street for her appointment.

Kayla was already seated in the lobby when Quinn stepped into the insurance agency. Expecting a snarky remark about her tardiness, Quinn was mildly surprised when her sister merely nodded and waited quietly for the agent to call them into his office.

"Ms. Baker, Mrs. Patterson, please come in. Can I offer you both some coffee?"

Quinn shook her head and saw Kayla do the same. They sat down in front of a big mahogany desk, so many photo frames arranged around the front that they could barely see over them to the man on the other side. Quinn chanced a quick glance at her sister, regretfully wishing they were closer, that she could offer a pat on the knee or a smile and that it would be warmly received.

"The results from the arson investigation on your grandmother's house have come back. The fire has been ruled an accident; it started in the basement and they suspect the oil furnace was to blame. It was old, the floor and surrounding walls were covered in oily residue. You couldn't have anticipated this."

Quinn closed her eyes. So many memories were made in that house. Happier times with Kayla and Nanny. Embarrassed, she accepted a tissue from the box the insurance agent held out. Kayla grabbed for one too and Quinn found she could not look at her sister for fear of losing what little control she had left over her emotions. They dabbed at their eyes, each reflecting privately on their loss.

"In addition to the market value of the home, we added what furniture and possessions remained at the time of the fire, based on a list we compiled from both your statements. As you requested, the total was split down the middle with a cashier's check made out to each of you." He pushed an envelope toward Quinn, nearly upsetting a picture frame in the process. The other he handed to Kayla.

"I know this has been a very rough year for the both of you, losing your grandmother and now your family home. But you're together now and that has to be a great comfort to you." He looked from one sister to the other, either unable or unwilling to see the distance, the tension between the women.

He stood, indicating that their appointment was over. Quinn shook the man's hand, thanked him for his time and quickly left the room. Kayla was right on her heels.

It was far too cold to stand and chat outside. Quinn thought about asking Kayla if she'd like to go for a coffee at the bakery, but she was too anxious to get to the drug store and buy a pregnancy test. She'd almost talked herself out of inviting Kay to the city when she realized her sister was not attacking her. She wasn't exactly friendly, but she wasn't hurling insults and making her intentionally miserable. If ever there was a good opening, this was it.

"Kay, I have a crazy suggestion," she began, licking her lips nervously. "I know Saturdays are your busy days at the salon, but what are you doing Sunday?"

Kayla's eyes narrowed and she began to frown. "Why?"

"I want to take you out. Just us girls. But not here. Manhattan. What do you say?"

"You want us to go all the way to the city for the day? What would we do?" The frown had been replaced by genuine confusion. Her sister didn't expect her to do something nice.

"What would you like to do? We could get our nails done, do a little shopping. You can get a jump-start on Christmas shopping for the girls. The toy store, FAO Schwarz, is just humongous."

"You've never asked me to visit the city before," Kayla whispered.

"I know. And that was awful of me. But I want to take you there now. It's not like I would have ever called it home, but I did spend quite a few years there. I've made some memories I want to share." Quinn held her breath as she waited for her sister's answer.

"You're driving. I've never even driven in Boston. And you're buying your nieces each an American Girl doll." Kayla threw down the challenge.

"I would love to."

They stood studying each other in the brisk, watery sunlight. The silence was awkward, but free of the rancor that charged their conversations of late. Quinn attempted a smile and was pleased when the edges of Kayla's mouth tipped up, ever so slightly.

"You'd better pick me up at six A.M. then. It's a four hour drive."

"I'll bring the coffee and pastries." Quinn waved as her sister turned and headed for the small parking lot behind the laundromat.

Well, that went ... pretty darned great. She giggled to herself.

Jonah had told her to take her time with this appointment, and try to spend a little time with her sister. But he was home watching Lily when he had jobs lined up. She needed to put the blinders on so she didn't head back to the baby boutique. She had one last errand to run. Hurrying toward her car, Quinn drove to a pharmacy one town over for privacy's sake, for something she thought she'd never have the chance to buy—a pregnancy test.

Heart in her throat by the time she reached the house, she carried the tiny paper sack inside. Jonah looked up from his recliner, where he and Lily were reading a book. He looked from the bag to Quinn, his smile nervous but eager.

"Should I wait?" he asked, this time looking from the bag to the hallway, where the bathroom was located.

"Um, no. You need to get to work." She left the pregnancy test in her room, where it wouldn't have the power to control her every thought.

When she returned, Lily was sitting on the couch with a bowl of graham crackers. The TV was on, some cartoon Quinn wasn't yet familiar with. Jonah was lacing up his work boots and shrugging into his heavy jacket. Before she'd met Jonah, Quinn never would have dreamed that she'd find grungy old work boots sexy. But on him? Yum.

"Will you call me?" He glanced at his daughter, absorbed by her TV show, and grasped both of Quinn's hands in his.

"Come on. You don't want to find out something so important over the phone." She snuck him a quick kiss on the cheek. "I'll tell you tonight."

He hesitated, his eyes boring deeply into hers. Without a word, he told her he loved her. And she got the message loud and clear. She nodded, hoping that her feelings were just as clearly reflected in her own eyes. Jonah smiled and she felt her knees grow weak. Oh, how she wanted a future with this man!

After he left the house, Quinn turned back to see that she, indeed, had a few minutes to herself. Lily wouldn't even blink until the next commercial. Taking a deep breath, she slipped into her room to retrieve the test.

"Lily, I'll be in the potty, okay?"

"Uh huh."

With shaking fingers she shut the door, turning the lock at the last second. Quinn opened the box, finding more paperwork than test. Was it really this complicated? She unfolded the paper and sat down on the toilet seat lid to educate herself on taking a pregnancy test.

In all her years of marriage she had never actually taken a test to see if she were pregnant. She had learned everything she could about online ovulation calculators. She'd become quite intimate with her cycle. She even had the charts to prove it. But every twenty-seven days, without fail, her period would start and she was forced to accept the fact that there would be no need for a pregnancy test that month.

Furrowing her brow, Quinn looked up from her reading to count back. How long had it been? Surely it was longer than twenty-seven days. It sure felt like it. Having charted for so many years, keeping track of her cycle was just something that became a habit. So it surprised her to be this unsure.

Paperwork studied, test taken, Quinn placed it on top of the toilet tank for the requisite three minutes. Three minutes. A blink of an eye. She stood up and paced the short length of the bathroom. She adjusted a slightly crooked picture frame. She sat down on the edge of the tub, drumming her fingers on the porcelain. Three minutes. It was a freaking eternity!

• • •

Country music blared from the speakers as Jonah tapped his fingers on the steering wheel of his pickup, his head nodding in time to the beat. It was a good day. For the first time in a long time he had no worries, no regrets.

Even if it turned out that Quinn wasn't pregnant this time, he knew, without being able to explain it, that the fault never lay with her. She was as fertile as the next woman. Oh, what he wouldn't give to meet that slimy ex who brainwashed her into thinking she was anything less than perfect!

The song on the radio switched to something a little more sedate. Jonah thought back to when he first opened his eyes this morning. He'd turned to the empty pillow beside him, empty for so long that it shouldn't have seemed out of place. But instead of feeling lonely, he pictured Quinn waking up beside him. Her long blonde hair mussed up and spread over the pillow, her sleepy brown eyes gazing at him with a mixture of love and lust. Jonah chuckled. Damned country songs really got him thinking things he had no business thinking when he ought to be paying attention to the road.

Whether he had a new mouth to feed or not, Jonah knew it was time to put his fear aside and talk to Blaise about that job. The man had said when he was ready, a job would be waiting. Well, he was ready. He'd finished the tiling job in Ms. Spencer's bathroom and, it being the start of winter, there wasn't much call for renovation or handyman projects. So with no further jobs lined up, he was on his way out to Blaise's building site, hoping the boss man was on duty.

The sun was sinking low over Perkins Pond as Jonah swung down out of his truck. His breath came out in big frosty billows and he rubbed his bare hands together to ward off the chill. He followed the pneumatic wheeze of a nail gun and the whine of a table saw to the hive of activity. Sure enough, Curtis Blaise stood in the center of it all, hard hat on his white hair, clipboard at the ready.

"Well, if it isn't my newest employee. You ready to jump on board, Goodwin?"

"I think I am, sir." Jonah stepped forward.

"Either you are, or you aren't. Which is it?" Blaise arched a brow, tucking his clipboard against his side.

Jonah pressed his lips together, held out his hand and said, "I would be pleased to come work for you, Mr. Blaise."

"Shucks, call me Curt. I knew your dad, after all." The older man's grip was firm, decisive.

"When can I start, sir, uh, Curt?" Jonah wanted to show his new boss he was eager to prove his worth.

"Tomorrow will be soon enough, young fella. Go on home to your two beautiful girls." Curt beamed.

"Oh, I just have the one daughter. Lily."

"And one of the prettiest live-in nannies I've ever laid my eyes on." The older man had the audacity to wink.

"Quinn's not … " Jonah shook his head, embarrassed.

"When you gonna make an honest woman of her, young man?" The look on his face must have been incriminating, because Curt let out a loud guffaw.

His new boss slapped him on his back and steered him back toward his truck, muttering something about small-town gossip and bucking up. He waved Jonah off, telling him he'd see him at eight A.M. sharp.

Jonah sat in his truck for a few moments before starting the engine. He'd spent his whole adult life avoiding Curtis Blaise because of his shameful secret. His own father had been gone ten years now. Curt was a good man. He'd make a great boss. But more than that, he'd make a good friend.

He was startled to realize just how starved he was for a buddy, a confidante, a role model, even. Curt brought back memories of growing up with his dad. He sorely missed that man.

It wasn't yet five o'clock. Quinn and Lily wouldn't be expecting him for another hour. Jonah knew he had big news to come home to. He was anxious to get there but he didn't want to arrive empty-handed. He'd watched Quinn turn her nose up at coffee this morning. Quinn, who would willingly give up breakfast in favor of her morning cup of joe. All the signs were there.

There was a store in town, wasn't there, that sold just baby things? He tried to remember where he'd seen it. Steering his car toward the center of town, Jonah swallowed his unease, praying that the person behind the counter had no connection to anyone he knew or had worked for. He told himself he was protecting Quinn's privacy. He could always say he was buying something for a friend. His neighbor, Thea, was as big as a house now. Wouldn't be long before her big day arrived.

He hesitated only briefly before gathering his courage and plunging inside, cringing only slightly at the tinkling of the bell that signaled his arrival. Everything was so tiny.

His breathing slowed and his throat felt thick as he thought of the very first time he held Lily in his arms. He'd been so afraid he'd break her. Then her eyes had opened and she'd fixed him with a look that he could only say was recognition.

Turning around to see what else he'd missed, Jonah knew the instant he'd found the perfect gift. Small and pink, it was just Lily's size. A plain-looking T-shirt with the words "I'm The Big Sister" written in glitter. It was perfect. It was sparkly, which Lily would love.

And because of Quinn, because of the woman he had completely lost his heart to, he could actually read what the shirt said. Jonah snatched his prize off the rack and carried it, like the cherished gift it was, to the register. He couldn't wait to show it to Quinn. They would give it to Lily together.

CHAPTER 20

Quinn fixed the most elaborate dinner she could think of. Pot roast with mashed potatoes and all the fixings involved a day's worth of preparation, buying the groceries, peeling and chopping the vegetables, and searching through the cupboards for a decent roast pan. Anything to keep busy.

With the roast in the oven and nothing left to do but wait, she got Lily up from her nap and fixed the little girl her favorite afternoon snack, ants on a log. She ignored the nausea that welled up the moment she twisted the lid off the peanut butter jar. It was nothing more than the surplus of emotions surging through her today.

She'd only just sat down beside Lily before Quinn was up again, wiping down counters and checking the roast. Must keep busy. Her chest felt heavy, painful, with the weight of unshed tears. Lily couldn't see her breakdown. Poor child. And Jonah didn't need to see her lose it, either. He'd been just as thrilled as she was, to think they were having a baby. *Don't go there, Quinn!*

"Hey, let's play Candy Land. I'll go get the box." Quinn hurried from the room, anxious for a few moments to recompose herself.

Eyes too bright and an excessively cheerful smile pasted on her face, she returned with the board game. Lily gave her a quizzical look that had Quinn toning down the "happy" a few notches. They played the game through twice, Lily winning both times. This only made Quinn want to cry even more. She was a freaking basket case.

Jonah wasn't due for another hour or so. Normally these quiet afternoons were a time for the girls to bond, enjoying each other's company. But today Quinn felt just like she had the first day she'd watched Lily, painfully reminded that this sweet child was not hers, that she was only borrowing time with her. The harsh reality, then and now, that she couldn't have her own children hurt like a knife wound.

When she was married to Andrew, she knew she'd been smart never to give herself false hope by taking a pregnancy test. She knew what she'd find. But this wasn't Andrew, it was Jonah. And Jonah made her believe in hope again, he'd made her believe in a future, a life that involved a big happy family. Only big happy families didn't happen when the pregnancy test turned out negative.

Quinn couldn't hold back the sob that slipped past her guard. She feigned a cough to cover it up. This was the longest day of her life! And the pregnancy test was only half of it.

During Lily's naptime, Quinn got a phone call from an editor in New York. They loved her fairy picture book and wanted to publish it. Did she have others? The woman talked contract details that didn't really sink in. How much better this news would have been if she'd already been celebrating. Instead, it was like getting good news at a funeral. Nice, but just not appropriate.

Peering out the window over the kitchen sink, the encroaching darkness hid the driveway from view. Quinn glanced at the clock and decided it was time to boil the potatoes. Unfortunately, this only required a quick twist of her wrist, and then her nerves once again had free reign to drive her to distraction.

"Daddy will be home soon." Lily smiled at her from in front of the fridge, where she'd been meticulously rearranging refrigerator magnets.

"I know, sweetie." Clearly she wasn't doing a good job of keeping this to herself.

Quinn set the table, taking the time to find a couple of tapers that had seen better days. She tried to smile when Lily clapped delighted hands at the flickering wave of light from the candles. But it fell flat.

Find your passion, Mom had said. Find your joy.

Grabbing a couple of sketchpads from the arts and crafts cabinet she'd set up, Quinn handed one to Lily and, since the table was already set, sat down with her back against the wall to draw.

A familiar peace settled over Quinn as she drew her pencil across the paper. The tight band in her chest began to loosen and ease off. As was her habit lately, she began to sketch a fairy. This one had Lily's pert little face, her dark hair curling on the ends. She wore a tiara and a tutu, with layers and layers of fluffy tulle, just as Lily wore so often.

"I wish I could be a ballerina," Lily remarked as she looked over at Quinn's drawing. "For real."

Quinn tilted her head, thinking. If Jonah would let her, she'd buy Lily ballet lessons for Christmas. Surely someone in town taught ballet? Goodness knew she had enough money, with the insurance money from Nanny's house and now selling her picture book to a publishing house in New York.

"I think that is a lovely idea."

"You and Daddy could come see me dance. You'd sit in the front row."

"Of course we would, darling."

"Quinn? Daddy says my mommy is up in Heaven, watching over me. She'd be happy that you were taking care of Daddy and me, right? She'd want me to have a new mommy." Lily slipped her hand into Quinn's, her need for reassurance humbling.

Unfortunately, this only served to remind Quinn that she had no business tying herself to Jonah and his little girl. As much as she loved them, and she loved them both so much it hurt, she had to back off and let Jonah find a real mother for Lily. She'd worn out her welcome. It was time to find a place of her own. Just as she came to that realization, the front door opened.

"Where are my two beautiful girls?"

"That's us, Quinn. Come on." Lily scrambled from the room.

Quinn stood up and immediately made a grab for the wall, the room spinning wildly. Just as quickly, she found a chair placed behind her and a large hand pushing her into it. What the heck was the matter with her? She smiled gratefully at Jonah, then remembered the news she had to tell him. Oh, how she wanted to shield him from the pain this would cause.

"Pot roast? Are we celebrating something?" He winked.

No, no, no. He completely misunderstood. Blood rushed in Quinn's ears and her muscles stretched taut. Now wasn't the time. She couldn't tell him in front of Lily. She forced a smile that hurt to wear.

"Yes, we are celebrating something. We are celebrating that I got a call today from a publisher in New York. They want to buy Lily's book."

Lily squealed and began to dance around the room. Jonah hesitated before offering his own congratulations. He watched her closely, like he was searching for more answers. Unable to bear the scrutiny, Quinn got up to check on the potatoes. Her back to the room, she stuck the large fork in several of them before deciding they were ready to drain.

Jonah took Lily to wash up for dinner while Quinn mashed the potatoes and finished up the preparations. By the time they came out of the bathroom, she'd set out big bowls of food, steam rising off the tops, the mingling scents setting everyone's stomachs grumbling. They took their seats and began passing food around.

"Well, I've got a bit of news to celebrate too," Jonah announced, once they had all started to eat.

Quinn paused, a bite of food halfway to her mouth. He certainly looked happy.

"I got a job, a permanent job. No more handyman stuff. I start on the housing development down at Perkins Pond tomorrow. I work for Curtis Blaise."

"Jonah, that's amazing!" Quinn found herself up and out of her chair before she realized what she was doing. She threw her arms around Jonah and dropped a loud kiss on his cheek.

Lily giggled, causing Quinn to blush and try to scramble away. Jonah had looped his arms around her waist, one big hand placed possessively over her flat stomach. She stared down at his hand branding her. He was watching her closely again. Quinn shook her head, fighting the panic that closed off her breathing. She squirmed free and rushed around to her own chair, resuming her meal with her head bent low.

After dinner, while Jonah put his little one to bed, Quinn chickened out of a conversation by sneaking off to her own room. If the door was shut, he'd leave her alone, right? Wrong. The soft tapping came all too soon after she heard him bid Lily goodnight. Quinn searched around and snatched up her latest book on mythology.

"Tired already?" He stuck his head in the door without waiting for her answer.

"Yeah. Just going to read a chapter or two and then hit the hay." She slipped her finger into the space created by the bookmark.

"Did you take all of them or just stop at the one negative one?" He sat down on the end of the bed.

"All of what?" Why didn't he just go away? She didn't want to have this conversation.

"You bought a package of three, right? Paige got a positive on the first one, but then insisted on taking every single one after. She just refused to believe the results, I guess."

"I only bought the one. Lucky for me, because it would have been a waste of money to keep getting that result over and over."

And then she couldn't hold it back anymore. The pain and grief that she had swallowed down all day came out in a rush of tears, blubbering, unintelligible speech and fists, pounding at his back when Jonah hauled her into his arms. He was strong, so much stronger than she, and he held on so tight while she poured out her heartbreak in great, wrenching sobs.

Her head heavy against his chest, Quinn took a deep, shuddering breath and found that she was just too exhausted to shed another tear. Jonah held her like a child, rocking back and forth and rubbing her back. The pain was still there, but she could breathe again. She wanted to pretend she'd fallen asleep. Then he'd tuck her into bed and stop insisting she take another horrid pregnancy test. She'd never take another one for as long as she lived.

"I'll leave you alone about this now. Get some rest." Would he stop getting inside her head?

"I'm going to look for a place to live tomorrow. I need to give you and Lily some space." A huge yawn stole the import that statement was supposed to have made.

"If that's what you want to do." He was pulling back the covers and settling her in for the night.

"It's what I have to do."

Jonah sat on the edge of the bed and leaned in close. He didn't look sad or in any way disappointed that she wasn't going to give him the child she thought he'd wanted.

"I love you, Quinn. The results of a pregnancy test won't change that. But if you need to put conditions on our relationship, then maybe you're right. I won't stop you."

He brushed the softest kiss against her lips and left the room.

• • •

"But you have a home. You live with us," Lily whined as she was dragged from the house to the car.

"That's your home, yours and your dad's. I've just been visiting until I could get my own place. We've talked about this, Lily. It was never supposed to be forever." Quinn buckled the little girl into her seat quickly, before her own tears reappeared.

Jonah had said very little this morning, knowing her mind was made up. He'd eaten quickly and left the house. She wished him well on his first day at his new job but he hadn't responded.

Wonderful. She'd alienated her own family, letting her pain and unhappiness over not being able to have children take over her life. She'd missed out on the cutest years of her nieces' lives. Now she was pushing away Jonah and his daughter. Those two had become just as close as a family could be, without blood ties. Moving back to Scallop Shores hadn't changed a thing. She was still running away from all her problems.

Quinn's plan had been to hit the pavement again, trying to find a place of her own. Normally, Lily was happy to tag along. Today she was moody, recalcitrant. Her second favorite person in the world was leaving her and Lily was not going to make it easy on her.

"You know I'll still be in town, right? And I'm still going to come over and take care of you every weekday." Quinn switched out her Andrew Lloyd Webber CD in favor of some preschool tunes.

"Daddy is happier with you around." Four years old and already a master manipulator when it came to emotional blackmail.

"Your daddy is still going to see me plenty. Lily, where are we going to go for lunch?" She had to get the topic off Jonah.

"I want ice cream." Oh, yeah, manipulator!

"It's November, it is cold and miserable out. You don't need ice cream."

"Yes, I do. Ice cream makes me feel better." Ah, now she was speaking Quinn's language.

"How about the bakery? We can stop in for pie a la mode."

"What's a la mode?" Finally, a genuine question without any of the whine.

They spent the next couple of hours trying out leads that Quinn had circled in the newspaper. Two of them had neglected to mention that they didn't accept pets. Two more were no longer available, the landlords not realizing they still had the ad listed. The one apartment that was decently priced was not somewhere she could envision herself living.

The kitchen had indoor/outdoor carpeting, something she hadn't even known existed until that moment. The rest of the apartment was covered in a 70's shag carpeting, the color of vomit. And the place smelled like a few tenants had done just that—several times.

Trying to cover her nose without being obvious, Quinn politely shook her head and trotted down the stairs as fast as she could, hauling in deep breaths of clean air while the landlord locked up behind them. The look on Lily's face was comical. She must have been struggling not to say something rude, but her face told the story just the same. Quinn bit the inside of her cheek to keep from giggling.

Oh, what was she going to do? This was the last place on her list. She'd have to expand her search to the surrounding towns in the area. But that wasn't what she wanted. She came back to Scallop Shores for the town, the history, the ambience. Port Kitt and Wellsmouth just weren't home.

Lily was right. It was time for ice cream. But she definitely wanted pie with hers. Pumpkin pie, to be exact. Buckling the child into her car seat once more, Quinn drove to the center of town and found a spot right in front of Logan's Bakery. Lily pushed the door open and waved at all the regulars.

Quinn was reminded of how isolated this little girl's life had been until just recently. Jonah had such a big secret to keep from the townsfolk. How unfortunate that it had to affect Lily's life as well. She had every right to be shy, clamming up around these people that she was only just starting to get to know. But brave little Lily embraced life. Even now she was flirting with the old men sitting on their stools.

"Hey, Quinn. I heard Lily say something about ice cream. You think she'll eat a slice of pumpkin pie with it?" Cady called from behind the display case.

"Let's give it a try. We're celebrating today. My second attempt at finding an apartment and no luck. And this time I don't even have Kayla to blame."

"Aw, sweetie, that's too bad. I'd let you move in with me, but there is barely enough room up there as it is." Cady pointed to the ceiling, referring to her tiny apartment over the bakery.

Quinn snagged a real estate freebie off the rack by the door and sat at a table by the window. She had a sizeable down payment from the insurance money for Nanny's house. She had a job and an income … How did that work, exactly? Maybe she didn't need to be wasting her time and money looking for an apartment. Maybe she could look for a house.

She thought about the new job Jonah just started. She liked the idea of living in a house that his hands had worked on. It would be the next best thing to living in his cozy little home, with the living room fireplace, large back deck, and a basement that smelled of sawdust instead of mildew. She'd have to look into that, see if every house in that new development by the pond was spoken for.

"So why is it we haven't seen you around town much before, little missy?"

Quinn looked up in panic as that question broke into her own thoughts.

"Daddy was hidin'." Lily was preening at the attention.

Quinn held her breath as she turned in her chair, ready to rescue Lily.

"Hiding, you say? Were you hiding too?" It was one of Old Man Feeney's cronies, and he scented a juicy bit of gossip. He wasn't letting go until he had it.

"Nah. I didn't care. Daddy couldn't read. He was 'barrassed. But Quinn teachded him so now he doesn't have to hide."

"Couldn't read?"

Oh, God! How had she known?

"Yeah, he used to make up my bedtime stories. Every night was a tiny bit different." She held up two fingers close together.

Cady hurried to the table with two plates of pie a la mode. Her features were pinched, her expression apologetic. Quinn looked from her to the little girl swinging in circles on the counter stool. Jonah's life, everything that he'd worked so hard to keep out of this small town's gossip mill, was on display.

"Okay, boys, time to leave Miss Lily to her pie. Let's not forget that her daddy was hiding for a reason and that reason better remain hidden." Cady crossed her arms and arched a thin brow at the gruff old men sitting in front of her.

Lily hopped down from the stool and hurried to the table Quinn held, completely unaware of the sensation she'd caused. At the moment she only had eyes for pumpkin pie and a dollop of vanilla ice cream. After a few bites she looked up at Quinn and smiled.

"Those old guys sure were friendly." She giggled as the men in question gathered their coats and headed for the door, tipping their hats to her and winking.

Was there any way this was not going to get all over town and eventually back to Jonah? Quinn mentally crossed her fingers. Peering out the window, she saw that Feeney's buddy had stopped to talk to an older woman on the sidewalk. They turned, as one, to gaze into the bakery window. And so it started. Quinn pushed her pie plate to the center of the table, wishing she could sink straight into the floor.

CHAPTER 21

They had been on the road a full hour and not one word was spoken. Kayla had turned the radio to an old '80s station almost immediately. The silence was uncomfortable. Quinn glanced over to find her sister studying the scenery as they drove south on 95. Swinging her eyes forward to focus on the road, she allowed her thoughts to wander.

It had been a couple of days since Lily's big declaration in Logan's. Quinn knew she should have come straight home and told Jonah. It involved all of them. And it wasn't her fault. She had no idea that Lily was clued in to her father's fateful secret. Or that she'd spill the beans to the town gossips, of all people.

They'd been busy dancing around the whole pregnancy scare. Scare? Quinn thought she was experiencing the answer to her prayers. The scary part was that now she was back where she'd been before, alone and living vicariously through others.

Kayla rooted around in her purse, beside her, and dug out an emery board. Their eyes met briefly before Kay bent her head to her task. Quinn frowned, knowing she had only herself to blame for this rift. They used to be so close. Trips in the car would have been filled with talk about boys, clothes, or the latest prank they had pulled on Nanny.

Nanny. A sob lodged in Quinn's throat. She couldn't believe how ridiculously emotional she was lately. Over-the-top emotional. She'd cried yesterday, at a dog food commercial. She needed to repair things with Kayla quickly.

She hadn't found an apartment and Jonah had no problem showing how pleased he was. When she mentioned buying a house instead, his smile had been indulgent. Was it the built-in babysitter aspect? No, that wasn't fair. He claimed to love her.

Quinn gripped the steering wheel tighter, fighting the urge to cry again. She was broken. She couldn't have children. What part about that was so difficult for him to grasp? Quinn deserved to be alone and the sooner he realized that and found himself someone he could build a family with, the better.

"So you were teaching him to read, huh?"

She should have been prepared for it, but the question came out of left field.

Quinn nodded.

"That's cool. That he could go to you like that." Kayla sounded sincere.

Quinn waited for some snarky reference to the fact that she hadn't been there for her own sister all these years. But it never came.

"I was a little intimidated, but he really needed help. And now he's built up enough confidence to get a job working for that big construction company in town."

"Will you two be getting married?"

This time Quinn spluttered. "Where in the world would you get that idea?" She kept her eyes on the road, passing a semi full of Christmas trees. Wow. They started earlier and earlier these days.

"You love him." It wasn't a question so she needn't answer. She bit her lip.

"And he loves you?"

"He says he does." This time Quinn snuck a look at her sister in the passenger seat.

"So why is it so preposterous to think you two might get married?"

"We haven't even officially been dating. I've only lived at his house because I had nowhere else to go."

Kayla had the good grace to lower her gaze to her lap. She may not have had anything to do with the fire destroying Nanny's house, but she had plenty to do with Quinn not being able to find suitable lodging.

"I thought you'd move back to the city," she mumbled, her voice subdued.

"I told you, I'm not going anywhere."

"I guess I needed to test that. Or push you away. I got used to your distance." Kay twisted uncomfortably in her seat and rested her head back, her eyes closed.

"I deserved that." Quinn flipped the visor down and cut off the sun's glare.

"No, you didn't. I was a bitch when you came back. I acted like a horrible, spoiled kid. The girls are lucky to have you in their lives. You're a great aunt … when you decide to be there." Kay leaned over and punched her in the arm.

"So what changed? Why suddenly be nice to me?" Now Quinn was the snarky one, but she couldn't hold it back. Kay really had been cruel to her.

"I may have made some assumptions about you. You stayed in New York. You never visited. It was easy to make up this whole life you'd had that was so much better than anything you could have gotten out of a visit to your pathetic home town.

"But I saw how you took care of Jonah's daughter, even though she wasn't your own. And then I heard that you taught him to read. The sister I'd made up wouldn't do those selfless things for someone else."

Quinn flinched as though Kayla had punched her. She'd had no idea that staying away had affected her sister like this.

"Nanny knew why I stayed away. Nanny answered my emails, my phone calls. If you wanted to know anything, you could have talked to her."

"She always liked you best." Kay began to chew on a nail she'd just finished shaping to perfection.

"Oh, please."

"I thought once you left town and I had her all to myself that she'd like me more. But all she did was talk about you. Quinn is such a success. Quinn is the first woman in our family to graduate from college. My own little blip in beauty school didn't seem to even make it on the map."

"I'm sorry. I had no idea."

"I was mean and petty to Nanny. I kept the girls away. Jake wanted to do Sunday night dinners, as a way of keeping the family that was in town as close as possible. I wouldn't let him."

Fat tears rolled down Kayla's cheeks. Quinn was flustered. She'd never seen her sister this vulnerable. Since she'd been back in town, she'd only seen the 'ice queen' side of her. Still concentrating on the road, she reached over and patted Kayla's knee. Kay gripped her hand and squeezed hard. She scrabbled in her bag for a tissue, the ensuing honk quite unladylike.

"I thought we had years left. Lots of years."

"It was a complete surprise."

Kayla turned back toward the window. It had cost her sister a lot to open up like that, Quinn could see. She felt an immense weight lifted from her chest. They were going to get through this. Struggling to get her own tears under control, Quinn focused on the exit signs whipping by in succession. Traffic was blessedly light the weekend before Thanksgiving. She'd enjoy this little pre-holiday treat.

"I'm sorry she played up the college thing. I had no idea." She whispered across the enclosed space.

"Don't be sorry. Be proud. You kicked academic butt! I guess I was just a little jealous because I didn't strive for more. Remember what Mom used to say?"

"Follow your passions and you'll always find happiness. But you did exactly that! You started your own business, Kay. That took guts, perseverance. If Nanny never acknowledged that, then that was her mistake."

"You never acknowledged it." Hadn't she? Quinn hung her head in shame.

"I guess I thought you knew."

"My name is Kayla, the-all-seeing-all-knowing." But instead of sarcasm, there was humor in her voice.

"I'm sorry."

"Thanks."

"I kind of got lost." Quinn chewed her lip at the admission.

Kayla looked around, bewildered. "We're still on 95. How could you get lost?"

"No, I mean with regards to what Mom taught us—following our passions. I got my degree but then Andrew saw no reason for me to work outside the home. He saw an art degree as a pretty piece of paper, nothing more."

"I never liked him. He took my sister, the sister I knew, and changed her. Made her sad and closed off. The person who came back to Scallop Shores was broken. And I blame him."

More broken than she realized. Quinn shook her head sadly.

"Okay, let's shelve this conversation for a later date." *Or never.* Quinn put on a wide smile. "We need a plan of attack for when we get into the city. Do we want to eat first? Hit a museum? Shop?"

"Where did you used to waitress? Can we have lunch there? Oh, and Rockefeller Plaza. I want to see the ice skaters." Kayla's eyes twinkled with child-like delight.

For the first time in years, Quinn actually looked forward to spending time with her little sister. They were almost through Connecticut now. Not much longer. She wanted to giggle. She had her sister back and everything was going to be okay.

• • •

Feeling strangely out of sorts because Quinn was gone for an entire day, Jonah prowled the house in search of something to do. He'd already finished the dishes and a couple of loads of laundry.

Quinn had been on his case about Thanksgiving and he'd put her off. Maybe he could plan a menu, invite her sister and her family. She'd be pleased. He sat at the table to start a grocery list. Thanksgivings had always been a pretty low-key holiday for him. What did people like to make, beyond turkey? Speaking of turkey, he'd never actually cooked a whole bird. He paused, pen raised above the paper.

Looking between the paper and the pen, Jonah grinned wide. This time last year he would have run into the store without a list, grabbed a little turkey breast, some cranberry sauce, and a box of instant mashed potatoes and called it a day. Now look at him … writing a grocery list.

Yeah, he'd do a whole turkey for Quinn. He owed her the world. He hadn't been comfortable with it, but she'd brought him out of his shell. And he would always be grateful. He added pumpkin pie to the list. He knew that was her favorite.

"Hey, Cuteness, throw some shoes on, we're going grocery shopping."

Lily had commandeered his recliner and sat surrounded by a ton of her books. When had she gotten so many? Jonah swore those things, like her stuffed animals, bred at night. She slid from the chair, dumping several books in the process. She didn't even notice. He shook his head.

She was so eager to get out and be among the townspeople. His daughter, Scallop Shores' own social butterfly. She definitely got that from Paige. Jonah was surprised to realize he no longer felt that familiar stab of blame and guilt when he thought about his late wife. Just a sad resignation. And that he could live with.

"How would you like to see Crystal and Zoe again?" He asked as he helped zip Lily into her coat.

"Yay! They're fun. They treat me like a big girl." Lily did a little dance in the foyer as soon as she was dressed for the outdoors.

"What, like you do each other's make up and stuff?" He grinned.

"No, Daddy! They talk to me and they don't say, 'Go away—you're a baby!'"

They headed out into the nippy November morning, Jonah thinking about lots of future play dates between Lily and Quinn's nieces. When he'd originally thought about finding a mom for Lily, it had purely been about having a woman's influence in her life. The woman he'd pictured didn't come with extended family, messed up self-esteem, or a jerk of an ex-husband. This was so much better than anything he could have imagined. Lily could have cousins.

He could have a brother-in-law. Jonah hadn't talked very long with Jake at Lily's birthday. But the man liked the Red Sox and the Patriots, so he was a good guy in Jonah's book. Hopefully, that is, if Quinn and Kayla's trip to New York City was the successful bonding experience she was hoping for. Otherwise, he might be sneaking around to spend time with Jake like Quinn had to do in order to see her nieces.

It was a clear morning, so half the town was out and about as Jonah pulled into the parking lot of Gifford's. A back corner of the tarmac was already roped off. They'd be getting fresh Christmas trees any day now. The local Boy Scout troops would stop by on the weekends, selling hot cider and donuts to raise money. The holiday season was already upon them. Jonah found himself grinning and whistling Jingle Bells as he and Lily grabbed a cart and headed inside.

"Oh, Daddy, flowers!" Lily pointed to a pretty table arrangement of chrysanthemums and a bunch of other flowers he'd never be able to name.

Eh, why not? Jonah set them in the cart. Quinn would appreciate a beautiful centerpiece.

Steering their way toward the produce aisle, Jonah nodded at a couple of old ladies who stood close together, conferring over the butternut squash. Their eyes squinted and they peered at him oddly. Did he have something hanging out of his nose? He looked down to see if Lily had noticed the strange looks, but she was busy stroking the velvety petals on the flowers.

He stopped in front of the potatoes, wondering how many bags he'd need to peel and boil, in order to make enough *real* mashed potatoes for his guests. He hefted a bag, turning it around, trying to see how many came in a five-pound bag. His brow furrowed in concentration.

"Anything I can help you with, Mr. Goodwin?" asked a gangly teenager with an unfortunate acne problem.

"Just trying to figure out how much I need to buy." He tried to tune the boy out.

"That says, five-pound bag of russet potatoes, sir."

"I know what it says, *junior*." Jonah wasn't sure if he was more annoyed at the extra attention or the title, given, no doubt, in deference to his age.

"Just wanted to help, s—, Mr. Goodwin."

Jonah threw two bags in the cart, figuring he'd sort it out later. He just wanted out of the produce department. The rest of the vegetables were going to come out of a can or the freezer. His guests would just have to deal with it. He motioned for Lily to hop on the back end of the cart and hang on tight. She giggled as he turned the corner.

They stopped in front of a big display of dinner rolls. So many choices. He tried to remember which ones Quinn had made that he liked. Did they even come from this section? Maybe she made them from scratch? He held up a couple of packages to see if they looked like the ones in the pretty bread basket she had covered in cloth and set in the middle of the table.

"Those are dinner rolls, dear. Are you looking for something in particular? I can help you." A young mom with several children in tow, stood at his elbow.

"I know what a dinner roll is. I don't get why everyone is going out of their way to be helpful today." He put the rolls back where he'd found them and tried not to glare at the woman, who was just being friendly.

"Of course you do, dear. How silly of me! It's probably the packaged food where you can't see through the wrapping that you have trouble with." She leaned in close, out of earshot of her children. "You have a hard time with the labels, you just come look for me. I'll help you." She smiled kindly and shooed her kids off ahead of her as they moved along the aisle.

Trouble? Hard time with the labels? What in the hell was she talking about? Realization hit him like a monster truck. All the color drained from his face before returning, tenfold, in a nasty shade of angry purple. Feeling like the last one in on the joke, Jonah's eyes closed to slits and he struggled to maintain a cool facade. He refused to give them any more to talk about than they obviously already were.

"Hey, munchkin, would you believe that your silly old dad forgot his wallet at home? Let's just leave our cart right here and go on back and get it." Taking carefully measured breaths, Jonah lifted Lily to his hip and strode for the front of the store.

The look on his face must have warned anyone looking to talk to him away, because patrons and employees both were stepping back and giving him a clear path to the exit. Lily, bless her heart, was waving and addressing everyone by name. When had she spent enough time in town to learn all these names?

Quinn. Quinn had taken Lily into town more times than he could count. Had Lily been there when she'd flapped her jaw and let the entire freakin' town know the shameful secret he had spent his entire life protecting? Of course she had. The townsfolk would judge him and that was just something he'd have to deal with. But to have his own daughter think less of him, look down on him because he was too stupid to speak up to his own dad and make reading a priority.

By the time they hit the parking lot, he was jogging for the truck. *Have to get away.* His lungs burned from the effort of holding back tears. Real men don't cry. But real men went to school, and real men learned to read before they were in their damned thirties. Have to get home. Home is safe. Home is just the two of us. And Quinn. Damn it, she betrayed him!

The phone was ringing when they walked in the door. Lily darted off to play with Grizzabella in her room. Jonah let it go to voicemail, not sure if he could trust himself not to rip the caller a new one, just because. He paced the kitchen, waiting for the chime that let him know he had a new message waiting.

It was Curt. He wanted to talk. He was asking to meet up at Smitty's for a beer tomorrow night. Jonah snapped the kinks out of his neck, fisting and unfisting his hands. He blew out a breath and stared miserably out the window. This wasn't a social visit. Curt had found out that he didn't have a high school diploma and could barely read. He was going to fire him.

CHAPTER 22

"I think my blisters have blisters." Kayla shoved all the bags she'd accumulated throughout the day into the booth ahead of her before she sat down.

Quinn did the same, resting her weary head against the back of the booth.

"You're going to have to talk to me on the ride home, keep me awake." She grinned.

"I'll try, but I don't know if I can." Her sister's yawn was so huge she heard her jaw crack.

They giggled. They hadn't had fun like this, just the two of them, since they were teenagers. Quinn opened her menu and skimmed the contents. It hadn't changed much since the last time she'd been here with Andrew.

She glanced briefly around the cozy restaurant. She had chosen this place to show Kayla, not because of the memories she'd made here with Andrew, because they were unremarkable, to be sure. She just really liked the food, the ambiance, even the detail in the decorating.

"How about a glass of wine?" She asked her sister, without looking up.

"Oh, not today. I'd slide under the table," Kay said, from behind her own menu.

She thought Kayla really loved her wine. Huh. Quinn ordered a bottle of sparkling water for them to share. Kay ordered an herbal tea. She couldn't remember ever seeing her drink tea before. Strange.

Quinn tapped her newly lacquered nails on the white tablecloth. She held them up, admiring the deep burgundy color against her pale skin. It was a nice autumn color, and it was bold, bolder than she'd ever gone before. Bold looked good on her, she decided.

"I have to bring Crystal and Zoe back to that American Girl doll store, someday. That was amazing."

"You think they'll like their new dolls?"

"I think they're going to especially like the matching nightgowns they'll open with them on Christmas morning."

"Thank you for spending the day with me, Kay. It means a lot to me."

"Oh, don't go making me cry again. I don't want to ruin this beautiful make-up job." Besides her nails, Kayla had also had her make-up done at the spa.

The waiter came to take their orders. Quinn ordered the chicken Marsala, handing over her menu as she did. Kayla opted for the pumpkin ravioli.

"Oh my God ... Look over your shoulder and to your right, about two o'clock. Isn't that Andrew?"

Seriously? A huge metropolis and she had to run into her ex again on the one day she was visiting the city with her sister? Quinn was starting to regret her choice of restaurants, realizing too late that it was also a favorite of Andrew's. Why shouldn't he come here with whomever he had moved on with?

She was probably beautiful. He'd want someone who made beautiful babies. She'd be tall and thin and ... She was a he. Quinn blinked. False alarm, it wasn't a date. It was just some boring business meeting. But then she saw Andrew lean in, his hand atop his dining partner's. It was a date! She turned back around in her seat, stunned, mortified.

"He was never good enough for you." Kayla's smile was sad. "Something always bothered me about Andrew. He wasn't who I pictured you with. And then you stopped visiting. I thought I was wrong. That he was all you needed in your life. I was so jealous."

"Things between us weren't ... well, you can see why we didn't work out."

"You don't have a penis." Kayla's words made her cringe, even though she'd been thinking the same exact thing. Her sister always told it like it was.

They sat quietly at the table for a few moments. Quinn wondered what Jonah and Lily were doing at that moment. She missed them. She couldn't wait to tell him about her day in the city. She patted the bag beside her that held an American Girl doll for Lily. She'd had so much fun picking it out. It looked just like her.

"Hey, so I have some news. I've been a little nervous to tell you about it." Kay twisted her napkin, her smile a little too tight.

Quinn tried to think of what it could be, that made her sister look so uncomfortable. They weren't moving out of Scallop Shores just as she was finally moving home, were they? What else could it be?

"I'm pregnant."

The floor felt like it dropped out from under her. Quinn's stomach plummeted, just as if she were on a roller coaster. She'd run from this before. In fact, her brain was screaming at her to get out, get away. She pasted on a congratulatory smile and hoped it looked far more genuine than it felt.

"That's amazing. You and Jake trying for a boy?"

"That's just it. We were done. This baby is a complete surprise. But a completely welcome one." Kayla beamed with pride.

She'd tried for years to get pregnant, with no success. Her sister managed to do it accidentally. Life wasn't fair.

"When I found out, I just knew, life is too short. I had to stop being such a bitch and trust that you were going to stick around for this baby. It's a second chance for us, Quinny." Oh Lord, she hadn't used that nickname since she was little.

"Of course I'm going to stick around. I told you I wasn't going anywhere. In fact, I'm thinking of buying one of those new houses going up by the pond. We can sell the land that Nanny's house was on and I can put down new roots, make new memories."

"But Jonah ... "

"Things just aren't going to work out between me and Jonah. He needs someone who can give him everything. I'm just not that person."

"But you love him and he loves you. What can't you give him?" Kayla looked perplexed.

"Children. I can't have children." The admission, coming several years too late, wasn't as difficult as Quinn had always imagined.

"Are you sure?" Her sister whispered.

"Andrew and I tried for six years. I'm pretty sure that if I could have kids, I would have gotten pregnant sometime during that period."

"I'm so sorry, Quinn." Kayla reached across the table and grasped her hand, squeezing.

"Oh, this explains so much. You weren't staying in the city because it was so much better than home, you were staying away because it was too hard to be around us. And I was so cruel." Kay took her hand away so she could dab at her eyes with a napkin.

"I should have told you a long time ago. I should have explained why I couldn't be around the girls." She chewed her bottom lip to keep from blubbering.

"No, I should have realized that you had a much more important reason than anything my stupid, jealous brain could come up with."

This time they both reached across the table. They were here for each other now. Quinn would stay and be a part of this new baby's life. And now that Kayla understood the reason for her sister's absence, she would be there to help Quinn get through the emotional heartache that not having children of her own would bring.

. . .

Despite what she said earlier, Quinn let Kayla sleep on the way back to Scallop Shores. Her sister had given it her best shot, but during a lull in the conversation, exhaustion got the best of her and she nodded off. Quinn was bone weary herself, but she was happy about the way things had turned out today. Glancing at Kay, she grinned wide. She felt at peace.

Turning on the CD player low enough not to wake up Kayla, Quinn hummed softly to an upbeat song from the musical *Evita*. Her flagging energy was slightly bolstered. She could make it another couple of hours on the road.

It would be late, but she hoped Jonah was still awake when she got home. She was finally ready to tell him that it didn't matter if they had no more children. She would love Lily like her own and the three of them could be a family. Well, that's if he wanted a future together. Quinn assumed that by admitting he loved her, he was thinking of a future that included her.

She hoped she hadn't pushed him away one time too many. She loved Jonah. She loved Lily. Yeah, it would hurt that they couldn't share the experience of raising a baby of their own together, but there was so much more to life. And now that she knew Kayla and her growing brood would finally be a part of her life, it was so much fuller.

The Andrew Lloyd Webber mix repeated a couple of times before Quinn dropped her sister at her front door. The lights were still on when she got back home, even though it was after eleven o'clock. She was getting her own bags out of the trunk when Jonah stepped out the front door, marching to the car.

"Leave them be. Get in the car." His voice dripped venom. *What the hell?*

"What on earth?" Quinn shut the trunk and slipped back into the driver's seat.

Jonah opened the passenger side door and climbed in. He held out his hand so she wouldn't talk.

"I don't want to wake Lily, or the neighbors, for that matter," he said, between clenched teeth.

He hadn't dropped his hand so she remained silent, staring at the man she'd come to love as though he'd completely lost it. He was priming for a fight. But on what grounds? Was he angry that she'd come back so late? It was a clear night. There was no chance of driving off the road.

"Did you think I wouldn't find out?" He hissed.

Okay, now he really had lost her.

"I trusted you. I trusted you with everything. I've worked my entire life to keep this town from finding out that I couldn't read. I kept everyone at a distance. And just when I think it's safe to make friends, to finally forge some relationships for me and my daughter, you come along and screw it all up."

Oh, God! In the excitement and emotional upheaval of the day trip, Quinn had completely forgotten about the fact that Lily had let slip Jonah's most sacred of secrets. She hung her head, ashamed that he'd had to hear it from someone else.

"Yeah, that's right. I can't believe I was considering a life with you, a future with you. You're nothing but a backstabber. You betrayed me!" Spit flew from his mouth as he spewed out his anger. He swiped angry tears away with the back of a large hand.

"I didn't—" she tried to speak but he cut her off.

"Oh, come on, let's not add lying to your growing list of crimes. You told someone, who told someone else. It doesn't matter how it got around. What matters is that you started this. You told the entire town something that I shared with you in confidence, something that you knew would crush me if it were to ever get out."

Okay, so he didn't know it was actually Lily who'd outed him. And since he refused to listen to reason ...

"I can only assume that since you insisted on dragging my daughter with you all over town, now she knows her father didn't learn to read when he was supposed to. You knew it was Lily I was hiding this from the most. You knew." His voice cracked.

"Lily already knew. She didn't judge you. You've been her hero all along and she knew."

"She couldn't have known, she's too little to understand. Did you tell her first? Is that what you're telling me?" He shrunk back against the passenger side door as though struck.

"No! I never told her anything. I never told anyone. Please, just listen to me. Your daughter is a lot smarter, a lot more intuitive than you give her credit for."

"Well, then she gets it from her mother. Maybe she didn't get my 'stupid' genes after all."

"Stop it, Jonah! You aren't stupid." Quinn reached out a hand, tried to touch his cheek but was rejected.

"Lily was chatting up the old men at the bakery. She's the one who told them. It wasn't me."

"Get out! I don't care where you go, but you can't stay here. I'll pack up your things and that damned cat tomorrow and drop them off at your sister's. You can pick them up there."

"But—"

"No—you don't try to use my precious daughter to manipulate your way out of this. I'm done. We're done. I don't want you ever to have contact with her again."

Jonah stepped from the car and slammed the door. Without a backward glance, he strode for the house. Stunned, Quinn sat for a moment, watching his retreating back. When the porch light went off immediately after he'd let himself in, she dissolved into tears. What had just happened?

Knowing how angry he was, and not wanting to deal with another confrontation if she remained in the driveway, Quinn pulled it together enough to drive. It was too late to knock on

Kayla's door and ask to spend the night. She'd park in their driveway for the night and sleep in her car. Ironically, it wouldn't be difficult. She was starting to get used to sleeping in her car.

CHAPTER 23

"Daddy? Where's Quinn? She promised me she'd bring me back a present from her trip." Shuffling out to the kitchen in her pink flannel pajamas, Lily scratched her head in confusion.

"You shouldn't ask about presents. It's rude," Jonah snapped from his spot at the table—where he'd been since giving up on sleep about four A.M.

He sighed, pinched the skin between his eyebrows and frowned down at his empty coffee cup. It wasn't fair to take his mood out on Lily. She'd done nothing wrong. She missed Quinn. Unfortunately, so did he.

"Quinn left me a message that it was so late, she decided to sleep at her sister's house."

"They're having a sleepover? Cool! I want to have a sleepover with Crystal and Zoe someday."

Which would be great—if he hadn't just killed any chance of Lily having a relationship with Quinn's nieces. His issue was with Quinn. The girls shouldn't have to suffer.

"How about some omelets this morning?" Jonah scraped his chair back and smiled down at his favorite little girl. "I think I've got some of that thick-sliced bacon you like, too."

"Okay, I guess. Then can we call Quinn and ask her to come home?"

"Tell you what, you can get the eggs out of the fridge for me." Trying to distract Lily with a chore she normally wasn't allowed to do, he prayed it would end this conversation.

He dragged himself to the stove, flinched when he slammed the frying pan down a little too hard on the burner and groaned, knowing he'd done it on purpose. He'd had no sleep last night, alternately steaming over Quinn's suggestion that Lily had been the one to betray his deepest secret, and worrying about sending Quinn out into the night. Just like he'd done to Paige. He'd kept his cell phone close, terrified of getting the call that Quinn had met with a terrible accident because she'd been out driving so late. He didn't care how justifiably angry he'd been. He never should have sent her away.

Wait a minute. This wasn't his fault. This was about trust and how his trust had been broken. He'd done what he had to do to protect his family. Lily had gotten too close to Quinn. He was going to have a hell of a time trying to explain to his little girl that her favorite adult in the whole world, other than him, just wasn't going to be a part of their little world anymore.

"Daddy, here ya go."

"What?" he snarled, turning just in time to see a startled Lily drop the carton of eggs.

Her bottom lip trembled and Jonah couldn't mistake the hurt expression in her tear-filled eyes. Calling himself all kinds of a jerk, he dropped to the floor, ignored the spreading yellow goo of egg yolk and motioned for his daughter to climb into his lap.

"I didn't mean it, Daddy," she sniffled.

"I know you didn't, Lovebug. Daddy's just being a real Crank Monster this morning, huh?" She nodded, hesitantly.

Closing his eyes, he breathed in the calming scent of her shampoo and cuddled Lily close. What to say? How to phrase it? She deserved the truth but he wasn't sure if she was old enough to understand. Remembering one of the last things that Quinn had said, about Lily being a lot smarter than he gave her credit for, he measured his words and prayed he was doing the right thing.

"So I guess you heard that Daddy didn't know how to read until just recently." He'd set Lily on his lap and looked directly into her eyes as he spoke.

"I heard Quinn giving you lessons one night. I had to go potty, so I went real quick, then back to bed," she added, as though this revelation would somehow get her in trouble.

"And you understood what we were doing?" His eyes narrowed as he tried to figure out if this was a line she'd been fed by Quinn.

"Yeah. You needed help and you tell me that when I need help with something, all I have to do is ask."

"How'd you know I needed help?"

"'Cuz you never read any of my stories the same. Every time you read one it was different than the last time. I 'membered. You just needed to find someone you could ask for help."

Lily smiled up at him. She'd known all along and she still treated him like he could do anything. Tears pricked at his eyelids and he tried not to completely shame himself by crying all over her.

"So when Quinn told my little secret in town, you already knew?"

"Quinn never told anyone you couldn't read." Lily slapped a hand over her mouth, her expression horrified, then lifted her palm enough to whisper, "It was supposed to be a secret?"

"What's the matter, Peanut?" Jonah's heart started to beat faster and he knew, with a sinking feeling, that he wasn't going to like the answer.

Lily hung her head, refusing to look at her father. She picked at the hem of her pajama top and rolled a pearl button between her fingers.

"I didn't know we shouldn't talk about it, Daddy. Honest, I didn't!" She swallowed hard and looked up, her face pale. "I told those men. At Cady's. They were being so nice. I didn't know."

She threw herself against his chest and sobbed her little heart out. Jonah held her close, rubbing her back and murmuring gentle reassurances. Oh, what had he done?

• • •

The town watering hole was no place for a kid, so Jonah made arrangements to drop Lily off at Thea's for a bit. Though it wasn't how he had envisioned presenting her with the gift he'd been working on, he brought it along. Seeing those happy jungle animals cavorting around on his cradle just reminded him of how much he missed her. He needed it gone already. While Thea's happy tears, hugs and gushed compliments should have given him a swelled head, without Quinn there to share the praise, it just made him uncomfortable.

Well, it was good while it lasted. Jonah stiffened his backbone, and shook his head as he heaved open the big oak door to Smitty's Pub. The jig was up. His secret was out and now he had to face his new boss and admit that he'd gotten the job under false pretenses.

But he wasn't a coward. And if Curt called him in to meet over drinks, then he'd take being fired like a man. Good that they would be in a crowded bar. There wouldn't be any dramatic scenes, no name-calling, well, not on his part, anyway. He knew when he was wrong. He should have gone in straight with the truth, offered to get his GED, start as an apprentice, and work his way up.

"You gonna stand over there all night or are you going to come share this pitcher with me?" Curt hollered from the other end of the room.

Snickers followed Jonah as he skirted his way between tables, nearly upsetting the tray of a waitress when she turned quickly away from a table. She gave him a dirty look then rolled her eyes as she stopped to let him pass. Curt kicked out a chair for him and he sat down, nodding his thanks.

"There's a menu on the table. You want something to eat?" It was the same waitress he'd just danced with on the way through the bar. "Wait, you're gonna need me to read it to you, though, aren't ya, sugar?"

"You want a tip, Wanda, you can drop that surly tone and leave my boy, here, alone. You hungry?" Curt raised a bushy eyebrow at Jonah.

"No, thanks. And I can read my own damned menu," he snarled at Wanda. Enough was enough.

"Whatever." She flounced away.

Curt topped off his own mug of beer and then poured a second, sliding it in Jonah's direction. He nodded and took several big swallows before setting it down and wiping his mouth with the sleeve of his green chamois shirt. *Working up to it. Poor stiff. He was a really nice guy and it probably killed him to have to can a single dad trying to work to raise his little girl.*

"You're doing some damned fine work up to the site, son," Curt offered in that old Down East accent that reminded Jonah so much of his father. "Fellas all seem to like you. I heard you even handled that Thurston kid without it coming to blows."

Yeah, that'd been fun. Stupid kid had shown up for work drunk. Jonah knew that it would have been Curt's ass if Thurston had picked up a power tool and hurt himself or someone else. Or if he'd done shoddy work that might not have been noticed until inspection, or later. He'd convinced the idiot to sleep it off. He'd even let him sleep in his own truck, with a spare blanket he kept behind Lily's seat for emergencies.

"You didn't need that headache," he mumbled.

"Nope, sure didn't." Curt took another swallow of beer and pointed the mug at him. "Foreman quit. Wife got hired on at some whiz-tech company in Boston. Said the benefits were too good to pass up."

"He can't commute?" Jonah reached for his beer and took a quick sip.

"Nah, something about family out there and finally being able to afford city living."

"Sorry, boss." He winced at the term, remembering the reason they were here. Concentrating on the drink, Jonah began to twirl his coaster around in circles.

"Anyway, job's open. I'm gonna order some wings. You want wings?" Curt flagged down the waitress and ordered a bucket before he could answer.

Okay, enough dancing around the subject. The suspense was killing him.

"I'm not trying to be rude, but can we just get on with this? You asked me here so you could fire me, right? I get it. But it's really difficult to chat and be all social when I know how this is going to end."

"Who told you I was going to fire you? That ain't why I asked you to meet me here." Curt's wrinkled brow suggested he was genuinely confused.

"I don't get it. Surely you've heard my big secret by now. Wanda sure knew." He drew out her name and spat it on the table.

"Son, I've known your 'big' secret since you were five years old and your daddy made the decision not to register you for kindergarten."

Rendered speechless, Jonah stared at the man, his mouth opening and closing, uselessly. Just to give himself something to do, he took a sip of beer, and then another.

Curt chuckled. "Floored ya there, didn't I? Come on, kid, you knew your daddy and I were close."

"I thought he wanted to keep it hidden. He could have gotten in a lot of trouble if the school ever found out I wasn't being homeschooled."

"Well, I can be discreet now, can't I?" The older man chuckled again.

The wings came and Curt tucked in, smacking his lips around the spicy barbeque sauce.

"But you," this time he pointed a chicken wing directly at Jonah's nose. "You are one stubborn son of a gun. I tried like hell to give you a job after your daddy passed. But you wouldn't take it."

"I didn't think I qualified. I thought as soon as you realized I didn't have a high school diploma, you'd feel like I'd cheated my way into your company."

"Heck no! I would have thought you were a smart young man, pulling himself up by his bootstraps and making an honest living with the skills his daddy taught him."

"I guess it took me a few years to get the street smarts I needed." Jonah reached for a wing and tore off a juicy bite of meat.

"A few years and just the right woman."

They laid waste to the bucket of wings, nothing but bones piled up on the paper plates Wanda had left on the table. The pitcher of beer was nearly gone and both men were patting their bellies. Curt burped, swiped at his face with an actual napkin this time, and cleared his throat.

"So, the reason I called you down here ... Foreman's job is up for grabs. I'd really like you to take it and I don't want to have to chase you down for the next several years before you do. Take the damned job."

"I'll take the damned job." Jonah's grin was wide. He set his elbows on the table and leaned across.

"Hey, I know you're building the houses and all, but do you have any pull as to who gets them? I heard the whole lot of them are nearly sold."

Not used to making impulsive decisions, Jonah was in uncharted territory here. But suddenly, his future seemed so clear. A future with the bigger family that he knew, with a certainty he just couldn't explain, was on the way. He'd have to sell his dad's house. He had nothing in the way of a down payment. Maybe he could work something out with Curt, have a portion of his newly padded paycheck go toward a house account? The possibilities set his head reeling.

"There happens to be exactly one left. You know someone who might be interested?" asked Curt, a wicked gleam in his eye.

CHAPTER 24

"I'm sorry, the last house in that development has just gone off the market. Blaise Contracting will be starting their next project this spring. I can put you at the top of the list for one of those." The perky realtor offered Quinn a winning smile.

"Thanks. I'd hoped to get into something a lot sooner."

"I can probably get you an older cape, closer to town." She shuffled through a sheaf of listings on her desk.

A cape. Just like Nanny's. That would remind her of her grandmother—and not in a good way.

"Actually, I was looking for a new construction." New beginnings. A fresh start.

Where moments before, the young woman behind the desk had been friendly, her smile megawatt, now she looked down her nose at Quinn. She brushed at an invisible piece of lint on her sweater. Just like she'd clearly like to brush Quinn from her office.

"Perhaps if you were a little more flexible in your housing needs, it might be easier to get you into something."

Quinn felt as though she were being spoken to like a stubborn child. And that made her want to act the part. She clenched her teeth and waited until the urge to go preschooler had passed.

"I've spent the past couple of months homeless, shuffling from one temporary residence to another. I have even slept in my car on two very memorable occasions. I would like to find myself a permanent home, and if you don't want my commission, I will gladly take my business elsewhere."

"But I thought you and Jonah Goodwin, you know … "

So she wasn't quite as anonymous as she thought she was. How could she keep forgetting that everyone knows everyone's business in a small town? Quinn sighed.

"Yes, I thought so too." Because thinking about Jonah again was only going to lead to more crying, Quinn leaned across the desk and reached for the stack of MLS listings.

"Could I bring these home?" At the woman's raised eyebrow, she rolled her eyes and amended, "my sister's home?"

The realtor passed her the papers and stood, extending her hand. The snootiness was gone from her attitude, replaced by ... *aw, crap* ... pity. Just what she did not need. *Don't think about Jonah. Don't think about loss.*

"Thank you. I'll be in touch."

"Take your time, Quinn. I'll be right here."

She left the realtor's office and headed toward Logan's Bakery, intent on a hot drink and something wickedly fattening. Her sketchpad was in her tote bag and she figured she could spend the rest of the morning deciding which fairies to add to which storyline.

Her contract was for the current book with an option for two more. At the time, she couldn't wait to get started. After being turned out by Jonah, it took most of her energy just to get out of bed in the morning.

Passing in front of Tiny Treasures, the baby boutique she'd so recently drooled over, Quinn found herself pausing. Her fingers reached up and touched the icy glass of the window. Her heart clenched and bile rose quickly to lodge in her throat. Only by force of will did it go back down to churn in her stomach, rather than cause an embarrassing scene on the sidewalk.

It was high time she got over the baby that couldn't be and got used to the baby that was growing in her sister's belly. Straightening her spine and taking a deep breath, Quinn pushed open the door to the boutique and prepared to do a little shopping for her niece- or nephew-to-be. Her head was on board, but her stomach still remained unsettled. Maybe it was food poisoning.

Carrying the little paper bag sporting the store's logo, Quinn left feeling proud of herself. She'd done it. She had gone inside, she had bought a gift for her sister, and she'd had a good time. She was going to be okay.

The weather had taken a turn over the course of the morning and fat snowflakes were now starting to fall. Quinn knew she had a while before it accumulated enough to make driving tricky. She decided to take a roundabout way back to the car. Lifting her face to the sky, she stuck out her tongue, like she'd watched Lily do during the last snowstorm.

Oh, how she missed that little girl! She'd briefly considered stopping by Jonah's to remind him that she'd been honoring a request from Nanny by watching Lily for him. But he had been clear in that he didn't want her to have anything to do with his daughter. She sure didn't think this is how Nanny envisioned things ending up.

At the corner of Main St. and Littlefield Lane, Quinn stopped to watch the children in the enclosed playground of a preschool. She gripped the chain link fence and watched them dance through the flakes, giggling and shrieking. There wasn't enough to pick up, but a couple of the girls made snow angels on the sparse dusting in the grass.

The grin on Quinn's face froze as she recognized Lily's little fur-lined pink coat amidst the gaggle of children. Maybe another girl had the same one. She pressed her forehead against the fence and stared hard. Familiar laughter reached her ears and wrapped around her heart. It was Lily. Jonah had enrolled his daughter in preschool. He didn't need Quinn anymore. They didn't need her anymore.

Quinn ran from the school before she was spotted. If Lily mentioned her presence to her father, he might think she was stalking his precious daughter. Tears froze to her cheeks as she hurried down Main St. to her car. All she wanted was to get back to Kayla's house. She had to get away from town.

The road was blessedly clear of traffic at this hour and Quinn was able to floor it. *Just get home. Just get back.* She pressed down harder on the gas and swiped at the tears blurring her vision. She passed the turn off for Tucker's Pass, Jonah's street, and was nearing the spot where she'd had her flat tire.

She tapped the brakes as she rounded the bend, just enough to get around on four wheels. It wasn't terribly slippery and she was anxious to get home to Kayla's. Then out of the tree line stepped a tall, proud buck. Quinn didn't have time to react. She couldn't hurt the poor animal.

She cranked the wheel and the BMW slid sideways on the snow-coated road. She prayed that the deer made it to safety even as she braced for impact with a huge oak coming up on her right. Her brakes shrieked, or was that her? The last thing she heard was the sickening crunch as the side of her car buckled in.

• • •

Her head was inside a metal drum and someone was beating at it with a sledgehammer. Every bone, every muscle in her body hurt. She couldn't hear over the roar in her ears. No amount of effort could open her eyes more than slits. But that was okay with Quinn. The lights overhead were piercingly bright and she much preferred the relative peace that the darkness brought. Going with it, she tuned out the banging and the roaring and allowed herself another nap.

The next time she woke, her headache had dialed itself back enough that she could hear. Snoring. Where was she? Bracing herself for another painful interaction with the fluorescents overhead, Quinn blinked her eyelids open slowly. A hospital room? How on earth?

Slowly it came back to her, driving the back roads to Kayla's, the deer coming out of nowhere. Oh, that poor deer. Deer …

dear. Quinn snorted. She must be on some good drugs because all of a sudden that just seemed wildly funny. She tried to lift her hand to cover her giggles but it was trapped beneath a heavy weight.

Frowning, she followed the length of her arm to the mattress and stared, stunned, at the sight of Jonah's head pillowed on her hand. Jonah was here. And he was snoring. Had he been the one to find her? Oh, God—the memories that would have resurrected for him! She wanted to pull him into her arms, reassure him that she was just fine.

But he didn't want her in his life anymore. He'd said so, quite clearly, the other night. And then again when he had signed Lily up for preschool, letting her know, in no uncertain terms, that her presence was no longer required. Why, then, was he here?

Quinn looked to the little table on wheels beside the bed. A large bouquet of bright yellow flowers sat next to a brand new sketchpad and set of pencils. He'd brought her a sketchpad. A peace offering, perhaps? A no-hard-feelings-let's-be-friends gift? Quinn sighed hard enough to lift the hair off her face before it settled back where it belonged.

"Hey, you're awake."

"And now you are. I'm sorry, I was trying to be quiet."

"Oh, please, I'm not the one who needs the rest, you are." The look on Jonah's face was anguish. He looked like she had felt, just moments before, when she wanted to pull him into her arms and take away all the bad memories involving Paige's accident.

"Were you the one? I mean, did you find me?" Quinn twisted the sheet between her newly released fingers.

"No, I'm not sure who it was, a client of your sister's maybe? Kayla called me."

"And you came?" She didn't mean to sound so flabbergasted, but she couldn't help it.

"Of course I came! Quinn, I love you. One night of me shooting my stupid mouth off doesn't change that."

"But you put Lily in preschool," her voice shook with unshed tears.

"I did, yes. Because you have a career to focus on now and because I can finally afford it. God, you don't know how badly I wanted your input on that. I wanted you there at the interview. I knew you'd ask all the right questions."

"But you told me to stay away from you and Lily. You didn't like the influence I had over her."

"Quinn, sweetheart, I'm trying to tell you I screwed up. I screwed up in the biggest way a guy can screw up." He pulled her hand to his chest and held it there with both of his own. "I found out a lot of truths these last couple of days."

He lifted her hand to his lips and kissed it gently. Quinn wished he'd offer her lips a little of that treatment.

"Scallop Shores is a small town. It was bound to come out that you'd taught me to read. I was an idiot to make such a big deal of it. I'm sorry I blew up at you."

"I'm sorry I didn't come to you the moment it happened." She offered up a conciliatory smile.

"Can you ever forgive me?" Those pale blue eyes shot an intense thrill straight through her, just as they had the first time they'd met.

"There's nothing to forgive." She patted the bed and waited as Jonah gently shifted in beside her.

He looked nervous, unsure, as though any movement might cause her more pain. Quinn snaked an arm behind his head, tangling her fingers in his hair and drawing his mouth down to hers. He was hesitant, so she took the lead, sweeping her tongue into his mouth and reveling in the moan that she elicited.

"Well, I see our patient is feeling much better," the doctor said as he breezed into the room. He pushed a small cart ahead of him.

Jonah scrambled off the bed and back to the folding chair he'd presumably spent the entire day in.

"You are one lucky woman, Miss Baker. I've heard I can't say the same about your car. I'm sorry. But you escaped your ordeal with a few cuts and contusions from flying glass."

"I don't understand. Why am I still here, then? Why am I hooked up to this?" She lifted the arm attached to an IV pump at the head of the bed.

"It's standard protocol when we're keeping an eye on you and the baby."

"I'm sorry, what baby?" Quinn's ribs complained as she began to breathe faster. She looked over in time to find a rather smug looking Jonah grinning between her and the doctor.

"You weren't aware of your pregnancy?" The doctor looked puzzled.

"I took a test. It was negative." Her jaw went slack.

"Unfortunately, that happens a lot. My guess is you probably took it when your body hadn't built up enough pregnancy hormones to register."

He wheeled the cart up to the side of the bed and lifted a wand from one end, squirting it with a clear gel. Turning on a small monitor, he waited as Quinn adjusted the sheet and her hospital gown so he could have access to her very flat stomach.

"Let's take a look at baby and make sure it isn't too stressed out from that crazy spin in the car today."

"Could I have hurt the baby? What if something's wrong?" To come this close to realizing her biggest dream, only to have it destroyed because she'd been driving too fast down a slippery road. She grabbed Jonah's hand and held on tight.

"I listened to the heartbeat earlier, while you were getting a little beauty sleep," the doctor admitted. "I thought actually seeing it on the screen, though, might give you more peace of mind."

Together, they watched as a black-and-white fuzzy picture emerged on the screen. It was hard to figure out what she was seeing. The doctor pointed out an area that appeared to be pulsing. Quinn was torn between looking at the screen and watching the doctor's face for his reaction. He leaned in close, concentrating. She bit her lip and waited to hear that everything was just fine.

"Well, I'd say you're about seven weeks along. Everything appears to look perfect. There's just one thing," he paused, smiling broadly. "There is the heartbeat ... of the first one. And here is the heartbeat of the second, right here. Congratulations, you're having twins."

Tears streamed down her cheeks as she stared at the two pulsing dots on the screen that would soon be sweet-smelling infants she could hold in her arms. "Jonah, what are we going to do? Your house isn't big enough for all of us."

"Well, it's a good thing I bought one of those houses in the development I'm working on."

"*You* bought the last one!" She laughed at the frustration she'd felt, only that morning, when she had learned she wouldn't be able to own one of Blaise's newest homes.

"It's good to have connections." He beamed down at her, tears of pure joy rolling down into his collar.

"You realize this sets the bar pretty high on Lily's Christmas wish fulfillment meter with Santa?" Quinn giggled.

"I'll try to get the stables built by next Christmas then."

"I have a more important project for you first." A mischievous twinkle sparkled in her eyes.

"Two more cradles, coming right up. You lending a hand again this time?"

"No way. I'm leaving the woodworking to you. I'll design the wall mural." They chuckled together.

They were so focused on making plans for their growing family that it was a while before they even realized the doctor had left the room. They were silent for a moment, Quinn settling back against the pillows, unable to keep from grinning ear to ear. Jonah moved from the chair back to his spot on the bed.

"I had intended to wait for Lily on this, but I think she'll understand. Quinn Baker, would you do us the honor of joining our humble family?"

Through a sheen of happy tears she looked up at the man that had made all her dreams come true. This was happening. This was real. Her heart felt so full it could burst.

"Nothing would make me happier."

About The Author

Jennifer DeCuir lives in the beautiful Pacific Northwest, a soccer and gymnastics mom, with a hopeless addiction to caffeine (in both coffee and chocolate form). Come visit her on Facebook (Jennifer DeCuir), Twitter (@JenniferDeCuir, and her website at *www.jenniferdecuir.com.*

A Sneak Peek from Crimson Romance
(From *Conveniently* by Debra Kayn)

Dana hitched up her dress, dodged the groups of people milling around in the lobby of the Timber Lodge, and ran for the long hallway. A crowd had gathered in hopes of catching a glimpse of one of the US men's downhill skiers, but what they'd gotten instead was a front row seat to the most humiliating moment of Dana's life. Positive the laughter in the room was at her expense, she only wanted to escape.

Escape from the embarrassment of wearing a wedding dress with no groom, no wedding, and no idea what she was going to do now.

A figure stepped in front of her exit. She bumped into a man's unmovable chest. Stumbling to the side, she gazed up into a pair of dark eyes. Her barricade stared at her intently, while holding her arms to keep her from falling.

"S-sorry," she mumbled, pulling away from him as he attempted to keep her there.

She spotted an open door, ran, and slipped into the empty banquet room. She gazed at the vases filled with pastel pink flowers atop the tables, the unlit candles, and the ivory colored lace draped over every flat surface. Everything perfectly decorated for a quaint reception. The guests who were coming had quietly slipped away after her fiancé, Jace Kendall, announced he'd changed his mind about getting married, because he wasn't in love with her anymore.

She removed the diamond necklace from the jewelry box that Jace had thrust into her hands, to soften the fact he'd dumped her on her wedding day, before he'd hightailed his way out the door. "I'm going to annihilate him."

She tossed the box to the floor, dug her phone out of the clutch purse she'd bought specifically for her wedding day—while dropping the jewelry inside—and rang her father. "Daddy. I've got an emergency and need you to do something for me."

"What's going on? You sound upset," her dad said. "Weren't you scheduled to get married right now?"

A knock sounded on the outer door. She raised her gaze, ignored the rude person interrupting her, and continued. "Jace walked out on me, said he didn't love me the way a man loves a woman and … " she sniffed, "I want you to fire him. Kick him out of his office, and make sure someone else takes over his job."

"He's one of my best employees," her father said. "You'll get past this setback."

She squeezed her eyes closed and opened them again at the accusation in her dad's voice. "But, Daddy. *He* left *me*."

The door opened and a man decked out in skiwear entered. He stood staring at her, and she glared while continuing to talk on the phone. "No, I don't want you to fly here from Italy." She paused to listen. "No, I don't want you to fly me away to Barbados. I want to get *married*. I want to become Mrs. Somebody today. That's what's supposed to happen. At twenty-five years old, I'm supposed to get married. At twenty-eight, I'm having my first baby. It's my life schedule, Daddy. You know how I've planned all the important events in my life. Jace ruined everything."

Her father sighed, sounding at a loss. "Do you want to come back home? I can send Pete there to run the shop."

Dana's father would never understand her need for order. Too busy traveling with his fourth wife and Dana's three half-brothers, he'd even failed to find time to attend the wedding of his only daughter from his first marriage. She blew out her breath. "No! No, I'm sorry I bothered you … just go do whatever you're doing. I'll handle this myself. Bye, Daddy."

She disconnected the call and turned her attention to the man standing in the room with her. "What?"

"Are you okay?" He stepped forward, studying her in what appeared to be a mix of fascination and trepidation.

She grabbed her bodice and hitched her dress, squaring her shoulders. He acted as if he'd never seen a woman whose whole world had crumbled into a gazillion little pieces only moments ago. "I'm fine."

Dressed in a two-piece gray ski suit, with goggles sitting on the top of his head holding back shoulder-length black hair, he let his gaze take in the full length of her dress. His eyes, the color of mahogany, were heated and intense. A quiver traveled up her spine, not exactly unpleasant, but definitely unwanted. Right away, she pegged him for a player.

"If you're looking for the lobby, go out the door, turn right, and keep walking. You can't miss it. It's that huge room that's packed with everyone laughing and talking." She tapped her foot, itching to shed the dress and throw away anything that reminded her of Jace.

"I came here to check on you." He held his hands out to the sides of him. "I'm the guy you plowed into when you ran down the hallway. You looked like you were in trouble. I thought I'd see if I could help you with anything."

"There's nothing you can do for me except go." She kicked off her shoes and reached behind her, searching for the hidden zipper on the floor length, eggshell white gown she'd had specially made a year ago for this exact day. "You can leave and shut the door behind you."

He tilted his head. "You're shaking. Are you sure you're all right?"

"Yes, dammit." She grabbed her elbow and forced her other hand further down her back, trying to reach the tiny hook on her dress. "This is all Jace's fault."

"Who?"

She clamped her lips together and muffled her scream. Her eyes burned with unshed tears, and anger bubbled to the surface. She would not cry.

"What can I do?"

"Nothing," she snapped.

He tilted his head and his gaze dropped to her dress. "Babe ... let me help. You're upset."

She studied him for a few blinks, turned around, and presented him with her back. "Fine. Undo my zipper for me, but hurry. I feel like I'm going to be sick, and I hate throwing up."

Her need to remove any remembrance of her planned marriage trumped any modesty she may have felt over standing in her underwear in front of a man she'd never met before. She wiggled her shoulders in impatience. "Please, hurry."

"I'll have you out of here in no time." His hand skimmed her back as he deftly undid her dress, including the eyehooks.

She shivered, blaming the chill on her emotions, and shimmied out of the wedding dress. The material pooled at her feet, and she was finally free from the suffocating dress that reminded her of everything she'd lost today. She glanced down at her body. The five-hundred dollar lingerie set that'd arrived yesterday from her stepmother was all wrong. There was nothing sacred or pure about her thoughts at the moment.

A low whistle reminded her she wasn't alone and the man wasn't leaving. She sighed in self-pity, because trouble seemed to keep jumping out and tripping her lately. She couldn't get a break.

Not in the mood to deal with another skier whose only goal was to screw every snow bunny that flooded the lodge this time of year, Dana tried to ignore him in hopes he'd go away. During the workweek, she had lots of practice pushing away the attention of men. Running the shop downstairs put her right in line to deal with every male in the lodge.

Except, as she paced the banquet room, she couldn't help glancing at the man who'd stayed to help her.

He was one of the sexiest skiers she'd seen visit the lodge. The long black hair hung haphazardly to his shoulders, the patch of whiskers under his lower lip accented full lips, and dark eyes surrounded with even darker lashes made him drool-worthy. Normally, his looks would've grabbed her attention.

If she didn't hate every single man on Earth at this moment.

She planted her hands on her bare hips. "You've had your fill. There's no more to see, so you can leave."

He seemed to gaze at her ivory colored lingerie with too much interest. She half turned. If he said one thing about the garter belt, the pantyhose, or her lack of clothing, she'd stab him with her four-inch Jimmy Choos.

He took a step toward her and stopped. "You're crying."

"I am not." She swiped her cheeks, upset to find wetness. She never cried. Not since she was twelve and broke her arm at Mount Shasta during ski camp.

He reached into the back pocket of his ski pants and extracted a handkerchief. She sniffed. Crying over Jace was a waste of good tears. She should be putting this energy into a backup plan.

"May I?" the skier whispered, motioning with the cloth, then stepping forward when she refused to answer and dotting her cheeks dry.

She gazed into his eyes and was surprised to find only concern. "What kind of man carries a handkerchief?"

"One that never knows if he'll meet a beautiful woman who'll need one." His gaze softened.

"Really?"

"No." His mouth curved upward. His perfect white teeth practically sparkled. "I use one to clean the moisture out of my goggles when I ski."

She wrinkled her nose. "Please tell me this doesn't have your sweat on it."

"Don't worry. I haven't hit the slopes yet."

"Oh." She dropped her gaze. "Well, thank you. That wasn't necessary, but it was … nice."

He hooked his thumb under her chin and lifted her gaze. "Will you be okay?"

The tenderness in his voice and the gentle touch undid her. She threw herself at him, burying her face in his neck, and sobbed.

She cried for her disappointing day, her pathetic wedding with no family and only the acquaintances from her father's business present to wish her well. Most of all she mourned for her failed life.

"Shh." He rubbed her back. "It can't be all bad."

Aware of the heat from the palm of his hand, Dana cried harder for her lost opportunity. She'd planned her life down to the most minuscule details in an effort to make sure she never ended up the way her parents had. Now it was over, and she had no idea what she was supposed to do next.

"Do you want to tell me what happened?" The man leaned back and held her by the upper arms, not letting her go.

"It doesn't matter. There's nothing I can do about it, not that I want to have that jerk back in my life." She blew her nose with the borrowed handkerchief. "Thanks for the shoulder and the h-handkerchief."

"My name's Juan."

"Dana." She inhaled a deep breath to compose herself. "I appreciate the help with the dress … and the hug. I'm okay now."

Juan frowned. She moistened her lips and tilted her head. He seemed familiar. Probably one of the men she'd sold equipment to, or passed by on her way downstairs in the lodge on her way to work over the last couple of months.

"Listen, I don't want to leave you while you're upset." He glanced around the room. "Why don't you put the dress back on, and I'll buy you a drink at the bar. It'll help you relax."

"Ugh." She walked over and sat atop a table pushed up against the wall. "I don't want to wear that *thing* ever again. I don't care if I have to walk up to my room wearing … " she raised her arms, "nothing. I refuse to have anything to do with Jace Kendall. Do you know him? Because I wouldn't be against you taking a bat to his car or decking him."

"No, I don't recognize the name." Juan cleared his throat. "You should forget about him. It sounds like you're better off with him out of your life."

"Yes, I am." But she didn't believe it. Jace had been the answer to her prayers for the last two years. "I suppose I better go up to my room."

"Dressed like that?" His brows rose.

"I'm not touching the wedding dress." She pointed to the floor where the yards and yards of expensive lace lay discarded. "Besides, I'm hideous."

"You're lovely, and I don't think walking out there into the lodge is wise considering the place is filled to capacity with men desperate to look at a beautiful woman."

"I doubt that." She shrugged. "Don't you think if men were willing to be with me, I would've gotten married today instead of being dumped at the front door?"

Juan winced. "He's a fool."

"He didn't even wait until we stepped in front of the minister before he chickened out. He screwed up my whole life. If I don't get married today, I'll never be able to reach my next goal."

He made a sympathetic noise.

"Not only that, Now I'm probably never going to experience what it's like to have a hon—" She clamped her lips together, then mumbled, "Never mind."

Juan shrugged off his coat, walked over, and sat beside her. She shook her head, unwilling to believe she was sitting here, when she should be slipping upstairs to enjoy her honeymoon. Jace could rot in hell for all she cared.

"Here. Cover up. You're shaking." Juan slipped his coat over her shoulders. "I've already missed most of my slope time. You can borrow my coat."

She pushed the sleeves of the coat to her wrists, noticing it was one of her daddy's products. "Thanks. I'm sure I won't be the only woman caught running up the back stairs in her panties. I run into at least one woman a week sneaking out of the rooms the Olympic team uses."

"Is that so?" He unzipped his pants. "You can wear these too, I have spandex underneath. It'll be safer. No one looks at a man half undressed going up the back stairs."

"I don't know why you're being so nice to me." Dana sighed. "But I do appreciate it. I'm not the spoiled brat Jace said I was. He was just … "

"An asshole?" He cussed, struggling with his zipper.

"Yes. Incredibly stupid and egotistical too." She glanced down at the front of his pants. "What's wrong?"

"Damn thing's stuck."

She pushed his hands aside. "It's the zipper. Happens all the time. Metal zippers rust over time, especially when subjected to the moist, cold weather the clothing is intended for … big mistake. That's why Reese Enterprise uses plastic or coated zippers in all outerwear clothing."

"Huh?" His hands stilled and he glanced at her.

"It's not important." She pushed his hands away. "Here, I'll help."

"We need a pair of scissors." He peered down at the front of him. "Or maybe you can rip it."

She tugged, but it only drew the zipper tighter, making it catch more. Without anything to use, she leaned over and opened her mouth.

"Whoa … " Juan sank his hands into the hair piled on the top of her head. "I'd like nothing more, but having your mouth on me when you're upset probably isn't the smartest decision."

She paused with her opened mouth above the zipper and gazed up at him. "You don't want me to try and bite the string in half?"

He chuckled and patted her head before removing his hand and leaning back. "Be careful with those teeth, babe."

She lowered her head, caught the edge of the material, and ground her teeth back and forth. It was harder than she'd imagined. She grunted and worked the string over to her eyetooth.

The zipper grew taut and she reached up and tugged at the material. She stilled with her hand against his crotch. There was a reason for the lack of space between the fabric and the man. A very big reason.

Warmth flooded her face. Her skin tingled. The bulge underneath the pants fascinated, yet shocked her. A heady sensation, considering she could almost feel the heat radiating off him on her cheek.

The door opened and a flash went off in the room. She frowned at the same time the string gave way and she jerked away from Juan, spitting the remains of the thread off her lip. She stood and glanced behind her.

A robust, angry man in a coat with the USA Olympics emblem scrolled across the chest stood inside the doorway. Two photographers snapped pictures behind him, blinding Dana from inspecting them any further. Juan jumped off the table and stepped in front of her, blocking her from view.

"Oh, shit," Juan muttered.

"What are they doing?" she whispered, zipping Juan's coat to her neck. She wasn't sure if that helped, because on the bottom half, she still wore her thong and garter. "Who are they?"

Juan straightened, keeping his hand on her hip to keep her hidden behind his body. "It's not what it looked like, Coach Lindhurst."

"It was exactly what it looked like, and it'll be on the front cover of *Sports Illustrated* in the morning thanks to your carelessness. You were supposed to meet with the press a half-hour ago. Looks like that won't be necessary. They've got their pictures, and I imagine more than an article or two to fill the damn magazine, thanks to you and your entourage." Coach Lindhurst growled. "I've warned you. Your sponsor warned you. One more scandal and your benefactors would pull their money. I'm going to have to put you on reserve, dammit. You've really screwed up this time, Santiago."

Juan stepped forward, stopped, and glanced back at Dana. He gave her a hint of a smile before turning around. "Yes, Coach. If I could request another meeting, I can explain what happened here. It's a simple misunderstanding. One that shows that the lady behind me is innocent, and shouldn't be involved with any gossip that comes my way. She's had a bad day, sir."

Coach Lindhurst shook his head in disgust. "You had one more month to return and win another gold, and you threw it away because of some woman who wants a piece of—"

"Stop. Seriously, don't go there, or we're going to have problems between us. I'll talk to Wyden. I'll get my sponsor back," Juan said. "Can you keep me on the roster until then?"

"It's out of my hands. You had two warnings. Three marks and you're out. Balden will go in your place. You're immediately on reserve." Coach stared Juan down, cursed, and headed toward the door.

She scrambled out from behind Juan. "Wait!"

"What are you doing?" Juan whispered.

She ignored him, stepped over, and picked up her wedding dress, holding it in front of her. "Juan's right. There's a simple explanation for what you saw. You see, we're getting married. He was helping me into my dress, and I was helping him out of his suit. You can go to the lobby. There's a minister waiting for us. We're already late though, so if you'll excuse us, we need to finish getting dressed."

Juan walked over and ushered everyone out of the room, a look of bemusement on his face. Dana crossed her arms and cradled her elbows in her hand. It didn't take a genius to figure out Juan was on the Olympic team, and he was in deep trouble. She owed him for being so kind to her.

The more she thought about actually marrying him, the better she felt. She'd stay on her schedule, and figure out what to do later when she had time to think over her rash decision. She'd prove to Jace and her father that she was not spoiled. She'd help Juan for the goodness of the United States.

"Thanks, babe, but I can take it from here. This is my fault and I only have myself to blame." Juan ran his hands through his hair and groaned. "I'll figure out some way to make it back on the team with a new sponsor. This isn't the first time I've had to go in front of the board and prove myself to them."

She took off his coat and pushed it into his chest. "Get dressed."

"What?" He slipped his arms in the sleeves. "I said you could take the jacket. I've got plenty."

"We'll have to hurry or the minister will leave." She stepped into her dress and turned around. "Zip me up."

"You're not serious?"

She patted her hair. "I take it you need an excuse for what that man saw in here today to get back on the Olympic team, and I have a deadline. We're getting married."

"We can't." He tilted his head and looked up at the ceiling. "This is not happening to me."

"Yes, it is." She grabbed his hand. "I'm Dana Reese. My daddy is Colton Reese of Reese Enterprise. You know, the owner of the most popular line of ski equipment. He'll sponsor you, and be happy you took me off his hands. Trust me."

"Are you serious?"

"More than you'll ever know. I won't let Daddy or Jace ruin my life schedule." She laughed hysterically. "Let's go get married."